RACHEL M. WILSON

Don't Touch

HARPER TEEN
An Imprint of HarperCollinsPublishers

HarperTeen is an imprint of HarperCollins Publishers.

Don't Touch
Copyright © 2014 by Rachel M. Wilson
www.epicreads.com

Library of Congress Cataloging-in-Publication Data
Wilson, Rachel M., date.
  Don't touch / Rachel Wilson. — First edition.
     pages cm
  Summary: "16-year-old Caddie struggles with OCD,
anxiety, and a powerful fear of touching another person's
skin, which threatens her dreams of being an actress—until
the boy playing Hamlet opposite her Ophelia gives her a
reason to overcome her fears."— Provided by publisher.
  Includes bibliographical references.
  ISBN 978-0-06-222093-6 (hardcover)
  [1. Obsessive-compulsive disorder—Fiction.
2. Anxiety—Fiction. 3. Acting—Fiction. 4. Self-actualization
(Psychology)—Fiction.] I. Title. II. Title: Do not touch.
PZ7.W69826Do 2014   2013043193
[Fic]—dc23   CIP
                                                                 AC

Typography by Torborg Davern
14 15 16 17 18   LP/RRDH   10 9 8 7 6 5 4 3 2 1
❖
First Edition

To my parents, Joe and Janet, who have always supported my most far-fetched dreams, and to my sister Laura, who gets it

ACT ONE

I am too much i' the sun.

—HAMLET, *HAMLET* (I.ii.70)

I.

"Cadence Finn? Take yourself right out there, hon."

The office lady points toward the academy's courtyard and goes back to her magazine: *Crafting for the Southern Home.*

"I think I'm supposed to get a Peer Pal?"

"Hon, yours is late. I'd stick you with another group, but you're our only new junior. You just wait right on out there."

"I can't wait inside?"

Outside, the air's thick and wet, the sun scalding. It's like the sauna at Mom's fitness club with the temperature dialed up to hell.

Instead of answering, the lady sniffs and sets down her magazine to pour me a Dixie cup of lemonade from a pitcher on the dividing wall. "You're not dressed for the heat," she says with a pinched smile.

That's an understatement.

It's ninety degrees out, but I'm wearing jeans, long sleeves, and a scarf. The humidity's plastered my hair to the back of my neck in a sticky shield. Alabama in August calls for pixie cuts and ponytails, but I don't dare leave my skin exposed.

Don't touch.

"I guess I wanted to wear my new school clothes?"

She holds out the cup, saying, "This will keep you cool."

I wait for her to set it down and move her hand away before I take the cup. Her smile's puckered into a knot with my delay, so I say my politest, "Thank you, ma'am," and head out to sit on the courtyard's brick wall, where I squint at the sun, sip watery lemonade, and shake.

Don't touch. Don't touch.

The words chime in the background, a constant and nagging refrain. The threat of touch pulses and swells the way skin gets raw after a burn. It's constant and secret and eager to catch me off-guard.

There's too much empty space behind me. My Peer Pal could sneak up, put her hand on my shoulder—or *his* hand! There I go shaking again.

If somebody asks why, I'll claim that I'm cold.

They probably won't challenge me, but I plan out the script anyway:

NOSY PEER PAL: *(eyeing my long sleeves)* What's with the shivers?

ME: *(throaty)* I guess I'm cold-blooded.

NOSY PEER PAL: There's something about you. What *is* it?

ME: *(confident, mysterious, a little tragic even)* I'm just me.

NOSY PEER PAL: You have *got* to try out for the fall play!

ME: That's part of my plan.

Ridiculous.

My life is not a play. I am *not* on stage.

People talk about stage fright, but life is what's scary. In a play, you know where to stand, what to say, and the ending's already been written. I've played crazy characters, emotional wrecks, but not one of them ever stopped breathing.

Don't touch.

The magic words help my pulse slow, if only for a second. It's like scratching an itch that won't stay in one place. I shouldn't give in, but thinking the words *feels* right, safe.

I almost want to call Dad—he's always been good at calming me down—but Dad *chose* to remove himself from our lives, and I'm going to respect that. I'm going to *respect* that choice till he feels what he's making us feel.

If I called, he'd play I-told-you-so: "This might all be too much for you, changing schools? Hanging out with a bunch of temperamental artsy types?"

So far, I'm not hanging out with anyone. The other new students sit in tight, buzzing rings among the statues on the courtyard lawn. There's a plaque explaining this sculpture garden as a student project made of recycled materials from Birmingham's old steelworks and mines. The statue nearest me has a wire frame filled with chunks of limestone roughly in the shape of a giant man. Small stones have been allowed to slip out in a pile at the giant's feet as if he's crumbling.

"Titan of Industry," the giant's called. Somebody passed his class in irony. I resist the urge to help the Titan by stuffing his stones back in his frame.

Maybe they couldn't find a Peer Pal willing to take me. Maybe I'm not supposed to be here—there's another Cadence Finn, a freshman one, and I got her acceptance letter by mistake.

And then Mandy Bower waves at me, an honest-to-God Peer—and I hope, hope, hope Pal. Mandy glides through the circles of freshmen as if barely tethered to earth, the half-human product of some Greek god's indiscretion. She's forever cursed to fraternize with the merely mortal, and it bums her out.

Still, Mandy smiles for me. A perfect Greek-goddess smile. "I'm your new Peer Pal. Aren't you so excited you could puke pink?"

She doesn't rush to hug me. That's a good thing, I guess, a safe thing, but Mandy used to squeeze me nearly to death every time we saw each other.

"Hi, Mandy."

This year, she's fashioned herself as a boho badass with rings of black eyeliner and a long, flowing skirt. She still has a ton of blond curls, but now there are streaks of pink on the undersides. Pointy sticks pretend like they want to keep her hair up, but it's an act. Messy curls fall in just the right way all around Mandy's face.

"What did your mom say about the pink hair?" I ask, knowing Mandy's pageant-obsessed mom would never approve.

Mandy pouts mischievously. "She threatened to cut it out. I told her I'd dye it back for competition but that if she cut it, I'd switch my dance to a dubstep."

"Can you *do* a dubstep?"

"No! But I sure can make an ass out of myself faking it."

She does a couple of twisty moves with her legs, some robot arms, and I laugh.

Mandy and I spent every possible second together from birth into middle school. We started drifting even then, but since she started at the academy, we've only seen each other at her family's Christmas parties or the occasional mom-daughter brunch.

We made plans.

They fell through.

Mandy bounces on her toes. "How's your life?" she

says as if it's been a few days and not a few years since we were friends. "Did you miss me?"

I'm afraid to answer: *Yes, of course, every day.*

"How's Bailey?" Mandy asks, naming the girl who became my closest friend by default after Mandy.

"She says Oregon is nice. She moved away in the middle of freshman year."

"Oh."

"How's Lena?"

"Beats me," Mandy says. "Lena was a capital B."

I want to holler applause, but I just say, "Ah," and nod.

"You still dominating the science fair?" she asks, and I sigh my assent.

Starting in seventh grade, thanks to Dad, I won four in a row. I love that Dad says the world needs more female scientists. I just wish he'd stop pushing me to be one of them.

"Okay, here's a fun game," Mandy says, hiking up her skirt to straddle the wall, her knees just a couple of inches away from me. Touching through clothes doesn't count, but having Mandy within poking distance still doesn't feel safe.

I scoot back, trying to pass it off like I'm just making room.

Mandy goes on. "The freshmen are split up by discipline. Can you tell who's who?"

She's always been good at filling up awkward spaces,

making things fun that weren't fun before. *Let it last. Please, please let this last.*

I scan the circles of freshmen. Any group of mostly girls is likely to be dancers, but the prevalence of bunheads and unnecessary stretching clinches it. When I guess, Mandy says, "No doubt."

I decide one group is studio artists based on creative wardrobe choices. One girl wears feather epaulettes like wings, and a guy wears a T-shirt that's been cut in half and stapled back together.

Mandy goes *"Annhh!"* like a game show buzzer. "Musicians," she says.

I thought the musicians would be more reserved. "How can you tell?" I ask.

"Context clues." She points to the girl with the feathered shoulders—who has her arm draped over a cello case.

"Oh, duh."

One circle screams theater, dressed to impress. There's a Louise Brooks clone with a bob and cloche hat, and a guy going for steampunk cowboy. This group's louder than the others, splashy and bright, but one sure clue tells me they're in theater: they've barely met, and already they're touching.

I take a deep breath—I *can* breathe—and hug my hands tight to my ribs. There's my chest moving up and down. An accidental touch is so easy. The words are my antidote: *Don't touch, please, please.*

I thought I'd outgrown this game or at least squashed it down into something I could ignore, but the moment Dad left, it started again, and this time it feels deeper and harder to shake.

Mandy never knew about my "games": See if you can hold your breath as we take the next curve or the car will fly out into nothing; try not to blink while you're looking at Mom or else she might get cancer and die. Touch another person's skin and Dad will never come home.

The danger *feels* even bigger than that. Touch another person's skin and Dad will *evaporate*. We'll never see him again. Mom will die of a broken heart. I'll have panic attacks, a complete and total breakdown, and get carted away to a hospital for crazy people. My brother will hate me forever and ever for failing him.

And I will be alone.

Every little thing in this world that has fallen apart will stay broken.

It's a lot, I know.

Dad would tell me to stop catastrophizing. Mom would tell me to drink some herbal tea.

There's a name for these imaginings: magical thinking. It almost sounds nice, but it isn't. The weirdest part is that I *know* my stupid games shouldn't have an effect on real life. But when I try to stop, the doubt creeps in—what if it *does* matter?

Dad left in June. I haven't touched a single person since.

10

"You okay?" Mandy asks.

"What? Yeah, I'm fine." I force a smile.

Mandy squints at the freshmen. "Let's find someplace more private."

Birmingham Arts Academy sits on the long ridge of Red Mountain, overlooking the city. Mandy leads me across the drive, past a row of flowering hydrangeas to the sloping woods. We're in the foothills of the Appalachians; I should be used to steep hills, but it makes me anxious to see the tops of trees angling downward so sharply.

Luckily, there are steps, a small amphitheater built into the side of the hill. If we sit on the bottom round of seats, we can't be seen from the courtyard.

The woods seem to close around us, a tangle of light-dappled leaves, mossy bark, and climbing vines. It reminds me of how Mandy and I used to build hideouts in the woods behind my house.

Mandy leaves space between us. My skin doesn't feel so *on edge* if I have room to maneuver, but the way Mandy keeps her distance makes me sad, too.

"I'm glad I got you," I say.

Mandy nods without looking at me. "Sorry I was late. Boy drama."

Always, with Mandy.

"What happened?"

She makes eye contact, so briefly, like she's checking

if it's okay to share. Then, just as fast, she looks away, through the trees toward downtown.

"Nothing worth talking about."

We used to tell each other everything.

Mandy lights a cigarette.

"Does your mom know you smoke?" I ask.

"Where do you think I got the cigarettes?" She absorbs my surprise with a flat smile and goes on, "She's convinced that it helps with my weight." She blows out a long stream of smoke, and I turn my head.

The sound of a slamming car door makes me jump. Mandy holds the cigarette low between her legs in a practiced way and twists over her shoulder to check the tree line. Getting caught might make me the first person in the history of the academy to get expelled at orientation. I want to grab the cigarette, grind it out on the seat between us, and bury it under a mountain of leaves, but Mandy just waits. No one comes.

"I was sorry to hear about your dad," Mandy says, picking up a shiny yellow leaf from the amphitheater's stage and twirling it by the stem. Her eyes stay on the leaf as if it holds more interest than my reaction, but I know better.

My mom must have told hers, and that makes it more real somehow, that other people know. I pretend I don't mind. I want Mandy to be my friend again. It's supposed to be okay for your friends to know what's going on with you.

"They're just trying it out," I say. "It's not like they're getting divorced."

Not yet.

I feel like I have to defend Dad. "One of his mentors from the University of Virginia wants his input on a study. It's a big honor. But, you know, it's temporary."

Mandy nods, but she still looks pitying.

"Or we might all move there," I say.

"Your mom would never leave Birmingham," she says. "Her whole life is here."

"She went away for college."

That's how Mom and Dad met. But Mandy knows my mom almost as well as I do, and I'm pretty sure she's right. When my parents moved here, Mom bought two rocking chairs for the back porch. When things were good, they would sit out there to watch the sun set behind the woods, have a drink, and chat. Mom always said she hoped that was how they'd spend their "twilight years"—in those chairs, side by side.

I don't want to leave Birmingham either, especially now that I'm at the academy. I want us all to stay happy in our same house, for Mom to get her "twilight years" wish. It seems like such a simple, small thing to ask.

Mandy goes back to twirling her leaf.

"Is your dad so pissed you're going here?" she asks.

I shrug.

My parents fought about the academy—a lot. They

fought about other things, but there was that one night in March . . . Mom had let me audition for the academy in secret, and when Dad found out—brutal.

Months later, when Dad said he had to go, Mom told him, "If you're leaving, you don't get to argue with me about Caddie's school," and I guess he agreed. I still worry he'll hold it against me—that even if he does come back, things will never be the same.

But I can't say that to Mandy.

"Do you still take dance?" I say. Friends ask each other things.

She purses her lips like she swallowed something nasty. "On weekends. Mom's got me taking voice lessons too. I'm supposed to be a triple threat."

"What's that?"

She smiles at my ignorance, not in a mean way, but it's a reminder of how much more time she's had in this world. "It means you act, sing, and dance. You have to be a triple threat to be on Broadway or do regional theater even and have a career. It's all musicals. . . . Here, watch me do a smoke ring."

The smoke comes out a shapeless mess and Mandy laughs at herself. "God, Caddie, I don't even like musicals." She inhales, then talks through her exhale. "They say movies are all waiting around, but I still think it'd be cool." Her eyes go misty.

"So go be in a movie. Tell your mom she can be her own triple threat."

Mandy laughs. I made Mandy laugh.

"I'm scared I don't have the look for it."

I've never known Mandy to be scared of anything, but I like her for saying it. "You're the best-looking person I know."

She laughs again. "No," she says. "I mean, even if I look all right here—and I think I look all right—this is Birmingham. We're tiny."

I follow her eyes to downtown, just visible through the tree cover. Our tallest buildings hardly scrape the sky, but they form a decent-sized grid stretching north and south of the train tracks. Most cities form around water, a lake or a river, an ocean port, but Birmingham's river was a railroad.

On the edges of the city are the smokestacks and furnaces. Now, a lot of these have been shut down. Graffiti artists have outdone themselves, tagging the highest pipes in jewel tones that complement the rust.

Most of what people call Birmingham is miles and miles of villages with names that play on nature words: "ridge" and "valley," "crest" and "dale," plenty of "red" for the iron. Toss in "Cahaba" and "Cherokee," the occasional "English" or "Avon," and you've got it covered.

Up here in Redmont Park over Avondale, the cicadas

sing louder than the downtown traffic.

Mandy's been still for a long time, but it doesn't feel wrong being quiet with her. Then she looks to me. "Caddie, why did we stop being friends?"

She doesn't seem worried by what I might say. It's a fact that we're no longer friends, and she says it like that, no emotion attached.

"I stopped taking dance; we went to different schools . . ."

We both know there's more to it than that, but Mandy doesn't contradict me.

I think *I* might have wrecked it with Mandy. I was jealous when she got the academy and *I* got panic attacks, afraid of her seeing how jealous I was and how strange I'd become.

Mandy's stopped twirling the leaf, and she studies me like she's making a decision.

"You're going to like the theater people," she tells me, and I feel like I've passed a test.

She holds her leaf out to me, but if I take it, our fingers will touch. I wave it away like she's handing me a milkshake and I'm watching my weight. I'm worried I failed that one, but she says, "Let's go," and the leaf falls down between us as we stand.

2.

As we climb the amphitheater's steps and cross the drive, words pour from Mandy faster than I can follow. "You have to get into *Hamlet* so we can go to Mountain Bard in January. We compete at the Alabama Shakespeare Festival in Montgomery. It's like the fifth largest one in the world and the only one that gets to fly the flag of the *Royal* Shakespeare Company. They've got this pond with *royal* swans— like *the queen's* swans—and they give out scholarships, and scouts from college programs come. We could share a room. I mean, we have to get screened, but we almost always win the whole thing. The only time I know of that we haven't made it was like five years ago when some kid got an asthma attack in the middle of playing Macbeth."

"Poor guy."

"Why? He wrecked it. I mean, take your medicine,

right? Or don't be Macbeth if you maybe can't breathe all the way through a soliloquy."

"But people are still talking about it?"

"You don't bother going to a fancy arts school to not be the best at your art. He messed it up for everyone."

And years later, they still hate him for it. Getting cast in a small part sounds better with that in mind, but Ophelia's not small.

It feels unwise to confide in Mandy that I've been dreaming about Ophelia, that I have all her speeches memorized, that Ophelia has a place on the wall by my bed. I printed a copy of this painting by John Everett Millais. Ophelia is lying in a pool of water, surrounded by leaves, a crown of flowers in her hair. Her back is arched, palms open, eyes staring. She's either dying and doesn't know it, or she's letting herself die. Her dress hangs heavy around her legs. Soon it will drag her down.

Mandy's still talking. ". . . And you have to try for State Thespians in the spring. Last year we went international."

"Whoa. Where does 'international' mean?"

"Lincoln, Nebraska, but it still sounds like fun. We can go together!" She squeals—actually squeals—about the two of us going on a trip at the end of the school year. She thinks we might still be friends then.

"And this is the real coup," she says. "The juniors have half a chance at some good parts because this year's seniors got into a whole drinking debacle in Lincoln, and they're banned from competing. Usually they *choose* the competition play specifically *for* the seniors, but this year it's all up for grabs."

As sad as that is for the seniors, it's good news for me. But that's not the best part. The best part is Mandy's excitement at having me here.

We tour the entire school: the giant lounge called the "green room," the visual arts studios, the special classrooms for dance and orchestra, and Mandy's favorite—the rehearsal rooms, which are completely unsupervised.

"I hooked up with Drew for the first time in here," she tells me. "He stood behind me, and I put one leg up on the barre while we were facing the mirror. I could see everything he was doing—totally hot."

I smile, but my stomach twists. Even if I could touch and be touched, I'm not sure I could handle that.

Our tour ends at the academy's theater for a talk from the department head. The space has that rich, dark glow that old theaters give off. Deep red carpets in the aisles match the velvet curtains around the stage, which is black, shiny, and flat, a blank canvas to hold whatever a designer imagines. But what makes the space feel endless are the lights. A whole world could fit under those lights. I could walk and walk and never fall off the edge of that stage.

The department head is Nadia, no last name. She doesn't need one.

Nadia's tiny with a pixie cut to match. Her clothing's . . . unique. She wears a weird apron dress over skinny jeans and lime-green heels with rubber straps. She was at my audition, but I mistook her for a student assistant. She'd been knitting, not paying attention, I thought.

Standing center stage, she still looks like one of the stranger students, but there's nothing "assistant" about her. As small as she is, she fills the whole stage. She pushes the microphone out of the way. Her voice doesn't need help to reach us, reach into us.

"Acting is about action," she says, "taking action on need. What do you *need* more than anything else in this world? Need as much as you need air?"

My throat tightens, and I tuck my hands under my arms. I know what it means to need air.

I *need* to not feel that way. I *need* to not touch anyone.

That's not really a need, that's a fear, but maybe if I'm lucky, Nadia won't be able to tell the difference.

After Nadia's talk, Mandy and I head back to the junior corridor. Banks of multicolored lockers—lavender, mint, and rhubarb—hug the halls, and murals fill the spaces in between.

"I don't think we're in Kansas anymore," I say, and Mandy laughs.

"It's like a rainbow exploded in here, right?"

"No, I love it."

A few students who clearly aren't being oriented camp out by their lockers, playing cards as if they're completely at home.

"What are they doing?" I ask.

Mandy gives me a look. "Playing cards."

"No, I mean, if school hasn't started yet?"

She shrugs. "Setting up lockers? Helping teachers get stuff ready?" Then she catches on to my confusion. "Most students actually *like* being here."

"They let people hang out in the halls when school's out?"

"Yeah, what are we going to do? Start an art riot?"

Mandy spots a tall guy at his locker and makes a face. "Hold on a sec. Me and Peter have talking to do."

Mandy mentioned boy trouble. Could this be the guy?

Peter's red-brown hair falls over his glasses—the hip, nerdy kind with the plastic frames. He's wearing a paint-spattered T-shirt, cargo pants, and work boots. He's broad-shouldered, not huge, but there's something about how he stands. Peter takes up space and doesn't seem to mind.

He's at home in his skin.

I feel like I *know* him or like I'm *supposed* to know him, but I'm sure we've never met. Mom's always said she's a little bit psychic—that every time she's met someone who's going to be important in her life, she's known at first sight. I don't really believe in all that, but there's some kind of energy shouting at me.

Crazily, I find myself hoping that Peter's *not* Mandy's guy—a stupid hope because it's not like *I* could be with Peter. Being with a guy generally involves touching a guy.

My pulse picks up and I feel a bit hot, but I don't think that's only from fear.

When Peter sees Mandy coming, he holds up his hands as if to say "don't shoot," and he smiles, guilty and loving it, totally game. Mandy steps close to him, and even though Peter's at least a head taller, the way she gathers herself into one charged column makes them seem equally matched.

"You. Do. Not," she says, each word a barb, "touch my car."

From the tirade that follows, I pick up the facts. Peter is *not* Mandy's boyfriend; that's Drew—yes, from the rehearsal room hookup. Drew lives across the street from the Birmingham Country Club. Last weekend when Mandy was at Drew's, Peter attached a winch to her car and towed it out of the driveway and onto the golf course—into a sand trap.

The more Mandy gets in his face, the wider Peter smiles.

"Drew's the one who gave me the idea," he says, and the air around Mandy sizzles and sparks.

For my benefit, Peter says, "Mandy wouldn't stop complaining about having to ride in Drew's truck."

His "ride" comes out "rahhhd." The most common

Birmingham accent squeezes vowels into nasal diph-thongs, but Peter's vowels take up wide-open spaces, true Southern drawl.

"That truck is an eyesore!" says Mandy.

"Ah-ah-ah." Peter holds up one finger. "Watch what you say or it's back to the sand trap for you, missy."

She pinches her fingers and thumb together like a beak and jabs his chest just below the collarbone. He groans, still laughing, and puts up a hand in defense.

"She should be thanking me," Peter says to me, "for settling the fight. See, she needed Drew's truck to tow her out, but he wouldn't do it until she said the magic words: 'Your badass truck is superior to my lame-ass car in every way, and I will never complain about it again.' Problem solved."

She goes for another jab, but he catches her wrists and holds her at bay so her kicks miss his shins. Mandy laughs too, but she doesn't stop kicking.

I step back and steady myself at the wall, ready to bolt if they swing around toward me.

In one swift reversal, Peter catches Mandy in a bear hug, pinning her back to his chest. Our eyes meet—Peter's eyes are green—and for one second it's me he's holding tight.

My breath catches. That kind of touching is definitely. Not. Allowed.

Mandy wrenches out of Peter's grip, and only then, when Peter's eyes drop, do I realize I'd been frozen. It couldn't have been more than a second, but it feels like so much longer that I couldn't look away.

I try to steady my breathing. *Each breath is enough. There is no need to struggle for air.*

Mandy and Peter face each other in a standoff.

"Truce?" Peter says.

"Payback," says Mandy, "when you least expect it."

"I live for danger."

Peter catches me staring and stares back as if we know each other well enough for that to be okay.

It's unnerving.

"Caddie," he says, like he's testing it out. I can't think how he knows my name, but I like the way it sounds in his voice. Does he have this effect on everyone?

He takes a step toward me— *Don't touch!*

"Excuse me," Mandy says, "I've got to check my hair for lice," and she stalks to the bathroom a few yards down the hall.

"I think she just said I've got cooties," Peter says. "That is so fourth grade."

"For us it was third," I say, surprising myself with how fast something flirty comes out of my mouth.

"So you were advanced. Way ahead of me."

He steps closer. I back up. No words come.

It's not comfortable holding eye contact for this long, but it's not safe to look away, either, not with him standing so close. I have no script for talking to Peter.

"So, do you do that a lot?" I say finally. "Steal people's cars? You could have gotten arrested."

Peter looks back over his shoulder. I can't tell if he's already bored with me or embarrassed by talking about himself, or maybe he's actually afraid the cops are listening. He seems like a guy who might have earned a spot on Birmingham's most-wanted pranksters list.

"I get a lot of great ideas," Peter says, looking back at me. "I'm just not always good at sorting out which ones are, you know, legal." Peter smiles the way cats stretch, easily and with his whole self.

"Hey, how did you know my name?" I ask.

"You know mine," he says.

"I . . . I heard Mandy say your name."

He raises one finger toward me and closes the distance between us. I step back and stumble.

"Maybe it should say, 'My name is Jumpy,'" he says.

His finger, too close, points at the name tag I'd forgotten I was wearing. There's space between us, but I *feel* the threat of his touch, potential energy between the tip of his finger and my heart.

I nod, rattled, like he's picked me up by the shoulders and shaken me. "I should check on Mandy."

I step far around him, keeping him in my sights as I back down the hall and through the bathroom door. I take extra time and when Mandy and I finally emerge, the coast's clear. Peter's gone.

3.

Dad taught me about potential energy.

It's the energy waiting to get used when a still object finally moves. A glass that's about to slip from a hand, a ball set to roll downhill, a car tipping over the edge of a cliff—all have potential energy.

Dad had it on the day he left. He stood in the den with his hands in his pockets and rocked on his heels, back and forth, as if he were standing in sand with the tide coming in.

All the tension, resentment, and whatever else made my parents split up sloshed around him like a wave and spilled closer to me, pooled.

The air felt unnaturally still—conditioned and vacuum-sealed to keep June outside. Dust motes hovered as if frozen in time, caught by the afternoon rays angling in through the den's big bay windows.

A body in motion remains in motion. That was Dad, going away to do research in physics at the University of Virginia.

A body at rest remains at rest unless something makes it move. That was me, not about to hug Dad good-bye. I didn't want any part of that bad-feeling wave. That's when the magic words crept back in: *Don't touch.*

Any second, Dad might have tipped forward, crossed the couple of feet between him and me, and taken my hand, wrapped me up in a hug.

But he didn't.

And I didn't budge from the big chaise lounge with its pillows stacked like sandbags, its high, wide arms two barricades. I felt powerful keeping my distance while Dad hugged Mom good-bye.

She sobbed, but not Dad. Not me. Mom says I'm "emotionally contained" just like him.

My brother, Jordan, on the other hand, exploded. He screamed in Dad's face, broke a vase, and ran into the woods, not to return until Dad was long gone.

It probably confused Dad that I wasn't clinging to him, begging him to stay. I thought, *Let him be confused.* Even if I tried to hold on, he's stronger than me. And even if he weren't, a person can't hold on to another person forever. At some point, their muscles give out, or the authorities get called.

Would he try to kiss me good-bye, squeeze my hand? Better not.

Or what?

Or this pain sloshing back and forth between us will be permanent, suck us all down. Touch another person's skin, and Dad will never come home. There will never again be enough air. This family will stay broken, drown.

Dad said, "Well, sweetie, this is it," and patted the chaise a few safe inches away from my feet. Even that felt too close, but I'd built a wall between us that he couldn't cross.

"Have a good drive," I said.

Dad looked surprised, maybe even relieved, at my calm. He didn't force things, didn't make me stand up and give him a hug. I almost wished he would.

The game might have been over as soon as it started.

But Dad didn't need a hug from me. He just waved.

4.

"Was it okay?" Mom wants to know as soon as I get in the car. She reaches over and squeezes my thigh.

Clothes make it safe. I take a deep breath. Touching through clothes makes me nervous, but it can't wreck the game; it's important to stick to that rule.

"It was good."

"How's your stress?" she says lightly, as if that's a question every mother asks.

"Not too bad."

It's not entirely a lie. I managed to keep breathing.

I return Mom's touch by placing my hand on her sleeve. She could suddenly shift, but it's a calculated risk. Mom would notice if I never touched her at all.

"How were the dog portraits?"

"Furry," Mom says with a grimace.

Mom has a small business photographing weddings, senior portraits, and, yes, dogs. She used to do artistic photography, too, but it's been ages since she did her own work.

Even though Mom shouldn't have meddled, I say, "Thank you for getting Mandy as my Peer Pal."

"I didn't do that," she says, turning onto the steeply curving road that will take us back down the hill. "I might have if I'd thought of it. That's lucky for y'all!"

Could Mandy have requested *me*? The idea makes me floaty.

The heat and humidity have been working up to a fight all day, one big pressure cooker. By the time we pull into the driveway, heat lightning's started lashing out and thunderclouds have a chokehold on the sun.

The trees whip and creak with the wind. Almost every year during hurricane season, one of the big trees surrounding our house topples over. Dad would always trim them back to protect the roof and power lines, but every once in a while, the wind helps them do damage anyway.

In the den, Jordan's watching a wrestling match in the dark. Mom goes straight for the lamps, and Jordan cringes from the light like a vampire.

"Jordan, what have we said about food on the couch?" Mom says, and he glares at us over a bag of potato chips.

It's almost cute how his floppy hair and the bag frame his glower. Almost.

"Dad eats on the couch," Jordan says.

"Nice try," says Mom. "Dad's not here."

She goes for the bag, but Jordan pulls back and it rips at the top. Yellow, greasy crumbs fly all over Mom's upholstery and the Oriental rug.

For a moment, there's a crease in Mom's brow—maybe she's going to let Jordan have it. Then she sighs the crease away.

"This is your mess to clean up," Mom says, heading for the kitchen.

"I *am* cleaning up," Jordan says as he picks potato chip crumbs off his shirt and eats them.

I flop down as far from Jordan as the sofa will allow, and he tucks his feet more tightly under himself. Sometimes, I think he can sense that I need extra space. More often, I think it's his own thing, his line in the sand that no one, not even me, is allowed to cross.

Mom returns with the mini-vac like I knew she would.

"I thought you were going to spend the night over at Connor's," Mom says.

"I was."

"And?"

"His brother goes back to college soon. They're going fishing, them and their dad." His face couldn't be more flat, but he's watching the wrestlers with an intensity that gives me the creeps, as if he'd like to try those moves on Connor—or maybe on us.

"You couldn't go?" Mom says. "I would have let you go."

"It's a *family* thing," Jordan says. He's being manipulative, but it works. Mom doesn't even fuss at him to take his feet off the table as she runs the vac under his legs.

"It's probably for the best," she says. "I wouldn't want you out there in a storm."

"People fish in rain all the time," Jordan mutters, but Mom's already on her way to the kitchen with the vacuum bag. Gauging by her stride, she's on a mission.

"Mom's in cleaning therapy mode," I say, hoping to shift Jordan's mood. "I bet if we ask nice, she'll let us get pizza."

Jordan doesn't even look at me, but I'm the big sister. It's my job not to let him get to me. "Mom, can we get pizza?" I call to the kitchen.

"Sure."

Dad says ordering out is a lazy man's waste of money. Mom says if we can afford it, why not treat ourselves once in a while? Since Dad left, we've been ordering out at least once a week.

"What did I tell you?" I say, but Jordan immediately ups the volume on the wrestling match. "I spoke a single sentence, and I'm trying to get you pizza." I keep my voice light.

"I don't care," Jordan growls. "I can't hear."

"You know wrestling's just soap operas for men."

"I don't *care!*" he says again. I'm not even sure he heard me.

I reach for the remote where it sits at Jordan's side, but his hand clamps down on it. I almost touch him without thinking, but I catch myself in time, tuck my hands under my arms in case the impulse strikes again.

"Was it really Connor's brother that made you not go?" I ask low so Mom can't hear.

The thunderclouds rumble outside, but Jordan stays mum.

"It's going to storm," I say. "Maybe the power will go out. We could get the sleeping bags."

Jordan always loved when the power went out. Dad used to let us set up camp around the fireplace and play board games by the kerosene lamp.

"I'm watching this," Jordan says.

"I've got a bunch of school shopping to do this weekend. You want to come?"

"You're way too excited about school," he says. "You don't even care that he's gone."

"Of course I care. I can be excited *and* care."

But Jordan's hit a nerve. It feels wrong to be excited for a good thing that's come out of something so bad. If Dad had stayed, he wouldn't have allowed me to switch schools. If he does come home, he might even make me switch back.

The space around my fingers presses thicker than empty space should. If I reach across the sofa and squeeze Jordan's hand, will that mean our fates are sealed? I'll stay in school, and Dad will stay gone, and we can all stop wondering whether it's final or not and move on?

But that feels wrong too. I don't want to believe I have that kind of power.

I don't want to test it and find out.

This temptation to break my own rules is a traitor's impulse, like how drivers can get the sudden urge to speed up and fly off a bridge.

Jordan surprises me by turning the TV down. I'm afraid if I speak first, he'll startle and run. Finally, he says, "I'm not fun anymore. That's what Connor says. He says I'm mean." Jordan pauses. "And his parents think we need a break."

"Have you been mean?"

Jordan shrugs and turns the TV back up, even louder than before.

I know how he feels. When Mandy and I first drifted, it destroyed me, but I had no idea what to do about it. Everything had changed so quickly. I didn't know how to be myself anymore, so how was I supposed to be someone's friend?

"You know," I say, "sometimes it makes sense to show when you're upset, and sometimes it's better to act like stuff doesn't bother you. People want to have fun with their friends. They don't want to be dealing with problems all the time."

"Is that what you're learning at your fancy acting school?" Jordan says. "How to act like our family doesn't suck?"

I exhale, trying to free some of the tension that's crept up on me during our talk. "Should I leave you to your misery?"

"Please!"

I get up and head toward my room, but as soon as I enter the hallway, Jordan flies past me, his eyes red and dark. I press my back to the wall.

He doesn't want to talk. I can't change anything. It's okay to let him be.

I am a terrible sister.

I lean against the door he just slammed. "Jordan, are you okay?"

If he opens the door, I'll want to give him a hug. I'm all covered up, but our cheeks might touch, our hands brush, and that's not allowed. I should be able to give my crying brother a hug.

I almost hope he *will* fling the door open and hug me tight so I can prove to myself that I know when enough is enough. I'll stand there and let him hug me and this stupid game will be over and done.

My breath rasps in my throat, the sound of panic.

It's enough to make me cringe—*please, please no.*

I haven't had a panic attack in months, not since Dad left. Now the feeling's back, swirling around and making me dizzy—water's rising and I won't have time to suck down enough air. Mom used to give me a paper bag to blow into when this happened because as much as I felt like I couldn't breathe, in truth I was breathing too hard, drowning in air.

I slide down the wall outside Jordan's room, force myself to slow down and take smaller breaths. Freaking out now can't help anything. Mom and Dad have their problems. Everything's already changed. If all the bad stuff has already happened, why do I still feel so scared?

I am *not* going to panic. Not going to drown.

And I'm not going to ask Jordan to open his door.

I push up to my feet, steady my breathing, and head to my room, where Ophelia's the first thing I see, the Millais painting taped to my wall.

Ophelia in the water, sinking.

My clothes pulse with stress, so I peel them off, peel off the sticker that told Peter my name. The stressy clothes go out of sight, out of mind, in the dirty clothes hamper. The name tag . . . *should* go in the trash, but it's wrapped up with Peter and throwing it out doesn't feel right. I stick it to my desk and head into the bathroom that Jordan and I share, making sure his door's locked.

The hot water washes the tension away. I breathe in the steam, and it helps my lungs open, unclench. Jordan and

Mandy and Ophelia, my parents and school all slide off, swirl around at my feet, and leave me alone—with Peter.

He made me feel . . . on edge, alert and alive. That I can't throw away the stupid name tag is a bad sign. I'm *not* going to be touching him, that's clear. But something happened when he looked at me.

When we locked eyes, the ease of his stare and the welcome of his smile made me feel like one of two fixed points in a hurricane. The building could have crashed down around us as he smiled, and I wouldn't have noticed.

That can't be good.

5.

Mom said she'd take me school shopping, but by noon on Saturday, she's still in bed with a migraine. When I crack the door to her darkened room to ask how she's feeling, she whispers, "Why don't you try Mandy?"

I obsess over this idea for nearly an hour. I'm way out of practice with friends. At my old school there were girls who included me in group stuff, but no one I could call on a whim. When I finally do text Mandy, my heart beats so fast, I get dizzy. But I do it.

She texts back within five minutes, saying:

PLEASE, YES. Dying to get out.

The honk brings me outside, but instead of Mandy's "lame-ass" car, the driveway is full of a humongous, tricked-out, bright-red monster truck. Mandy leans out the passenger-side window, peering over giant sunglasses like a movie star.

"Like my ride?" she asks in a put-on Southern belle drawl.

"Ahem. My ride," says the driver, a hulking guy.

"Darlin', you *are* my ride," Mandy teases.

"That's enough, Scarlett," he says. He's handsome in a WWE kind of way—beefy muscles, square jaw, sleepy-cow eyes. He's got Birmingham man-hair—thick, side-swept hair grown a little too long all around, like it dreams of becoming a mullet but doesn't quite dare.

"This is Drew," Mandy says.

Even though he's smiling, Drew makes me nervous. His hands are as big as my face.

The truck is a Frankenstein—the paint job's meticulous, but it covers a jumble of parts that look like they're itching to reassemble themselves into a more comfortable arrangement. There's a huge gash in the passenger side that I pray came from a former life and not from Drew's driving.

I climb in behind Mandy and buckle myself in.

"Will your mom care I'm not driving?" Mandy asks. "I told Drew he should park up the block, but he was being stubborn." She squeezes Drew's bicep and he winces.

"Ow. Hi, Caddie, nice to meet you. How are you doing? I'm fine." He says it like an etiquette robot, programmed to give Mandy a lesson. She goes to pinch him again, but he catches her hand and presses it flat to her leg. Drew reaches his free hand back to me, and I burrow into my sleeves. I wave Muppet-like, side to side, and drop my hand back in my lap.

Drew's sleepy eyes look right through me in a way that makes me want to pull a bag over my head. He smiles like he knows all my secrets and finds them funny.

"I don't think Mom would care," I say, "but she's in bed anyway."

Only then does Mandy flash her lightning smile. "It's good to be hanging out with you again, Caddie. I've missed you." Relief washes through me.

I always felt like I needed Mandy more than she needed me. She's good at taking care of herself, never lets a problem get too big before she solves it. Mandy says what she thinks, does what she wants, and doesn't look back, whereas I have to check and recheck to make sure what I'm doing is safe.

It takes me a long time to say back to her, "I missed you too."

Drew attacks the curves on Cherokee Bend as if we're in an armored tank. Every year, at least a couple of cars fall off these winding roads. A cross will mark the broken place in the undergrowth where one crashed down toward the golf course, or a ribbon might ring an enormous tree in memory of a car that wrapped itself around its trunk.

If I hold these ugly images in my brain for too long,

they might happen to us. I need to erase them, so I breathe deep and imagine the bad thoughts floating away. It's an old game, one that comes so automatically I barely notice it anymore.

Mandy's telling me about the different juniors in theater. There are "the musical fiends . . . Hank's in with them, but he likes us better"; a trio of "melancholy babies" who are "all about the harshness of life. . . . It's like they live in a vampire novel but it's no fun because the vampires aren't even hot"; and a group Mandy calls "the show ponies . . . You know, the kids with the crazy stage moms who do pageants and spokesmodel contests and all that?" To distinguish herself from them, Mandy says, "Except they actually like it."

If Mandy quizzes me later, I'll remember every word. I'm a good listener, even with the mental background noise.

Drew takes a sharp curve, and we shift as his tire skirts a broken place at the edge of the pavement. All my muscles clench. *Please let us be safe.*

"Could you maybe slow down, just a little?" I ask, but Drew doesn't hear me, and I don't have the guts to ask again. Once we're on Highway 280, it's better. Drew still drives too fast, but at least he's got a straight lane to do it in.

He takes us to Little Professor in Homewood because they've got a good theater section. When we get there,

Drew goes in search of some guitar chord book while Mandy leads me to the plays. There are eight different editions of *Hamlet* to choose from, but we're supposed to get one that keeps the original punctuation.

"Which version are you getting?" I ask.

Mandy waves a CliffsNotes *Hamlet* in my face.

"Haven't you read the actual play?"

She shrugs. "I get what happens. Dude wants to avenge his father's death. Dude says, 'To be or not to be.' Dude fights some people. Dude dies."

"There's more to it than that," I say, picking up a special edition that looks straight out of Elizabethan England, old spellings and all.

"I know, but I don't care about Hamlet. I want to be Ophelia. She gets to go crazy." My heart beats too fast, and I feel like Mandy's dropped a boulder in my stomach, but of course she wants Ophelia.

"There are never enough parts for girls." I flip to a speech of Ophelia's. I've read it over and over, but the old-fashioned spellings give it new color.

"Nadia casts girls as guys all the time," Mandy says. "I mean, as a new person, you're more likely to be a page or something, but it won't be because you're a girl."

This is what I've been listening for but not wanting to hear—that I'm too late to the party and don't even have a chance at a good part.

"I know what I want," I say, closing the book. "If

you're done, we can go."

"Yeah, I'm ready," Mandy says. She tosses the CliffsNotes, grabs a copy of the special edition, and tucks it under her arm like she planned to buy it all along.

"Sure that's not going to hurt your brain?" Drew asks when he sees Mandy's book, and I bristle. Mandy might not be a *scholar*, but that's choice, not a lack of intelligence.

Mandy smiles at me. "Caddie thinks it's good."

She links her arm through mine, pulling me close. Her hand slides down close to mine, and I gasp, jerk away.

"Whoa," says Mandy, like I'm a horse, "easy, girl."

My heart wants a breath for every beat—so much air—but I won't let it trick me. I make my voice gentle, no stress. "I don't like anyone to touch me lately." The best lies have a little truth in them. "It's weird, but I laid out in the sun the other day . . ."

Mandy knows my pasty skin never tans.

"It was dumb, but I thought with school starting . . ." I let her see me embarrassed. Making it part of the act takes its power away. "I got sun poisoning." Her eyes dart to my super-pale hands. "I mean, I wasn't even out long enough to burn, but I got these red bumps. That's why the long sleeves. So gross. And it still hurts."

"Yowch," Mandy says, happy to keep her distance now that we're talking about skin bumps. "You've got to take care of yourself, girl."

I nod. No kidding.

Mandy decides our next stop should be Ragamuffin, a consignment shop in Southside where we can get rehearsal clothes on the cheap. Drew speeds through the Red Mountain Expressway Cut, the rust-red corridor that was blasted from the mountain, and there's Vulcan, the Roman god of the forge. If a pagan can be a patron saint, he's Birmingham's. He's the largest cast iron statue in the world, and he towers over his anvil wearing only an apron so his naked butt moons Homewood.

As he drives, Drew shifts his hand back and forth between Mandy's thigh and the gearshift. They touch so easily.

"Peter says hi," Mandy says.

"What?" My voice cracks.

Mandy's fiddling with her phone. "I texted that we were out shopping. He says hi."

"He's the one who messed with your car, right?" I try to sound nonchalant.

"Ri-ight," Mandy says, eyeing me with suspicion, and I immediately realize how stupidly fake I must sound. Mandy watched me meet Peter yesterday, and it's not like I met a billion other people.

"You heard about the Great Car Caper," Drew says, laughing.

Mandy twists around to stare at me. "You like him," she crows. *"You! Like! Peter!"*

I shift my eyes toward Drew—*Hello, male in the car.* In the rearview, his eyes are amused.

"I don't like him. I mean, I don't *dis*like him. I don't even know—"

"Lies! You like him. Now talk. How can you be attracted to Peter?" asks Mandy.

"I never said I was."

"But you *are*," Mandy says. "That's clear."

I sink deeper into my seat.

"He's tall," she says. "I'll give you that. He's got a certain boyish charm."

Drew clears his throat.

"I'm just trying to empathize," Mandy says. "Please. I could never go for someone so—what's the word I'm looking for? Cocky?"

"Peter's not cocky. Peter's a nerd," Drew says.

"I know! Where does he get off being nerdy *and* full of himself? It's like he thinks he lives in some kind of alterna-world where nerds are cool."

"He does," Drew says, smiling wide. "It's called arts school." And I wonder—what's a monster trucker like Drew doing in arts school anyway?

Mandy rolls her eyes, but she smiles, too. "Okay, *that's* not the problem. The *problem*—" Drew doesn't slow for the turn onto University Boulevard, and Mandy has to swing forward to absorb the curve. She rights herself and goes on. "The *problem* is that Peter's nutty."

"I said I'm not interested, so it doesn't even matter." But I would like to know what qualifies a person as "nutty" in Mandy's book.

"Don't be bitchy, Mandy," Drew says, and he looks bummed by whatever he expects her to say.

"I hate that word," Mandy says.

"That's why I used it."

The what-happens-next? of the moment works like a vacuum, swallowing all sound, all breath.

Mandy zaps Drew with one of her lightning stares. He should be a sizzling pulp melting into the seat, but I guess he's immune. Mandy turns back to me, and the next moment floods in.

"You're talking about stuff that's private," Drew says, but Mandy holds firm.

"No," she says. "*You* are. All *I* meant was he's a goof, like that crap that he pulled with my car. But now that you mention it . . ."

"Mention *what*?" I ask.

Drew eyes me sternly in the rearview mirror. "It's Peter's own business."

"Not if my friend's thinking about dating him," Mandy says.

"*Peter's* your friend," Drew says.

"*Nobody's thinking about dating anyone,*" I say, but I can't help asking, "What 'stuff' are you talking about?"

Drew says, "It's from a long time ago."

"Not that long," says Mandy. "He had to go for counseling."

She doesn't know I had counseling for my panic attacks in middle school, back when Dad first threatened to split. What would she think of that?

"Mandy, Peter's my best friend," Drew says. "He's a good guy. Can we drop it?"

He zooms into Ragamuffin's parking lot, completely ignoring their speed bump. It makes my teeth clack.

"I love Peter," Mandy says, "but can we agree that he's not well? You *saw* what he did to my car!"

"*My idea!*" Drew growls, shaking Mandy's thigh. It's playful, but he's frustrated. "You can't hold a grudge against him for that."

"Fine, then I'll hold a grudge against you," Mandy says sharply. She hops down from the truck but says, "Ah-ah-ah," when Drew opens his door. "You, Mr. Idea Man, can wait outside. The ladies have shopping to do."

"You've got to be kidding me."

"Consider this your punishment for calling me 'bitchy,' *and* for telling me what I can talk about, AND for my CAR."

"Mandy, play nice," Drew says.

"Lady time," Mandy says with a flourish and sashays toward the store.

Their fight came on so quickly, I feel like I caused it somehow. I turn to give Drew a sympathy smile, but he's in his own world, fuming.

Inside, Mandy seems oblivious to the tension we just left. "Peter's not a bad guy," she says as we navigate the narrow aisles. "Drew's right about that."

"It doesn't matter because I'm not interested."

Mandy smiles knowingly. "You're not *that* good of an actress, Caddie."

Then I'll have to get better. I already feel like I'm one touch away from having all my craziness exposed. The last thing I need is a public, puppy dog crush on a guy who shows affection through wrestling. I'd fall to pieces if he shook my hand.

And then I see the gloves.

It's not healthy, something in me whispers, but it's better than being exposed.

"What do we think of these?" I ask, pulling on the evening-length lavender gloves. I push up my sleeves to make room.

"Ooh, *très chic*," Mandy says. "What are you, going to the opera?"

"They're kind of fabulous, right?"

She reaches out and runs her fingers along them, down my forearm to the back of my hand. The gloves work like armor. Everything's covered up safe.

"What if I wore them at school? They could be my thing—a signature."

Mandy laughs. "You afraid of not being weird enough for the artists?"

"Says the girl with pink hair."

She fingers her pink streak and grins. "Oh, I'm *aware*. But I like it."

"Maybe I like the gloves."

"Then go for it," she says. "You know, the pink hair was partly inspired by you."

"What?"

"Remember that time you suggested we wear pink for a week, just to see if people would notice?"

"Which they did on the very first day."

That hadn't been one of *my games*, just a game, in fifth grade. Mandy played along, and we weren't the least bit afraid of people making fun because together we were so cool.

"You were always good at that," Mandy says, "coming up with the zany thing nobody else would dare do."

That doesn't sound like me now at all, but I like that it's how she remembers me.

I hold up the gloves. "You won't tell anyone that I only started wearing these in time for school?"

"What? Caddie's always worn gloves! She's a real trendsetter. You watch. It's going to be all evening-gown gloves at New York Fashion Week this year."

"Don't overdo it."

"Who? Me? Never."

Mandy takes my gloved hand and swings it between us like we're kids again. The gloves are more than protection. They're a secret, and secrets work like glue between friends.

6.

"You're not wearing those to school, are you?" Jordan says, indicating my gloves.

"Is this a Mandy-Caddie thing?" Mom asks.

We're eating dinner together on the night before school starts, "like a family." We're doing our best impression. Mom's lit the candles in the dining room, poured a glass of wine for herself and sparkling grape juice for Jordan and me. The pork tenderloin rests in Dad's place at the head of the table.

I nod, yes, a Mandy-Caddie thing, like wearing pink for a week. It makes Mom happy to think that Mandy and I are getting closer again.

We are. If I can keep from messing it up.

Mom lifts her glass. "I'm so excited for you."

I clink glasses with her—super classy in my gloves. "Me too."

I make myself smile, but inside I'm a mess. What if Mandy's friends don't want me to sit with them at lunch? What if they don't care, but there's no room at the table? What if the only seat's next to Peter? What if I choke in acting class and Nadia says, "There's no hope for you"?

And on top of all that, there's the guilt. I wouldn't have this opportunity if Dad had stayed.

I've been so fixated on Mandy these last few days, as if being friends with her might bring me back to normal. As if it might be like before . . . before middle school, before stupid games in my head, before Dad even thought about leaving.

But here we are talking about Mandy and me over dinner, and Dad's still so gone.

There's a missed call and a text on my phone when I get back upstairs.

The text is from Mandy:

Can't wait for tomorrow! Happy first day!

I text back:

Thx! Can't wait.

The call . . . is from Dad.

I sense it before I check.

There's a voice mail, but I already know what it will

say: *Have a great first day. Wish I could be there. I'm thinking of you.*

Something from the "good dad" lexicon.

But it won't mean anything. He doesn't get to be Dad of the Year at a distance.

Mandy would delete it without listening, and she wouldn't think twice about it after.

But what if it *is* a real message?

What if he's in trouble, and my number was the last one he dialed? He went off the road, missed a curve on the highway, and drove into a wall. He's got night blindness— it could happen.

What if he's sick and needs help? He's too delirious to dial 911, but he managed to type in my name?

What if he's calling to say he was wrong, the move was a terrible mistake, and he needs my advice about how to convince Mom to take him back?

All my what-ifs steal my breath, compel me to check. I dial voice mail and tap in my password.

"Hi, sweet." Dad's voice sounds garbled on the message, like he's calling from underwater. "I wanted to check in. Your mom reminded me it's your first day of school."

Of course she did.

"I never missed a first day before. It feels strange, if I'm honest."

Good. That's exactly how it should feel.

"I'd say call me back, but it's almost eleven. You'll probably be getting to bed soon—or maybe you already are."

I check the time on my phone. He was an hour off. Dad keeps forgetting the time difference, like wherever he is, it must be that time everywhere.

"I just wanted to wish you luck and say I hope you'll be happy with your decision."

Well, that's big of him, but it's so passive-aggressive, like he's saying, you probably won't be happy, and when you're not, let's remember who told you so.

He's trying, a kinder part of me whispers.

He goes on, "When you decide to stop punishing me, Caddie, I *would* like to talk. Remember, Daddy loves you."

End of message.

I feel a bit of guilt. We haven't spoken more than a couple of times since he left, and only when Mom forced the phone into my hand. But guilt's what he wants me to feel. Dad's good at that, making the whole world feel sorry for not being who Charles Finn wants them to be.

I take two deep breaths, slow ones like I've learned.

Dad didn't have to leave. Even if he and Mom did need a break, that's no reason to move so far away. How are they supposed to fix things when he's in a whole other state?

I think about the night of our big fight last March when he disappeared, and immediately shove that thought down. *It's in his nature,* something in me whispers, *to go far away and never come back.*

Dad moved here for Mom's family, but we barely ever saw his—once a year, sometimes less. Dad and his father fight. He calls his mother weak-willed. His sister split the country ten years back. It always worried me that such distance could grow up between people who were supposed to love one another.

Dad is totally capable of trading an old, banged-up life for a shiny, new one.

I curl up on my bed and place the phone on the nightstand. It would make him happy if I called. It might even be nice to talk to him, to remember that he's still alive and out there in the world, that he hasn't been sucked into some dark abyss.

Outside, crickets, cicadas, and frogs sing in chorus. A train whistle sounds.

Dad used to read to me before bed when I was little, and if we heard the whistle, Dad would say, "A train's coming to bring you good dreams."

Tonight the whistle just sounds lonely. I don't think I'm going to be falling asleep anytime soon.

7.

The academy's halls shake with bodies swinging one another around by the arm, bodies colliding and losing their balance so I have to dodge, press myself to the wall. Mouths kiss, limbs crush.

One couple shuffles down the hall, the guy's arms wrapped around the girl from behind so they can barely move. A dancer does a pirouette into two of her friends, slides down their legs, and grabs at their ankles. They drag her, pretending not to notice, for maybe ten feet, while a couple of guys use her butt as a pommel horse.

Artists. They want to touch everything.

A tremor that starts in my stomach makes my legs go shaky, my hands ten times worse, so I clasp them together, close my eyes, force my face to reflect a calm I don't feel.

There is plenty of space, lots of space, between my skin and theirs.

I win the most-clothes contest, with jeans and long sleeves that cover the tops of my gloves. It makes sense everyone's nearly naked—it's still sweltering outside—and compared to my old school the dress code is . . . lax. One flock of girls has cleared out a space in the hall to stage a hip-hop dance. They wear nothing but tank tops and booty shorts, no shoes even, so maybe they have dance class first? Or maybe that's just the academy.

If the actors dress like this, I'm in trouble.

I squeeze against the lockers to pass them, some kind of campy superhero with my gloves on, scaling a wall.

At the far hall where the juniors and seniors have lockers, not everyone's dressed for the heat. The seniors are dressed for a Renaissance Faire. The girls mostly have on long skirts, but they're showing extra cleavage to make up for it. Posters every few feet say, SENIORS RULE THE FALL! LIFE'S A CARNIVALE! and FAIRE OR NOT, WE'VE REACHED THE TOP!

I slip through the mass of bodies, trying to find my locker without getting sucked in. I realize I'm scanning the crowd for Peter's face, but I'm not sure whether seeing him would be good or bad.

One tall senior girl blocks my path, corset-squashed boobs uncomfortably close to my face. "Who leaked the theme?" she says, grabbing my hand. The shock of the touch rattles me before I remember I have armor.

"No," I say, pulling my gloved hand out of her grip. "I—no one leaked. I just wear these."

She breaks into a relieved laugh. "Dang it! Am I paranoid or what? All right, well, good morrow to ye!"

The idea of me wearing gloves, just because, doesn't faze her. She turns away but keeps talking, "Wait, what does 'morrow' mean? Morning or tomorrow? I'm not going to make any sense all day!" If I didn't know better, I'd think she was drunk.

Mandy's squeal—"Finally! Where were you?"—makes me turn. She's waiting by my locker. Drew slouches beside her, going over his schedule.

"I was afraid Boob-a-licious was going to suffocate you in her cleavage," she says.

"Thank God!" I say. "I was starting to get dizzy."

"I thought I'd missed you. Don't go into lunch without me. We'll go together so you can sit by me."

Drew finally looks up and says, "Mandy, she's not an infant."

"It's not *your* first day," Mandy says.

"Thank you, thank you," I tell Mandy, opening my locker. If the halls are any indication, lunch will be anarchy.

Drew's eyes skate over me like he's not aware, or at least not concerned, that I can see him looking. "Still with the gloves?" he says, his eyes crinkled with humor or scorn, I can't tell. Mandy promised not to tell that the gloves are a new thing, but Drew sure didn't.

"I can't believe you're actually here," Mandy says. "My academy friends are great, but it's not the same as that person who's known you forever, you know?"

Drew makes a show of clearing his throat.

I nod, trying not to let on how stupid happy she just made me.

A bell rings, and Mandy says, "We'd better get going. I'll see you at lunch, and in acting, of course."

With people streaming toward class in both directions, the hall seems to narrow and press. Mine and Mandy's schedules are entirely different except for our block of theater at the end of the day.

Drew takes my schedule. "We both have English first," he says. "Here, I'll walk you."

"Oh, you don't have to."

"I do, kind of, since we're both walking in the same direction."

He rests his elbow on my shoulder, which tugs at my hair, making my head tilt toward him. I want to wash the touch away, but it isn't skin touching skin. I can't let this get worse or I'll have to start wearing a hood.

Let it go, let it go.

"You're shaking," Drew says, dropping his arm. "Are you that freaked out?"

"I get nervous," I say. "I'll be okay."

"Everyone here is some kind of freak," Drew says. "You'll fit right in."

"Um, thanks?"

"I'm serious," says Drew. "Mandy's in love with you, so you must have something going for you."

"We haven't been friends for a long time." I can't believe I'm confiding in Drew.

"That's not how she talks about you," he says. "She talks like you're her long-lost twin who got kidnapped by pirates and finally she's found you again."

"Really?"

"And truly."

At the top of a staircase, Drew gestures toward our classroom door like a true southern gentleman. As I pass, he says, "Watch out for Mandy's feelings, okay? She's missed you."

There's a hint of warning in his fixed jaw, but then he looks away. I wonder what Mandy's told Drew about me, whether she's missed me the way he makes it sound. I'm at a loss for words, but I nod, slip past him, and find an open seat toward the back. He sits beside me but keeps his eyes forward.

At the end of class, Drew smiles like we're old friends. "You've got chemistry next? Mr. Kiernan. He can be fun. I'll point you in the right direction."

He walks me to the nearest staircase. "Take a right at the foot of the stairs, and straight on till morning."

"Hey, that's . . ."

"*Peter Pan.*" He smiles at my surprise. "Saw the musical in eighth grade. Changed my life."

"*Peter PAN* changed your life?"

"In middle school, I was such a jock. When I told my buds I was applying to BAA, they lost it and asked if I was gay, but I said, 'You know where there are a ton of straight girls fighting over a limited supply of straight dudes? Theater.'"

"And that worked?"

"No, they kept being total dicks." He winks. "More fun for me."

As he turns and walks away, it hits me: I might just have made friends with Drew.

Acting class hasn't started, but this is my first acting challenge—to act like I'm comfortable entering the lunchroom at Mandy's side, sitting with her friends. And the gloves are just for fun. I'm the kind of girl born to quirkiness, who spreads whimsy like the common cold.

Like Livia. She's first to the table, having brought her own lunch, a plastic container of earthy orange paste and a bag of what look like giant bronze grapes.

Livia's dressed all in green—always, according to Mandy—and it brings out the warmth of her dark skin. The black girls at my old school mostly stayed together—a lot of Birmingham is still weirdly divided by race—but looking around the dining hall, it's cool how everybody's mixed in together. Livia wears her hair in big swirly loops like an avatar from one of Jordan's video games. Little-girl green barrettes frame her face.

"Hi, Mandy," she says, and then locks on to me. "I know who you are."

Does acting work on other actors? I'm about to find out.

"You must be the one who wears green," I say. "Livia, right? I'm—"

"No, don't tell me." She holds her fingertips to her temples like she's going to pluck my name out of the air.

"This is Caddie," Mandy says, interrupting Livia's trance.

"Caddie," Livia says as if I'm not so much a person as a concept. "Okay, here's the impression I get . . ."

"No, Livia," Mandy says. "It's stressy enough being new."

"It's a good one," Livia says. "I like her, first impression." She's about to reveal the mystery of me to me. "You want to fit in, do the right thing. It can make people uncomfortable," she says, "but I find it refreshing."

So, I come off as desperate, which she finds refreshing—like wet wipes, or cucumber salad. Being friends with Mandy means making friends with this hippy-dippy girl who's annoyingly . . . perceptive.

Mandy rolls her eyes and digs into her "South of the Border Salad," which is actually nacho chips slathered with processed cheese and salty ground beef. "Livia's on a 'living on impulse' kick."

"You try to shut off all your filters," Livia explains. "When an idea comes to mind, you speak it. When the impulse comes to take action, you take it. It's harder than it sounds."

"No," I say, "that sounds hard, impossible even—"

Before the words fully leave my mouth, Livia has placed one of her grape things in her spoon and launched it across the dining hall directly into the back of a guy standing in line. He's got heavy eyebrows and a distinct lack of lips. The skin where his lips should be curls back from his braces as if simply closing his mouth might hurt, making his teeth look even bigger than they already are.

"That's Oscar," Mandy says.

"Wait, was he in—?"

She nods. He played Lance Dalton's son in *Monkey Boy*. If there's a kid who gets to do that in all of Alabama, it only makes sense that he's Mandy's friend.

Oscar looks around until he finds Livia waving, then gives her a mock-threatening fist pump, mouthing the words, "I'm coming for you."

"Sometimes, impulses can get you in trouble," Livia says, but she looks thrilled. *I'm* thrilled to be sitting across from the girl who just pegged a weird fruit at a guy who played the son of a giant movie star.

"What are you eating?" Mandy asks, pointing to the battle grapes.

"Scuppernongs," Livia says. "They grow in my backyard. Here."

I decline, but Mandy says, "Don't be a wuss."

Livia scrapes the mushy insides from the skins with her teeth. I cut mine in half with a fork and knife first so I won't have to take off my gloves. The jelly inside is sweet and tangy, but the seeds are bitter.

Even Livia's food is out-quirking me. Livia hasn't said a word about my gloves.

The rest of the group takes seats one by one. Hank is handsome, and also a bit sly. With a slick pompadour, he's old-timey movie-star classic. "We've heard so much about you," he says, holding his hand out for mine. When I reach out to shake, he bends down and kisses my knuckles. I feel pressure and a warm breath through the gloves, but that's okay.

"Classy," he says of the gloves as he lets me go. "And what have you heard about me? Did Mandy warn you how deadly handsome I am?"

He *is* handsome, and it might be deadly, except that he makes my gaydar go bleep.

Instead of waiting for an answer, he launches into a blow-by-blow of his attempt to get Nadia to consider producing *Avenue Q*, a Broadway musical where puppets in New York City sing about racism and have puppet sex.

"She says it's too raunchy. I mean, puppets! It's not like anybody's going to get turned on by that!"

"I don't know," says Drew, shoving his tray between Mandy's and mine and hovering behind us, "I always had a thing for Miss Piggy." He pinches Mandy.

"Tell me you're not comparing me to a pig!"

My fork digs so hard into a corn chip, it breaks through and cracks against my plate. Mandy gets enough harassment from her mom about her weight. She doesn't need it from her boyfriend.

Mandy pouts at Drew and he laughs. "Because you're both bossy! That's all I meant!" he says, crouching down beside her and trying for a hug. She shoves at the top of his head. "And violent."

"Bite me," Mandy says.

He does, on the meat of her shoulder, with a lot of growling from him and squealing from her until she holds a milk carton over his head. It rattles me, seeing them play like that, and it's not just the touching. My oldest and probably best friend in spite of the time lapse trades saliva on a regular basis with this person who looks like a man. Drew has a five o'clock shadow, and it's only eleven.

Instead of sitting in one of the empty seats, my new buddy Drew swings a chair around from the table behind us to place between Mandy and me. It doesn't quite fit, so he grabs the back of my chair and scoots it—and me— over to make room.

"Rude," Mandy says, but it's clear that she thinks he's adorable.

Before I can fully settle into my new spot, hands clamp down on my shoulders.

I shriek, which makes everyone laugh.

It's Lance Dalton, Jr. He's made it through the line and put his tray on the table behind us in order to have his hands free to maul me. He's not touching skin, but it still makes my breath rasp. "God, you scared me."

"Oscar Morgan," he says, swinging his tray of nachos over my head.

He braces his hands on the table to clamber over the back of the chair on my Drew-free side, rocking the table so hard Livia's juice sloshes out the top of her glass. He barely makes it over, almost wiping the bottom of his sneaker on my face. Then, he plops down, face too close to mine, and beams like he planned it that way.

"And you are?"

"Caddie."

He holds his hand out, so I shake, and it takes muscle to keep him from using the handshake to lean even closer. "I saw you in that movie," I say.

"Ahh, yes," he says. "Thanks."

"She didn't say she liked it," says Mandy.

"Oh," he says. "Well, Caddie, did you like it?" But I get the sense he doesn't have a sliver of doubt what I thought.

"You were funny."

"They cut my best scene," he says. "There used to be a dramatic part where I cried." I get the sense everybody else at the table has heard this many times over. "Mm-hm," he says. "I can cry on command. It's how I booked my first commercial. 'Band-Aids make it better.'"

He crumples his face, takes both my gloved hands in his, and just as Mandy says, "Not again," he starts weeping, actually weeping, in front of me. If everyone at this school already knows how to cry on command, I'm done for.

"He's trying to impress you," says Drew.

"Sensitivity is one thing," Hank says, "but nobody wants a crybaby."

Livia bangs her hands down on the table, making me jump, and says, "Impulse!"

Nobody else even looks at her.

"I'm not a crybaby," Oscar says to Hank, feigning hurt. "Dude, that's acting. Maybe you should try it sometime."

"You're just mad I don't find you attractive."

"I am," Oscar says, switching gears fast to play this new game. "Hank, you got me. I'm a mess about it. I cry myself to sleep."

"That's not acting. It's a party trick," says . . . Peter. He's standing across from Oscar, less than three feet away. Our eyes meet, and his smile falters for a second, then goes back to normal.

Is that surprise to find me sitting here? Good surprise, or disappointment?

"Hi, Jumpy," he says.

Why should he care if I sit here or not? It's all in my head.

"Oh!" says Oscar, waving his arms in front of him like he's gearing up to wrestle. "Peter's looking for a smackdown. Tell us, then, oh enlightened one, what is acting?"

"Acting requires empathy," Peter says, playing along, "some emotional engagement, listening to your partner."

"Acting," Oscar says, "requires doing what the director asks you to do *when* he asks so that you can get paid."

"Or she," Livia says. "Your director might be a she!"

"All right," says Peter to Oscar. "Just don't let Nadia hear you say that."

"I'm not an idiot," Oscar says. "You know what else I won't do? I won't ask her to write me a check for every time that Band-Aid commercial ran either."

"A hit, a very palpable hit!" Peter says, quoting *Hamlet*. He fakes like Oscar stabbed him and falls into the seat across from us.

"Nerd," Mandy says.

"You've been studying," says Oscar.

"Don't doubt it. So, Caddie," Peter says. "First day, and you've landed here." He shakes his head like I'm in trouble—the kind of trouble that leads to bear hugs? I contract with the teasing rush of that idea.

Do. Not. Touch.

"Let's all make her feel *welcome*," Mandy says threateningly.

"Oh, she's *welcome*," Peter says. "I feel sorry for her is all. Girl doesn't know what she's gotten herself into."

"I do," I say, feeling brave. Sure, he's teasing me, but that's part of belonging here. "I've gotten into an on-command-crying, impulse-following, Shakespeare-joke-making, puppet-sex-watching cult of theater nerds, and I'm actually pretty happy about it."

Peter smiles at my verbal gymnastics. On the rare occasions when my brain lets me speak without thinking, it's one of my special skills.

Livia motions to me. "Are you coming to Bard?"

"Of course she is," says Oscar.

"*If* I get cast."

"But even if you don't, you can do a scene," Livia says, like it's a given that any scene I might do would be good enough to make it. Maybe that *is* a given for anyone else here. "Hank and I placed second last year with *Romeo and Juliet.*"

"We were *lovers*," he says dramatically. "I was very convincing." Livia giggles and reaches up to stroke his hair. Hank pretends not to notice Livia's hand as it crawls across his cheek, and it turns into a game. Her fingers pet his lips as he mumbles through them, "What part do you want?"

I keep my eyes on Hank, but I swear I can feel Mandy's eyes on me. "I don't really care," I lie. "I'd be happy with anything."

Hank nods. "You should read for Ophelia." Then he says to the table, "She looks like she could go crazy, doesn't she?"

He means well, but that's the last thing I need to hear.

"I bet Caddie wants Gertrude," Mandy says. That's Hamlet's mother. She's just married Claudius, her dead husband's brother and also—surprise—his murderer. It's a good part, but it's not Ophelia.

I lie. "Yeah, I'm not sure what part I want."

"*You* could be a good Gertrude," Mandy says to Livia, and it feels like she's taken Gertrude away from me as punishment for not going along.

"Give me devious," Mandy says. Livia purses her lips and screws up her eyes.

"I think I want one of the man parts, though," Livia says. "Or maybe Ophelia."

Mandy's face stays cool. "I think you should go for the friend guy." She makes it sound like a compliment that she thinks Livia could handle such a good part.

"Horatio," I say. "Hamlet's friend?"

"Yeah, that guy," Mandy says. "We should cast the whole thing right now and see how close we get!"

"Hey, what kind of a name is Caddie?" Oscar says. It's as if he's physically wrenched the conversation back in his direction, but I'm grateful for it.

"It's short for Cadence, family name."

"Ah, I was thinking maybe your parents were golfers." Oscar puts on his best country club voice, stands, thrusts his pelvis toward me, and says, "Hey, Caddie, want to carry my club?" He mimes gripping an optimistically large "club" and swings his hand around in the air between us.

Everybody laughs, more at his idiocy than at me, but still, they're all watching to see how I'll respond. I should say something clever, should *not* care. My face shouldn't be going hot.

Drew's sleepy smile taunts me—this wouldn't faze Mandy—while Peter leans in and says, "He can't help himself. He's not used to girls speaking to him. Mostly they just cry and run."

Oscar's thigh knocks my shoulder.

"Could you give me some space?" I sound snobbish, restrained. I can't laugh like the rest of them do—it's on my face like a billboard, I'm certain, how odd I am.

Mandy still has her arm around Drew. She's letting me fend for myself. Why shouldn't she? If I can't handle her friends, maybe I'm not meant to be one of them.

"I'm sorry," Oscar says, putting on another character, a lovelorn one, "I just want to be close to you," and he comes in low, balancing his hands on my thigh.

It's not about me anymore. It's about Livia and Hank, who are giggling, Mandy and Drew, watching and waiting, and Peter, who isn't impressed enough yet with how far Oscar's willing to go for a laugh.

Oscar squeezes between me and the table, slides himself onto my lap so I'm pinned to my seat, and pushes me closer to Drew, who says, "Dude, watch out," through laughter.

I can't let Oscar touch the places where clothes shift and fail.

Peter's exactly across from me. He looks annoyed, but everyone else is showing their teeth. It's hilarious—stupid, but hilarious. Hank snorts milk from his nose. Livia drops her face in her hands.

I'm a clenched fist trying to pass for an open palm. Smiling hurts. My teeth grind. Even the little muscles beside my ears feel tight.

"Wow," Oscar says, "your thighs are really—hard. No, wait, sorry, that's something else!" He half-stands to straddle my thigh.

I'm supposed to say something funny to put Oscar in his place—that's what Mandy would do—but my brain's blank. Oscar rocks like a kid getting a pony ride, except that he groans and yips, "Giddy-yap!" and "Yee-haw!"

Livia gives a half-hearted, "Oscar, enough," and Mandy finally speaks up.

"Oscar! Stop being a jackass!"

Without any input from my brain, my elbow jabs into his ribs and my free foot kicks at his leg. He curses and grabs my thigh to balance himself.

"Get *off* me!" comes out of my mouth before I can remember to be cool, to be one of them, and I shove at him.

Oscar grabs my hands, but the gloves twist in his grip, and one of the seams where the thumb meets the first finger tears. Like a burn, his thumb presses my skin.

I pull the other way, and he's small but he's strong and it's not enough.

Someone, Peter, yells, "Hey! Let her go!"

Oscar releases my hand, but before I can push him away, he catches my cheeks between his fingers and thumb, squeezing the flesh against my teeth. "That hurt," he says. "I don't let guys or girls hurt me. Okay?"

I do not nod or speak. I bring my arms up between us, twist away. My hand pulses where he touched my skin, my cheeks hurt where he squeezed—the wave of panic threatens to choke me, spill out at my eyes, but I'm not about to cry in front of him.

Peter's come around to our side. He drags Oscar off my lap and says, "You're not as funny as you think you are." He holds Oscar by his shirt, and Drew looks poised to come between them.

"Stop acting all Superman," Mandy says to Peter. "Caddie can handle herself."

Peter lets Oscar go and kneels down by me. "Are you okay?" he asks, and reaches for the place between my finger and thumb where Oscar pressed—a splotch of red has flown up to the surface to see what's up here, what's going on? I yank the hand away. He's too helpful, too kind. He could be the kindest person in the world and I still couldn't let him touch me.

"I've got to go," I say. Time's rushing forward. If I can wash Oscar's touch away, maybe whatever's set in motion will reverse itself. I *have* to believe that can work or else I've lost.

The table's gone quiet. My reaction to Oscar, the rawness of my voice when I pushed him, was over the top. He was just playing. That's what this group does. They play.

Drew looks amused, but in a secret way. His smile floats in the air. Mandy's annoyed, but I can't tell with whom. Maybe with all of us.

Oscar's rubbing his ribs where I elbowed him. Peter hovers. And my frenzied mind is telling me, *Get out of here, hurry, please hurry!*

"You don't have to leave," Peter says. "He can leave."

I shake my head. I want to be part of their group, not split it up.

How many other tables are paying attention to my scene? The panic ripples, eager to swallow me.

"No, it's not— I just realized what time it is." I stand and pick up my tray. "Y'all, thanks for letting me sit with you." I smile at the table. "I'll try not to cause more than one scene a week."

Livia smiles to reassure me. All of them laugh except Peter.

"Oscar," I say, because I have to say something. The tension's too high to breathe if I don't. "I'm sorry if I hurt you, but that was too much."

Drew does a Miss Piggy voice, "Hi-yah!" and karate chops the air.

Oscar looks at me like I'm an alien, but he nods and says, "Okay, yeah, sorry." I think he's mostly sorry about getting in trouble with Peter, but he'll be keeping his distance at least.

"Okay, later. I'll see y'all in acting." I've been avoiding Mandy's eyes, but I can't resist glancing at her before I leave.

She looks worried.

8.

My eyes in the mirror seem too far away, and the air pulses in tandem with the blood in my temples, my wrists. Touching the wall, touching the faucet takes effort. If I stop thinking about breathing, I'll stop doing it.

This energy has to go somewhere. I could break the mirror, slam my hand against it, scream. I reach for the water instead and turn it as hot as it will go.

I used to do this all the time back in middle school when I'd lost one of my games and couldn't accept the consequences. I would wash away the game and my fears until my skin turned red and raw. Sometimes it would bleed.

The hot water burns, but that feels right. *Okay, it's okay.*

I start with my hands, then move on to my face. Washing doesn't take away the sense of a seal being broken, of

Pandora's box being opened and the monsters spilling out, but I have to believe it can help, or I'm lost.

I can't afford to start doing this again—it takes up a suspicious amount of time for one thing, and it shows. The cracked and bleeding skin made Mom and Dad take me to a doctor in sixth grade—for allergies, they thought, but I'm not allergic to anything.

"It's so strange," Mom said. "What else could be causing it?"

I managed to change the game before they could figure it out, replacing the washing with silent thoughts up in my head—a prayer, *please, don't touch.*

If the washing comes back, I'll know I've really lost control.

I should make it a rule that accidental touching doesn't count, but my body's telling me it does. That it *might,* which is just as bad.

The girl in the mirror touches her face, presses the red places under her eyes, smoothes her brow and tries to wipe the tension from her skin.

I look crazy in the mirror. Ophelia has nothing on me.

As I'm rubbing the liquid soap into my cheeks for a second round, Mandy opens the bathroom door. Our eyes meet in the mirror and I hurry to wash the suds away. I feel her watching me, and sure enough, when I straighten to pull a couple of paper towels down to pat myself dry, she's still staring.

"Are you okay?" she asks.

"Yes."

"Your face is all red."

"I just washed. Oscar smeared my makeup and I looked splotchy."

Mandy nods, but I don't think she buys it. "I'm so sorry," she says. "Oscar was totally out of line."

"It's not your fault."

"If you want, I can tell him to find someplace else to sit and he will. He's afraid of me." She smiles, and I smile back. "I think he's a little afraid of you, too."

"I elbowed him pretty hard."

"Well, yeah, but what you said to him . . . Oscar's used to being treated like he's famous. It turned his world upside-down that you called him out."

"Good."

"Caddie . . ."

Here it comes.

"Is something else wrong?"

No, of course not, nothing is wrong . . . besides the insane monster stress of trying to make a good first impression, of knowing my first acting class is still to come, my family is falling apart, and, oh right, I'm crazy.

"No, I'm good."

Mandy waits a long time before asking again. I would brush it off, leave, but she's blocking the door, so I try to stay calm, wait her out. "You looked so upset," she says.

"I thought maybe something bad happened this morning, or, like, with your parents?"

Something bad might be happening right now because of me.

I shake my head. "The house isn't tense all the time now. It's great."

Again, the skeptical nod.

"Look," I say, "I'm stressed out. It's my first day here. I want these people to like me, and I completely freaked." I let the tears come. "I have plenty to be upset about without thinking about my parents."

This is true. It's also true that the only thing I could think about when Oscar ripped my glove was the two of them calling it quits, giving up, because I slipped.

It wasn't my fault.

I'll make sure that it won't be my fault if my family stays broken.

I turn back to the sink, wash my hands one more time.

9.

Acting class meets in a giant room that's part classroom, part stage. An afternoon thunderstorm pounds at the windows, but heavy curtains muffle the sound. A couple of stage lamps cast a dim, honey glow on the floor. With the rain sounds and the dark, I feel swallowed. A number of students are sprawled on the floor like starfish. They hum.

I tiptoe around arms and legs to get to the risers of seats where I drop off my bag. Stepping down to the main floor, my ankle catches in one of my bag's straps. I grab at a chair, making it clatter, and barely stop myself from tumbling down on top of the nearest starfish, a tall Indian girl. She opens her eyes to check that she's safe, shoots me a quick glare, and then shuts them again fast.

I step across her, but just as I do, she draws her knees up—several starfish have their knees up and are rocking them side to side—and I jostle her. She keeps her eyes closed this time but stops humming. I tiptoe around the others to a clear spot at the back and sit down.

Peter walks in and drops his backpack on a pile by the door. Nobody else bothered creeping over all the bodies to get to the chairs, which we probably won't even use. I'm still sitting up when he sees me. He walks straight to me, timing his steps to clear the starfish knees with no problem. He smiles and stretches out flat on his back with his eyes closed.

His bare hand is inches away from my leg. Behind his glasses, his eyelids have that liquid sheen—there's the tiniest space where the upper lids meet the lower. They flutter open and he stares back at me.

I flop down on my side to talk as close to his ear as I dare. "Sorry. I didn't mean to stare. I'm just trying to figure out what I'm supposed to be doing."

Someone shushes me.

Peter doesn't speak, but he doesn't look away, either. He rolls up on his elbow and reaches one finger toward my shoulder like he's planning to give me a push.

And he does. Without touching me, Peter pushes the bubble of air surrounding me, so there's less space to breathe—I lie down fast. I stretch my left arm out like everybody else but keep my right hand with the torn glove safe against my chest. Peter lies down and hums with a sense of purpose meant to tell me to join in. I do, but it gives me the giggles. I keep the sound breathy, try not to laugh out loud.

I whisper, "Sorry," but I can't stop giggling.

The shusher shushes again, and that makes Peter laugh too. He hisses it out, "Sh-sh-sh-sh," but we're both shuddering, trying to stay silent when a click of heels and a rattle of keys make us freeze.

"Something funny?" It's Nadia.

The silence must satisfy her, because she keeps clicking into the room. I stay down but let my head fall to the side so I can see Nadia spilling the contents of a giant tapestry bag onto the teacher's desk. She sorts through the mess, pulls some books to the side, and stuffs the other things back in: a pair of bright yellow sneakers, a length of fabric like a sari, a coil of electrical cord, two cans of Diet Coke, handfuls of makeup and tampons.

"When you're ready, stand up. Roll onto your side; use as few muscles as possible. Let the movement be easy."

All around me, bodies roll up, heads loll, knees drag. It's a room full of zombies. Some of them groan, "huh-hum-mmmmmmm." I make myself a zombie, too, try to groan with the best of them.

Once we're all up, a tight circle forms. Peter stays next to me. It's my imagination, has to be, that the heat off his skin is warming me. Nadia approaches and a space opens up just for her.

People want to look at her the way I want to look at

Peter. You feel it, the way they turn to face her without being asked. No one speaks.

Then she smiles. "I'm happy to see so many familiar faces." Her eyes land on me. "And one new one. Thanks for playing along. I'll give you an outline of the warm-up we use to start class. It won't be so funny after you've done it a couple of times."

My face goes hot, but Nadia doesn't seem mad, just . . . curious. It's like being watched by a tiger at the zoo.

My eyes meet Mandy's, and she widens hers in warning. *Keep it together, Caddie.*

"Y'all know how I work," Nadia says. "If you fall behind, this train doesn't stop. You'll notice this class has shrunk since last spring." Tension seeps through the room as people turn their heads, counting, trying to place who is missing. "Some of you will be working on *Hamlet,* but that doesn't mean you can slide. When you're out in the world as working actors, you will be overcommitted. You will be tired. You will book your first national commercial and find out it shoots the same weekend you're under contract to a theater, and you will have to figure that out without pissing everybody off."

The faces around me are apprehensive but hungry, too. This is what I've been wanting, a teacher who takes acting seriously, who understands that we don't just want to stop with the school play, we want to spend our lives making theater.

"All right, impromptu assignment," says Nadia. "Take a seat at the edge of the stage."

We scramble to do as she says, sitting on the edge of the lowest platform with our feet on the floor. I sit in the middle so as not to be first on either end, and I cover the hole in my glove; it's amazing how naked I feel with that one tiny circle of skin exposed.

"One by one, you will walk to center, turn, and face us. Stand in the space. Tell us your name and then exit. That's all."

She steps through our line and up to a chair.

It sounds too simple.

Nadia waits for us to start the exercise on our own. When Oscar, a couple spots down from me, stands to go first, I want to elbow him all over again. If we go in order, I could be going third. He takes a flying leap into the playing space, does a spin, and bows. "My name is—"

Nadia cuts him off. "That's not what I asked for. Go back."

"Points for creativity?"

"This exercise is not about creativity. Again," Nadia says.

Oscar stands at the edge of the space, takes a deep breath in and out.

"Again, without the breath."

"Are we doing this because you forgot our names over the summer?" he asks.

"Again, Oscar."

He composes himself and walks back to the edge. He starts forward with his head down, a man on a mission.

Nadia stops him again. "Now you're *acting* like a person who's walking to the center of a stage."

"What? That's what I am. That's what I'm supposed to be."

"No. Somebody tell Oscar what he's supposed to be."

Mandy raises her hand and tilts her head back to see Nadia nod. "A person walking to the center of a stage."

"That's what I just did," Oscar says.

Mandy goes on. "Not a person *acting* like a person walking to the center of a stage."

"Thank you, Mandy."

Livia makes a crowing sound then says, "Sorry. Impulse."

"No, that's good," Nadia says.

"I've been living on impulse all summer," Livia says.

Drew makes an audible sigh, and Nadia clears her throat.

"What? That was *my* impulse!" says Drew.

For that, she makes him go next, but eventually, Nadia calls on me.

She notices right away that my left hand's pressed over my right. "Drop your arms," she says. "Go back."

I do it, but I'm still too stiff.

"You're clenching your fists. Can you feel that tension?

You look like you think somebody's going to hit you."

"I'm sorry."

"Don't be sorry. Stop making a fist."

I walk to the center of the stage with my arms hanging down and my hands open wide, my face blank. I say, "I am Caddie Finn," and Nadia says, "No, you're not."

Maddening.

She turns to a small red-haired girl and says, "Go hit her."

The class laughs, but the girl leaps up.

"Can I try it by myself one more time?"

Nadia shakes her head. "Try it my way."

Peter's eyes burn me, watching to see if I'll fail.

Mandy watches too. She looks nervous for me, which is nice in one way and not in another because clearly she thinks there's a reason for nerves.

The red-haired girl might touch my neck or my face.

"Don't make it hard. Just bop her one." The girl smiles, asks permission with her eyes; then she swings her arm sideways into my shoulder, making me wobble. I shake out my hands, trying to release tension.

"See, that wasn't so bad," Nadia says. "Tension is self-protection. It's fear. Ask yourself what's the worst thing that can happen?"

Getting bopped by a classmate is hardly the worst thing I can think of, but I don't dare say that to Nadia.

At the end of class, she leaves us with this: "We all

did some acting today. Most of you are still acting right now. Acting like you weren't disappointed if you failed the exercise. Acting like you agree with me, nodding your heads extra hard so I'll see."

She nods her head in an exaggerated way, zeroing in on Hank, who laughs at himself.

"You're acting like students who care what their teacher is saying. So you're making yourselves sit up straight."

Several bodies instantly slouch.

"Or you're slouching to show that you wouldn't be caught dead acting."

The room goes still.

"Anybody can act in that sense of the word. We do it all day, every day. We *need* to do it. But to act in a play, you have to learn to strip those defenses down. It's scary to be your simple, lonely self onstage, but it is required of you."

10.

With my first day at the academy over, all the tiny supports that have been keeping my stress at bay crack and give, and the weight of the day crashes in. I let Mandy and the others surge ahead as we enter the stream of students flooding the hall. It's like pushing my way down a river, current dragging at my knees, feet slipping on algae and silt.

A tug on the strap of my backpack nearly sinks me. It's Peter, and my heart beats at my ribs.

"Why so sad, clown?" he says.

"What?"

"You look so sad. Look up. You're missing out. There's nothing on the floor."

"Dust," I say as I back away, pulling my hair forward to cover the skin near the strap, skin that he almost touched.

He smiles. "Dust's okay, but people are much more interesting."

He's trying to be friendly, but it feels like he's making a thing of my weirdness.

Peter stands between me and the after-school rush and holds out a hand like he means to pull me back into the stream. Even with gloves, that hand is a dare I can't take. *Don't touch, don't touch.*

All my muscles are tight, and a headache threatens. Tension is self-protection, Nadia said. Necessary.

And it hurts.

"I hope you didn't let Oscar get to you," he says.

I feel too aware of the hole in my glove, like if I can't stop thinking about it he'll be able to read my mind.

"No, I was just thinking." My hands clench the straps of my backpack.

When *don't touch* first came back, I thought about the possibility of meeting a guy at my new school and what that would mean. I thought, *This is from stress. It won't last.* When weeks passed and the game kept mattering, I thought, *I'll be busy with school. Chances are I won't meet anyone I like anyway.*

"Well, far be it from me to disturb anybody who's thinking," Peter says, "but you'd better be thinking about something good."

His hand drops, and he jogs to catch up with the others. *Please don't let Peter be able to read my mind, pluck this something-good-something-bad thought from my brain. . . .* Sharp and guilty, it sears at my fingertips and my heart, burns my cheeks red and easy to read.

I'm thinking about Peter's hand, Peter taking my hand in his, touching me.

In the car, I try to judge whether the breach in my armor has done any damage.

Mom seems stressed but that might be because Jordan keeps kicking the back of her seat.

"If you let me play football, I wouldn't have so much extra energy," he says.

"It's a distraction, Jordan. Your grades weren't so hot last year."

"That's what Dad says." He's kicking her seat again. "I thought Dad wasn't in charge anymore since you're getting divorced."

I wait for Mom to correct him: it isn't a divorce; it's a separation. But the correction doesn't come. Maybe something happened between Mom and Dad because Oscar touched my skin. Or maybe my stupid game is just that—a game. If that's true, how will I know when to stop playing?

"I can sew that up for you," Mom says, and I realize I'm picking at the hole in my glove, making it bigger.

"I know how to sew."

That night, I place the stitches as close together as I can. I reinforce the thumb on the other hand too, for good measure. Once I'm done, I can tug at the seams and barely see space between stitches. It was a bad idea to rely on a cheap costume seam to keep myself safe. But I can't show up to school in chain mail and gauntlets.

I'll have to be more careful.

ACT TWO

. . . best safety lies in fear . . .
—LAERTES, *HAMLET* (I.iii.48)

II.

You'd think people would notice the way I protect myself, but I'm getting better at choosing my moments to touch over clothes. And with fall coming on, long sleeves don't stand out as much.

People who touch with abandon draw attention to themselves, but the absence of touch . . . people hardly notice.

Mandy's crowd is slowly starting to feel like my crowd. One weekend, we go to the Scratch to play pool. Mandy has a fake ID, but for me, she says, "She's my older sister," and bats her lashes.

The guy at the door rolls his eyes but says, "Y'all don't go trying to buy drinks now," and lets us in. The great thing about pool is that no one comes close when you're taking your shot, and the threat of the cue keeps Oscar at bay.

Another weekend, we pile into Drew's and Peter's trucks and drive about an hour north to the Ave Maria Grotto in Cullman. In an old quarry, a Benedictine monk made miniature versions of famous churches and other holy buildings out of all sorts of materials—concrete and tile but also trinkets, tiny shells, and beads. The Temple of the Fairies features cold cream jars.

Livia poses like Godzilla about to crush St. Martin's Church, and a grouchy old lady yells at Mandy and Drew for making out in front of St. Peter's Basilica.

I notice our Peter sitting alone for the longest time staring into the grotto itself, a false cave with marble statues, a mosaic altar, and handmade, cement stalactites. I promised myself I'd keep Peter at a safe distance, but he's all alone, so I walk up and say, "What do you see?"

"My parents came here a long time ago as part of the road trip they took on their honeymoon. I have a photo of them standing here. I was trying to picture it."

"Their honeymoon?" I ask.

"No," he says, smiling up at me, and I know before he says it: "I'm trying to picture how they were ever in love."

He gets up then and walks on toward Little Jerusalem.

Mom's taking on more photography jobs lately, and she's been making field trips for artistic work. One night, she drags me down to her darkroom in the basement to show me a series she took near the Irondale Café.

It's a place locked in time. Train tracks run right past the restaurant. Once, we saw an engineer stop his train there so he could hop down and get a sweet iced tea to go. Then he hopped back on the train and took off again.

Mom hands me a set in which the sides of abandoned boxcars scale like birch trees so that patches of color pop out from the rust.

"Mom, these are gorgeous."

Lit from the side by the red lamp and smiling, Mom's cheeks look hot and shiny, like a person with a fever. She says, "I *know*. I'm really proud of these. It's been so long since I've done something that feels like *mine*. Does that make sense?"

It does—and it worries me. The more things change before Dad comes back, the harder coming back will be.

On Jordan's thirteenth birthday, Mom gets him a cake from a place that prints photos in icing with a picture of her holding him as a baby. Jordan smears it with a knife before we can sing "Happy Birthday," saying "Don't act like this is some great family memory when we all know how it turns out."

Mom makes excuses for why Dad couldn't come: "You know he's a workaholic. He goes into mad scientist mode and loses track of the rest of the world." She calls it "mad scientist mode" to make it sound cute, but it isn't.

Jordan speaks to Dad on the phone, but I decline.

I say to Mom, "Tell him he should have been here for Jordan."

She purses her lips and says, "He knows," but I'm annoyed. There ought to be something she can do.

I make Jordan a card that reads, "I know it hurts right now. This won't last forever." I'm not sure I believe my own words, so I'm not surprised when Jordan sets it aside with no comment.

Later that night, though, he stands in my doorway and says, "I hear you practicing all the time."

Ophelia. I hoped I'd been quiet enough that he and Mom wouldn't notice.

"I think you can stop practicing," he says. "You're good."

"Thanks, Jordan. That means a lot."

He shrugs and heads back to his room for some serious video game slaughter.

I always get to school early so I won't miss the before-school shenanigans. It doesn't surprise me, knowing Mandy, that her friends are really good at shenanigans.

One morning, Peter arranges a sit-in in front of the main office to plead for "mouse rights." I don't think he's even for real, just pushing buttons, but he convinces the principal to switch to cruelty-free traps.

The next day is all about Livia leaving a fake love note for a classical guitarist ex of Mandy's who "scorned" her.

The guy skims the note, looks straight at Mandy, and says, "Ha-ha. Very funny." For that, we're all late to first period.

A couple weeks into September, I dare to make my first proposal: a flash mob where at the exact same moment, a bunch of people freeze and stay frozen for three minutes straight. "There's a performance group called Improv Everywhere that did it in Grand Central Station, and the crowd's reactions in the video are amazing."

"Yes!" Peter says. "But it's going to take some planning." He immediately drops to the floor and starts drawing up a list of recruits who can be trusted to pull it off.

"Look what you've started," Mandy says to me. "This is all we're going to hear about for a month!"

I kneel beside Peter. The veins on the back of his scribbling hand stand up like a web of inverted rivers. I imagine a finger tracing one, slipping over to a tendon and following that all the way to the fingertip.

"Don't forget whose idea this was," I say. "I want creative control."

"Of course," Peter says. "Think of me as your production assistant."

"You can be more than that," I say. "You can direct. I get nervous telling people what to do. Just remember who hired you."

He smiles, and I try to keep my face friendly and easy

like his, to *not* seem like a crushing idiot, but I wonder how readable I am.

On my way out of acting, hands grip my upper arms, making me squeal. I'm spun off my path, yanked around the corner, and shoved through the open door of a dark utility closet. I fling an elbow back in defense, and Mandy yelps.

"Calm down," Mandy's voice whispers as she shuts the door. "You hit my boob."

"Sorry! What are you doing?"

It's freaky to be in the dark where I can't see her hands.

"God, you're jumpy. You're like my mom when she gets off her beta-blockers. It's time for an intervention."

Intervention? Oh, Lord.

Mandy has always been pushy. If she pushes too hard, I'll fall.

"I'm going to set you up with Peter."

I'd thought maybe she knew about *don't touch*, but this might be worse. Mandy doesn't push; Mandy shoves.

She goes on, "We're practicing for auditions tonight at my house. We split up to work on scenes . . . we leave you alone by the pool . . ."

"Please, please, no."

"I saw you flirting." She puts on a high-pitched voice: "Direct me, Peter. Make my flash mob dreams come true."

"Mandy . . ."

"And he was flirting back."

"He was not."

"Well, he sure was eager."

"He was eager about the flash mob. Because flash mobs are awesome."

"Okay, it doesn't have to be about Peter. It could just be fun. This might be the last weekend it's warm enough to swim. Oscar wants to play strip Marco Polo, of course."

"Strip?"

"You have to wear extra clothes in the pool, or else everybody's naked too fast."

"Naked?"

"You can't see much underwater."

"I can't."

"Look, you don't have to play, and you don't have to make out with Peter. Just come. It will be good for practice."

Practice at being normal is what I hear, but my brain plays catch up. Auditions, she means. The idea of Mandy seeing me try for Ophelia makes me cringe.

"No, I have this thing with my mom. She has a special meal planned." None of that is a lie. Mom plans a meal every night for this special event we call dinner.

"This is for school. Your mom will understand."

"But I have lots of homework."

"We all have homework, Caddie. We're all going. You want to be one of the group? This is the group. If you want friends, you've got to, you know, put in the time."

I made too many excuses to Mandy back in middle school when I felt like I was losing it and didn't know how to be around her—or anyone—anymore.

They can't really mean to play strip Marco Polo, can they? That's not a real thing high school students in Birmingham, Alabama, do, is it?

"Fine, yes, you're right. I'll go."

12.

Oscar is naked.

Buck. Naked. And doing the backstroke smack-dab in the middle of Mandy's pool.

I want to run after Mom's car, but she's already halfway down the steep drive. The Bowers' bright, Tudor-style home sits almost at the top of the ridge, presiding over a neighborhood of equally gorgeous, old houses. Their yard feels like some secluded, medieval glade, but from the highest point, you can look down on the entire city.

"Caddie! You made it!" Mandy squeals, and I hold up my hands in defense. I've got my gloves, jeans, and long sleeves, but there's lots of exposed Mandy flying my way. At least she's wearing a bikini.

Mandy squeezes me, pinning my arms to my sides and resting her cheek on my shoulder, too close to my neckline.

Don't touch, please, don't touch.

Her wet suit soaks through my shirt, just a bit. *Water that touched Mandy's skin is touching mine.* Water's a conductor; it feels like that should matter, but I push the thought down. My magical-thinking mind could make up rules all day if I let it. *No new rules.*

I squirm out of Mandy's grip and say, "You're actually playing strip Marco Polo?"

"Marco!" Oscar calls suggestively, but there's nobody else in the pool.

"No!" Mandy says. "But this is Oscar pouting." She flaps a hand toward him and he flips into an underwater somersault, his butt cresting the water like the shiny skin of a humpback whale.

"I am scarred for life," I say, shielding my eyes.

Peter's laugh pulls my focus. He's sitting poolside with his feet in the water. His swim trunks are neon yellow— *warning, slow down*—and he's not wearing anything else.

These are the things I can process.

I keep my eyes up, on his, which are friendly, but below them is his chest.

Stop. Looking.

The others are scattered around the pool. Drew's got wet hair, but he's wearing a T-shirt and has a towel around his neck. Livia and Hank lounge in twin chairs facing the pool and clearly haven't gone in at all. Still, they're dressed for this last blast of summer. Livia's in her sundress and flip-flops; Hank's in board shorts and a stripy tank. We've got a breeze, but it's far too warm and humid for all my clothes.

"Are we going to work inside?" I ask.

"Caddie's a task master," Mandy says. "Should we start?"

"Come swim," Oscar says, smacking the water to splash my legs. The chill of it actually feels nice, but there's nothing nice about sitting around in wet jeans.

"Oscar," I say, "I have something to confess."

"What's that?" he asks, folding his arms on the edge of the pool, everything else thankfully hidden underwater.

"I've never seen a naked man before."

All of their eyes turn to me. It's a chance to play the way they do, to show that I *can*.

"Well, congratulations, Caddie. Today's the day."

I keep my voice innocent. "Oh! You thought I was talking about you! Oh, this is awkward. No, I was just sharing. I've *never* seen a naked man," I deadpan. "Still."

"Da-amn," Oscar says. "Ice. Cold."

Peter starts a slow clap, and they all join in.

"Aw, come *on!*" Oscar says. "That was so not worthy of a slow clap."

Hank and Livia start a standing ovation, and Mandy doubles over laughing.

"Fine," Oscar says in a goofy growl. "Fine, fine, fine." He flips back from the wall to float on his back and claps with his arms stretched high, making zero effort to hide.

"It's kind of gross out in all these clothes," I whisper to Mandy. I hold out my arms and I'm stiff, barely bendable.

"Yeah, okay," Mandy says quietly, "I know how to get them inside," and then louder, "Y'all, my mom said we could make margaritas if nobody's driving for a while."

Oscar's out of the water before she's finished speaking.

Livia says, "Yes, please."

"But dry off first."

The swimmers duck into the pool house to dress— even Oscar, thank the Lord—and Hank offers to get things started inside. Mandy brings me up to her bedroom to hang out while she changes.

It's a lot like I remember. The pristine white carpet is the same and so is the canopy bed with translucent curtains all around, but the pastel bedding has been replaced by jewel tones, rich teal and plum. There's a new-looking elliptical machine in the corner facing the flat-screen TV that sits on Mandy's dresser.

I guess Mandy's rich. My house is full of old family treasures from Mom's parents. Mandy's house has those, but also investments: paintings by fancy artists, antique furniture too delicate for sitting. The house itself is old— on the historic registry—but it doesn't *feel* old because it's kept up so well.

"Do you like my new torture device?" Mandy waves

at the elliptical machine then steps behind her closet door to change. "I'd rather run outside, but Mom says it's not ladylike to be sweaty on the street."

"Whoa." Even for Mandy's mom, that's impressively Victorian.

"I know. She thinks she's in another century, like all my gentleman callers will bolt if they see me in sweatpants."

"Lord," I say. "Does she really not mind if we drink?"

"As long as I use the sugar-free mix." Mandy pauses and then confides, "She did this with my big sister, too. She says she wants our house to be cool."

"Your mom's stuck in high school," I say.

"Tell me something I don't know."

It's weird to think about our moms being besties back in the day. They both lived in Mountain Brook, with its high school sororities and senior year coming-out balls.

"Coming out" still has its old-fashioned meaning in Birmingham—debutantes in white dresses parade into ballrooms on young men's arms to show that they've entered society. Mom says it's an archaic, patriarchal ritual that I don't have to submit myself to.

Mandy's mom says it's the best time of a girl's life. And that's the biggest difference between Mandy's mom and mine.

After college, Mom and Dad stayed in Virginia. They only moved when her father was dying and Meemaw was losing it with stress. Mom jokes that she "tricked" Dad into the Deep South. "He should have known that once I got him here, there was no going back," she'd say.

Meemaw always called Dad a "Yankee" even though he's only from Maryland. She still teases him about the time he ordered a side of green beans and said, "I think they mixed some ham in here by mistake."

I'm not sure Dad was ever truly comfortable here.

"I think this is good for Ophelia," Mandy says as she primps in the vanity mirror, freeing a few tendrils of hair. "It's romantic, right?"

When I don't answer, she says, "Earth to Caddie. You ready?"

"Sure," I say, and we head downstairs.

When we reach the kitchen, Hank and Livia are wrestling with Mandy's giant Newfoundland over a puddle of spilled margarita.

"Sterling, front!" Mandy shouts, and the dog lopes to her, sits, and stares up into her eyes. She scratches his head and then sends him to lie down at the edge of the room.

"Sorry," Livia says, "I didn't get the blender screwed on right."

"I'm good at screwing," Oscar says, and Mandy punches him in the arm.

"Enough with the double entendres," she says.

Oscar puts on a terrible French accent, "Ohn-hohn-hohn, Madame, but you *French* so well." He waggles his tongue with his eyes closed, so he doesn't see her finger coming up to flick his tongue, hard.

"Ow!" he cries. "Mean!"

"You're lucky I don't cut it off," Mandy says, and goes to help Hank and Livia.

"Caddie, do you think this is enough room?" Peter calls.

I step through the breakfast nook and down a couple of steps to the humongous den. Drew and Peter have pushed the sofas and coffee tables back to create space in front of the fireplace. It's as big as our classroom.

"I think this will be plenty," I say.

"We want it as accurate as possible," Drew says. He seems like he wouldn't care, but clearly he does.

Peter smiles. "Showtime."

I perch on an ottoman to signal I'm in no rush to go first. "So, how does this work? Do we do monologues or what?"

Oscar appears carrying a ginormous glass full of frozen margarita. I think he's actually drinking from a vase.

"We audition with scenes," he says, "more like a callback." I know that a callback means a second round of auditions, but I've never been to one. Oscar says it like he has a callback every Tuesday.

"Scooch over," he says, meaning to squeeze in beside me on the ottoman.

"There's room for twenty people on these sofas," I say, gesturing to all the empty seats.

"But I want to snuggle," Oscar says.

"I'm taking out a restraining order," I say, crawling backward into a chair with huge arms but only room for one butt.

"You're no fun," Oscar says, taking the ottoman.

"I'm a huge amount of fun," I say. "I just haven't figured out how to have it with you."

Oscar narrows his eyes at me—I've won this round—and slurps from his vase.

"Can I go first and get it over with?" Livia says.

She and Hank each have a tray full of drinks. When Hank brings me one, I try a little sip. There's a pungent flavor that reminds me of morning breath and the bitterness of fake sweetener.

"I can make you a virgin one if you want," Mandy says as she takes a seat near me.

"Caddie *is* a virgin after all," Oscar says. "She just told us so. I mean, if she's never seen a naked man—"

"Shut up," Mandy says.

"It's kind of sweet," says Oscar. "Of course, I'd be more than happy to help you change that, Caddie."

"No, that's okay," I say in answer to Mandy, though it works for Oscar as well, and take another sip.

"It takes some getting used to," Mandy says.

"So do I," Oscar says.

"Do you never stop talking?" says Mandy.

"People," Peter says, flourishing his glass, "let us begin."

Drew's leaning in the doorway to the kitchen with a glass of straight tequila on ice. Since I've hardly had more than a sip of sherry my whole life, it's probably not the best idea to join him, but I can't blame him for making the trade.

"Me first! Me first!" Livia says.

"What's it going to be?" Peter asks. He waves a folder full of photocopied scenes.

"Let me try Ophelia," Livia says, and Oscar volunteers to go with her.

As they look over their scene, Peter sits cross-legged on the floor between Oscar's ottoman and Mandy's legs, just a few feet away from me.

"How do we know which scene we'll have to read?" I ask him.

"For Ophelia, it's a pretty good bet you'll do the one in the hall of mirrors."

"You saw the Branagh version." That's the one with the mirrors.

"Yeah," Peter says, like that goes without saying.

It's my favorite scene in the play. King Claudius and Ophelia's father, Polonius, think maybe Hamlet's crazy with love, so they get Ophelia to break up with Hamlet to see how he reacts. Ophelia goes along with it, but then Hamlet turns mean. He might be acting because he knows the king's watching, or he might really be crazy, but whatever it is, it's awful. He denies they were ever a thing, says he never loved her, but there's one part where he lets his guard down. He says, "I did love you once," and Ophelia says, "Indeed, my lord, you made me believe so."

That line, "I did love you once," that's the part that kills me.

Livia and Oscar do well. Oscar's goofiness drops away, and he seems like he's actually interested in what another person has to say. I think Livia's too strong for Ophelia, but it depends what Nadia wants.

Mandy and Hank are pretty great too. By the time Hank's ranting at her, Mandy's breathing has changed, and she's contracting her whole body with his words. It's physical, and it makes me feel for her—with her. Maybe I shouldn't have quit dance.

Peter and Drew try Hamlet and his friend Horatio, switching off parts. Peter's better at both in my opinion, but I might be biased. Drew has a huge presence on stage, but the language keeps tripping him up. Shakespeare's hard even for professional actors, and it's clearly not Drew's forte.

I peek at Mandy, and her lips are a tense line. She catches me looking and whispers, "I offered to practice with him, but he's too proud to let me help."

I give her a grimace of sympathy. Each time Drew messes up, his next words come out sounding frustrated, whether or not that's how his character should be. On their second time through the scene, Drew ends it early. "That's enough for me," he says, and heads back to his tequila, eyes on the floor.

We've been at it for more than an hour when Peter says, "Caddie, you're up."

I twist a pillow in my fist and try to send all my nerves into that squeeze.

Mandy's eyes are on me, and she still looks tense from watching Drew.

"I don't think I'm going to go," I say.

"Ohhh!" Peter sounds like a sports announcer reacting to a boffed play. "Don't be shy," he says. "If you're nervous to do it here, think how nervous you'll be at the audition."

"I'm not nervous," I say. "I'm just . . . I don't know what I am."

"Nervous is good," Peter says, and he holds the scripts out to me. "You're nervous because you care."

I don't want them to know how *much* I care, but of course he's right.

"Okay," I say, "but I don't know what to read."

"Don't be that way," Peter says. "You'll read Ophelia."

"She can pick whatever she wants," Mandy says.

Peter's clearly going for Hamlet. Maybe he *wants* me to play Ophelia opposite him, but no, because then he says, "Every girl wants Ophelia."

"Gertrude's a bigger part," Livia says. "I might rather do that."

"Caddie looks like an Ophelia," says Peter.

As much as I want to play Ophelia, I don't love the idea of "looking like" her—because what does that mean? Crazy? Breakable?

"I'll read with you," Hank says.

Peter hands me the scene.

"Okay, but I've got to run to the bathroom real quick," I say, and I scurry to the guest bath in the hall.

Behind me, Mandy asks, "Who needs a second round?" and I bless her for keeping them occupied. I'd hate to picture them all sitting silently, waiting on me to perform.

At the bathroom mirror, I smooth my brow. Even though I haven't made any blunders, I'm tempted to wash. Oscar was sitting close to me. What if my pants leg rode up, and his hand brushed the skin at my ankle but I didn't notice?

Stop it, I think. *Don't freak out.*

There's no touching required in this scene. Performing in front of them has nothing to do with my game. If I start scrubbing myself every time I feel anxious, I'm going to get caught. Lady Macbeth is Shakespeare's obsessive-compulsive hand-washer, not Ophelia.

I take a deep breath, blow it out, and run my gloved hands down my sides as if I might press myself back together. I picture myself walking into the den and showing what I can do, being one of them.

Be brave. Be brave.

When I get back to the room, Mandy's sitting in Drew's

lap, and he's playing with her hair. Livia's arguing with Oscar about whether or not a magazine ad featuring an impossibly skinny girl is sexist.

"Just because it's sexist doesn't make it less hot," he says.

"But it *should*!" she says.

Hank's laughing at them.

Only Peter looks bored, like I've kept him waiting.

"Ready?" he asks. He's smiling, but it feels like he's my director. I'm late for my audition and I've got something major to prove.

"Yeah, let's get it over with."

"I'll be gentle," Hank says, and reaches toward my arm as if for a reassuring squeeze.

I jerk back and he laughs breathily in surprise.

"Sorry," I say. "I think I've got stage fright."

"Happens to the best of us," Oscar says, "which would be me!" He raises his glass.

"Take it from Hamlet's last line before her entrance," Peter suggests.

And Hank starts, "Soft you now! The fair Ophelia!"

Ophelia's being watched, like me. She would be nervous too. "Good my lord, how does your honor for this many a day?"

"I humbly thank you," he says, "well, well, well."

She wants to seem strong. I make my voice hard: "My lord, I have remembrances of yours, that I have longed long to redeliver." I hold out my script like it's a gift.

"No, not I," Hank says. "I never gave you aught."

Now some of the emotion should seep through. I let my voice quaver, plead with him:

"My honored lord, you know right well you did; and, with them, words of so sweet breath composed as made the things more rich—"

"You're acting," says Peter.

"What?" He didn't stop anyone else like this.

"Sorry, I just—you were in the scene at first, but now you're overthinking it."

"Let her get through it," Mandy says.

"No, he's right. Can we go back?"

We do the first part of the scene over again. I still can't think about anything but them looking at me, about how bad a job I'm doing. At the same spot, I stop and say, "I'm sorry, Hank."

"That was better!" Peter says. "Why did you stop?"

"I was just saying the lines. I wasn't feeling anything."

"That's better than fake feeling. You sounded honest." Peter hops up to talk only to me. "You've got to let go of some of that control," he says, "that tension, like Nadia says. It isn't helping you." Peter takes me by the shoulders and shakes me, not hard, but I'm so stiff it jars me. His face is so close. His eyes are so *green*.

I say the first thing that comes to mind, "My phone," and slip out of his grip, pretend I'm checking a message.

"Sorry," I say, avoiding Peter's eyes by looking at Hank. "I got a text from my mom. She has to come get me earlier than she thought."

"Oh no!" Mandy says. "Here, let me text her. One of us can give you a ride."

"No, she's already almost here," I say, "and we've all been drinking. . . ."

"I'm sober," Drew says, but I remember how fast he took those curves when he *wasn't* under the influence.

"You're going to miss all the fun," Mandy says. "After we practice, we play games."

"Next time," I say. "Okay?" I go for my bag.

"You're leaving *now*? Don't you want to at least wait till she's actually here?"

"I have to meet her at the bottom of the driveway."

"That's crazy," Mandy says. "It's a super-steep walk and it's dark out."

"She gets scared of backing down it."

"Fine." Mandy untangles herself from Drew and stands. "I mean, if you have to go, you have to go."

"I'm sorry," I say.

She's not looking at me, but she leads me toward the front hall.

"Bye, everybody. I'll see you Monday."

They all mutter good-byes, but nobody other than Mandy seems particularly concerned that I'm leaving. I'm afraid Peter sees through my lies. He waves the stack of scripts at me and smiles as if to say it's too bad I'm such a scaredy-cat.

Or maybe that's all in my head.

"Wait here," Mandy says in the entrance hall and ducks into the kitchen, coming back with a pack of gum. "We don't want your mom to freak out."

"Right," I say. I didn't drink much, but I'm sure Mom would smell it.

Mandy opens the door and looks glum as she says, "Do you want me to wait with you?"

"No, I don't want to take you away from things," I say. "I'll be fine."

She looks toward the ceiling, *almost* an eye roll. "I thought this would be a good chance for you to bond with everyone."

"And I got to," I say, "a little bit."

"But Caddie," Mandy says, "it's not cool to watch everybody else put themselves out there and then leave."

"I know, but my mom—"

"I know, I know," Mandy says, sounding exasperated. "Look, it's not you. I'm just worked up about auditions."

"You were great," I say. "You're going to do great."

"Thanks," she says, but she's looking at the floor. "Hey, do you remember the last time you spent the night over here?"

"Um, I don't know." That's another lie. I remember it too well.

"You had to go home early then, too."

"I did?"

Mandy leans on the door, pausing a second before opening it. She looks out into the dark. "This is old, stupid stuff. I'm sorry I'm being weird." She turns back to me and there's the smallest reassuring smile. "You can't help if your mom says you have to go."

"Thanks for understanding," I say. I should squeeze her arm or give her a hug.

But I don't.

As I make my way down the hill, I turn to wave and see Mandy shutting the door.

At the base of the drive, the trees mostly block the light from the houses. Stone columns with lamps mark the end of Mandy's driveway, but that light blinds me to what's farther off in the woods.

The creepiness isn't enough to send me back to the house, though. Being scared of the dark is so normal. Why couldn't that be my thing?

I should have texted Mom when I first pulled out my phone. It will take her at least twenty minutes to get here. I'll have to hope Mandy's not watching to see when she actually comes.

That last night at Mandy's was her birthday, seventh grade. She'd invited a bunch of girls from dance for a sleepover. There was Lena, a wiry girl who was daring and smart about guys, but who could be mean. There was

Britt, whose mom didn't let her go anywhere until she'd curled her hair with a hot iron. And Bailey.

Bailey had the clean-scrubbed look of a girl who preferred apples to candy. She always seemed to be going along for the ride, and it could be easy to forget she was there. Mothers loved that about her.

Mom and Dad had been fighting all week, and *don't touch* kept ricocheting around in my head. By the time we climbed in our sleeping bags, I just wanted to sleep.

But Lena had made up a game called Truth or Spoons. There'd be a bunch of spoons in a circle, one less than the number of players. We had to lay down cards in a sequence, and whenever someone got rid of all her cards, everybody had to grab a spoon.

Whoever failed had to answer a question from the girl who was out of cards. "And it has to be the truth," Lena said. "Cross your heart and hope to die."

If she hadn't added that last part, I might have been all right, but what if I lied and I really did die? It might not happen right away, but when it came, maybe years from now, I would know I had brought it on myself.

Each time someone played her last card, hands would fly into the center, but I couldn't risk touch. A couple of times, a spoon went flying and I grabbed it, but mostly I kept losing.

The questions were easy at first.

"If you could go anywhere on vacation," Mandy asked,

"where would you go?"

"Boring," said Lena. "Ask something interesting."

"I don't want to be mean," Britt said, when it was her turn to ask.

"It's not mean," said Lena. "It's part of the game." But Britt asked an easy question too.

Finally, Lena said, "I think Caddie's losing on purpose. We should ask her something good—for punishment."

And the next time she won, she asked, "Who do you like?"

I knew she'd make a thing of it, but I named a guy in our class: "Dev Lakhani."

Lena cackled and said, "I cannot wait for Monday," but Mandy stuck up for me.

"We can't play a game with secrets if we can't trust each other to keep them," she said.

"Fine," Lena said, but the mocking threat in her eyes never went away. The next time I lost, she said, "Tell us about your parents."

"That's not a question," Mandy said, her voice sharp.

But Lena said, "I hear they fight all the time."

Mandy started picking at the carpet. Lena had never been at my house, and I'd definitely never told her about my parents' fights.

Lena rephrased. "Do you think your parents will get a divorce?"

"I don't know."

"Your best guess," Lena said. "You have to answer."

"I told you, I don't know," I said, but was that true? Answering either way felt dangerous. If I said yes, that might make it come true. And if I said no, that might be a lie.

I had cut back on the washing by then, but when a game had a consequence that I couldn't accept, washing gave me an out, a clean slate and a second chance.

"I have to use the bathroom," I said.

"I'm guessing the answer is yes," Lena teased as I stepped through the tangle of sleeping bags to get to the door.

In the bathroom with the door locked, I washed all the way to my elbows. I don't know how long it was before Mandy knocked. "Caddie," she called, "are you sick or something? Can I come in?"

"Just a second."

I finished and dried off. Then I opened the door.

I said, "Sorry I'm taking too long."

Mandy looked concerned, but disappointed, too. "I really like Lena," she said. "I want her to have a good time."

Do you like her more than me? I wanted to ask but didn't dare.

"Why would you talk to her about my parents?" I said.

"It just came up," she said, and then, "Can you not be weird?"

She knows. She knows, played in a loop in my head. I followed Mandy back into her room and tried to look cheery and ready to play.

"Since you hate my question," Lena said, "I thought of an alternate: What were you doing in the bathroom for so long?"

My face went hot, but I couldn't speak. Eons passed. New species developed, flourished, then died. My limbs wouldn't work, my jaw wouldn't move, even if I had known what to say.

"You have to answer," Lena said.

I tried to tell myself it was okay to lie because Lena was mean, but no lie came. Part of me wanted to spill my guts about my games and the panic and ask them to keep it a secret, *but tell me I'm normal, please, tell me I'm not as freakish as I think I am.*

I didn't have it in me—to lie or to tell them the truth.

"I just—shouldn't be here," I mumbled, before I knew what I was saying. "I need to go home."

"Are you sick?" Bailey asked.

I nodded, but Lena wouldn't let up. "We would have heard if she'd gotten sick."

"It's just a stupid game," Mandy said, and she sounded desperate for us not to ruin her party.

"You're shaking," Britt said, and I was. My teeth were chattering, my hands . . . I pressed my fingers together but couldn't hold them still.

"Caddie," Mandy pleaded, "don't freak out. We don't have to play anymore." There was frustration in her voice, in her eyes, that and something else too—contempt.

"She has to answer," Lena said. "Those are the rules."

"No, she doesn't. You don't have to," Bailey said.

"Just answer," Mandy said. "Lie if you want. No one cares." She was begging me to behave, to keep being her friend, but our friendship died, right then. I felt it go.

"I'm sorry. I want to go home."

"My parents are asleep," Mandy said, but I left the room and walked down the hall to the master bedroom. The door stood open a crack. "Caddie, don't," Mandy shout-whispered, but I pushed the door open.

Her parents looked weirdly exposed with bare feet sticking out from under the sheet, her father's arm across her mother's hip. Mandy's mother must have sensed me—she sat up gasping, clutching her husband. Mandy's father lurched to sitting, a defensive reaction, and they stared at me with something like horror. That changed to annoyance as soon as they got their bearings, but horror felt like what I deserved.

My parents were called. Mandy's father put on a robe over his hairy chest and boxers—I hadn't wanted to see that—and sat up with me in the kitchen, not speaking, waiting for Dad to come.

The next week, Mandy asked if I felt any better, but there was a wall up. She told me Lena had invited her to spend the night that weekend, saying something about it being a shame that I couldn't come too, but that Lena's mom only let her have one guest at a time.

We still sat together at lunch. Mandy still told me secrets, but she didn't ask me to share mine. I never spent the night at her house again.

13.

Auditions make everyone crazy, but it comes out in different ways.

Mandy shows up reeking of smoke. "I had the windows open on the way here and everything," she says. "It didn't matter."

"You're not going to have any voice left if you don't take it easy," says Drew. He's in his usual slouch against the wall of lockers, thumbing through a car magazine.

"Aren't you nervous?" Mandy asks.

"What's the point?" Drew says, but it's clear he's on emotional lockdown. He doesn't look up from the magazine, and he flips the pages with so much force you'd think they conspired to give him paper cuts.

At lunch, Livia's extra-impulsive. At one point she lunges for the saltshaker and rains salt down on Oscar's chicken-fried steak. He eats it. For a laugh. Then he opens his mouth in my face to show how dry the salt made his tongue.

According to Oscar, once you've been in a movie with Lance Dalton, nothing about a school audition can make you nervous. He feels bad for the rest of us. Really bad. He tells us so about fifteen times.

Hank wanders around singing Hamlet's lines to the air.

And Peter. Nervous looks good on Peter.

I see him once in the hall singing Billy Joel. When a girl laughs at him, he goes down on one knee for a serenade.

At lunch, he asks if we want more fries, and before anybody can answer, he's up and jogging to the front of the line. He comes back ridiculously fast with a huge mound of fries—the lunch ladies, the students he cut in front of, all charmed by him. Nothing and nobody gets in his way.

"How are you in such a good mood?" Mandy says, diving for the fries and biting the ends off of four all at once.

"I'm excited," says Peter.

"How are *you* so calm?" she asks, glaring at me. I'm anything but.

"I'm nervous," I say, stabbing a fry with my fork and nibbling, even though the sight of food makes my stomach wobble.

"Could have fooled me," she says, and her eyes drop to my hands. "You *could* take your gloves off to eat."

"I could," I say, and I swallow the rest of the fry. It goes down in a lump.

I should show my nerves—nerves make us normal—but one crack might open the floodgates. I'm a wreck, and I hide it too well.

Peter's eyeing me. I meet his gaze, and for a second I'm caught there, not able to move or to breathe. His eyes drop to my gloves, then away.

We enter the theater together, a tribe. A girl with porcelain skin and white-blond hair guards the base of Nadia's stage. She looks fragile and cold and untouchable.

She looks like Ophelia.

"Sign your name here and pick up your sides," she says.

For a second, I think she means, "pick sides," like we're going to have to battle one another to make it to the stage, but no, by "sides," she means copies of the scenes we'll be reading.

"Hi, April," Mandy says to the girl, and April smiles—a sharp line that's more like a grimace.

"I'll go ahead and hand you these," April says, giving her the Ophelia sides.

April is a senior—her attitude gives her away—the senior who would be playing Ophelia if she hadn't gotten caught drinking in Lincoln.

"Cute gloves," she says, and it's a real talent she has as

an actress for saying nice words while making the subtext so clear: *I hate those stupid gloves, you weirdo poser who wants to steal my part.*

I sign my name but hover over the sides marked "Ophelia." It scares me how much I want it.

"Read for Ophelia," a voice whispers. It seems to come from inside me, except for the warm breath at my ear, too close, making me shiver. I shrink and twist around to find Peter standing over me.

He leans past me and reaches for the Hamlet sides with no hesitation. April smiles for Peter. She can't help herself; his smile's contagious.

As he straightens up, he says, "You want to play Ophelia, right?"

I stare at the sides. "Maybe I want a man part."

"Yeah?" He picks up another set of the Hamlet sides. "I bet you could give me some competition."

I shake my head.

"Do you want to play Gertrude?"

"No."

"Then you read for Ophelia." He hands me the sides, and it's done and decided. No stress. No embarrassment.

He turns and finds a seat at the end of a row, where he starts reading over his lines.

I do the same. It's easier than facing Mandy with the sides in my hand.

The front of the theater fills up quickly. At precisely

3:15, Nadia crosses the stage to stand center. All this space is hers—we won't forget.

"Welcome," she says, at normal volume since all talking stopped the second she entered. "I know you have scripts, but try to make physical choices." She holds out her hands and waves, cuing the audience to speak, and they do, in a chorus I haven't learned yet: "Don't be boring."

Nadia steps down from the stage to April's table, scans the sign-in sheet, and sits a few rows back. She calls the oldest students first. There are a couple of senior girls who either missed Lincoln last year or didn't participate in the partying. One handles the language well, the other trips over the words, but neither seems strong enough to play a lead.

Of our group, Mandy and Drew are called first for the breakup scene. Mandy's all about physical choices. She circles Drew like a stalking wolf, runs her hands down his chest.

"Too sexy," Nadia says. "Ophelia represents everything pure and innocent. All the things Hamlet's lost faith in."

"See, but I don't think Ophelia's so innocent," Mandy says, and Drew rolls his eyes to the rafters. "In the Branagh version, she and Hamlet have sex and he's all about it, but then he turns into a hypocrite."

I told Mandy to watch the Branagh version, but I didn't think she actually would.

"Mandy, cool it," Drew mutters, but she goes on.

"He thinks she's this perfect angel, but the second they do it, she's a whore."

"Welcome to the history of Western literature," Nadia says. "I like that you want to make the character complex, but we still need to see Ophelia vulnerable."

"Okay, can we try it again?"

Drew sighs, but they go back to the beginning. Drew's stiff, but Mandy looks at him with love and seems hurt when he says, "I loved you not."

Her "I was the more deceived" breaks hearts. I feel silly for competing with her.

Then Drew starts in on Hamlet's "Get thee to a nunnery" speech. He delivers it more to the audience than to Mandy, doesn't even start to make physical choices. It's like he's not even trying anymore. At first, Mandy acts affected—she puts her hands to her head, contracts as if she's been hit, but eventually she gets frustrated.

"I'm supposed to be hurt by this, Drew," she says. "He says that women make men monsters! You've got to *be* a *monster*!"

Drew goes red, and Nadia says, "Actors don't direct other actors, Mandy."

"But he's not being physical. He's hardly talking to me."

Nadia studies Drew's face. "There's some Hamlet anger. Take that speech again, Drew."

He starts, and he does sound angry, but he's still just as stiff.

"Mandy," Nadia says, and it sounds like she's having a lightbulb moment, "you're a dancer. Pretend you're doing choreography, and put Drew in a shape you think works for the scene."

Mandy's eyes burn with new power. "I can just move him?"

Nadia nods, and Mandy pulls Drew down so he's on top of her on the floor. A couple of students snicker. Mandy takes Drew's script away and moves his arm so it's pressing down against her collarbone. Drew more or less goes along, but he makes his body floppy and heavy to move.

"I think, like this . . . ," Mandy says. Drew looks more and more irritated as she wiggles his shoulders, requesting more tension.

"Speak from there now, Drew," Nadia says. "Where he says, 'Be thou chaste as ice.'"

"I don't have it memorized," Drew says.

"You don't need to. Just say that much."

Drew holds his position for a second, puffs out air, then bends down and grabs his script, holding it beside Mandy's face. He reads the line, but the words don't come out any differently. For Mandy though, her voice comes out desperate and strained by the shape she's chosen.

"Better," Nadia says. "You can leave the stage. I've seen enough."

Drew takes the stairs to the audience two at a time.

Mandy tries to make eye contact with him, but he keeps his head down.

"We can't try one more time?" Mandy says.

"Mandy," Nadia says, "sometimes when a director says they've seen enough, that's a good thing."

Mandy nods and keeps her face composed, but on her way offstage she seeks me out and pops her eyes wide—did I hear that? She's in.

I promise myself I'll be happy for her when she gets the part.

"Peter, come on up," Nadia says, and he jogs to the stage. He bounces on his feet while Nadia scans the audition list. I get a feeling right before she calls me, so it's less a surprise that it's me and more a surprise that my feeling was right.

All my nerves fire at once, and my legs go wobbly as I stand. Already, my hands are shaking. I take a deep breath before walking the aisle to the stage, looking down, not at Peter. He's probably worried about reading with me after I messed up at Mandy's.

It will be okay. There's a character to play and words to be said. In a way, the scene's already happened. We all know how it's supposed to end.

I stand across from Peter, and he gives me a nod, his lips already pressed in a grim line, eyes guarded but full. He holds my gaze, the papers at his side—he has the scene memorized. So do I, but I'm afraid to let it show.

Nadia says, "I'd like to hear, 'To be, or not to be,' from you, Peter."

My instinct is to search out Drew. He's just been told, basically, that he isn't being considered for the part. I resist looking, but it makes me cringe.

"So, Ophelia," Nadia says, "wait in the wings and listen to the speech. Let that inform how you enter."

I nod, but she's humoring me, giving me notes on how to act offstage so that I'll feel like I've done something when she cuts us off halfway through the scene.

Peter goes into the speech, and it's clear he understands the choice Hamlet has. Is it better to stay alive and suffer, or to let his "sea of troubles" drown him? He's afraid that what comes after life might be worse, so it's safest not to act at all.

"—Soft you now! The fair Ophelia!"

Ophelia's just heard her boyfriend say he would kill himself if he weren't too afraid. I try to compose my face. Ophelia's an actress too.

"Good my lord, how does your honor for this many a day?"

I focus on Hamlet, on saying what I came here to say, and that gets me into the scene, but soon I catch myself pushing again.

I take a breath to refocus. I'm breaking up with Hamlet even though I love him. I can imagine loving Peter. And my whole family's just broken up. It's not Ophelia's story, but it's better than thinking about how the words sound.

I repeat the line about returning Hamlet's gifts. It's good I know the lines—my hands are shaking so hard I'll never find my place again.

Nadia's voice chimes in, "What do you want to make him do, Caddie?"

My frustration comes out when I answer. "I want him to feel bad," I say. "I want him to stop acting like everything is normal."

"All right, then, say the line again."

I do. This time I watch for Peter's face to change, for him to break and let me see if he cares. I don't think I'm doing terribly, but I shouldn't be *thinking* about how I'm doing at all. I should *be* Ophelia.

Peter gets scornful, and it takes me off-guard. He's so good, so real, that for a second I forget he's acting. He's not, in a way. I'm pretty sure this is how Peter looks when he's angry. "Ha, ha! are you honest?"

He takes a step toward me, and I back up. "My lord!"

He reaches for me, reaches for my face, "Are you *fair*?" and I duck away, raising a hand.

"What means your lordship?" My voice cracks, but from real fear this time. He means to touch Ophelia. *Physical choices,* she said.

Peter answers, "That if you be honest and fair, your honesty should admit no discourse to your beauty."

He steps away again, smiling, which confuses me. I

want him to turn around.

"Could beauty, my lord, have better commerce than with honesty?"

He advances, and as he speaks, he reaches for me again. I step away, but he moves faster, grabs me around the waist with one arm, his other hand on my shoulder. No skin's touching, but the wave is crashing in. I can't have a panic attack on stage, but my breath rasps.

"Ay, truly," he says, "for the power of beauty will sooner transform honesty from what it is to a bawd . . ." He claps his hand down nearly on my backside, pulls my hips toward his, our faces so close . . . I make a noise, push back against his chest, but he goes on: ". . . than the force of honesty can translate beauty into his likeness . . ." He relaxes his hold but keeps his hands at the backs of my elbows, keeps me close, looks me straight in the eye, so unguarded, so in need.

No one has ever looked at me this way before.

"I did love you once," he says.

And he reaches one hand toward my cheek.

Ophelia would let him. I'm Ophelia, but I'm Caddie, too. I'm not sure what's real anymore.

I lift my gloved hand to catch his wrist. It feels strong in my hand, and his fingers, his palm, burn an inch away from my already hot cheek. The wave rises over our heads. I breathe in once, twice—it's hard to get enough air. His hand floats so close but doesn't move closer. It would be a choice to let him touch me. I almost want to pull his hand to my face, close the gap, and let go.

Nadia's voice, from a great distance, gives me my line: "Indeed, my lord, you made me believe so."

It comes out a whisper. I have to stop for breath between phrases.

Peter drops his hand then, drops me, and I sink to my knees.

"You should not have believed me," he says, "for virtue cannot so inoculate our old stock but we shall relish of it." He says it with disgust: "I loved you not."

"I was the more deceived." The line falls from my lips. I don't know where I am anymore. I'm crying, but I'm not sure why. Because he almost touched me? Or because he stopped? Or because I'm her and she hurts?

Peter's gone on with his speech. When I'm brave enough to catch his eyes, there's hesitation there, concern that belongs to Peter. Or maybe Hamlet feels that too, that he carried the act too far.

Over the next few lines, my breath hitches, and I sob before I'm able to speak. It's either the best or the worst acting I've ever done—both at once. Nadia should stop us. It's too much. I'm a mess.

At the cursing part, Peter gets much more physical than Drew. He crouches and squeezes my shoulders. "Be thou as chaste as ice, as pure as snow, thou shalt not escape calumny."

I backpedal away from him, and he lets me go, delivers the rest of his lines out to the audience. I don't know if it's a choice, or if he's too worried about me to touch me again. It's all I can do not to ask to stop, but it wouldn't be fair to Peter to wreck his audition more than I already have.

He finishes his lines, "we will have no more marriages; those that are married already, all but one, shall live; the rest shall keep as they are. To a nunnery, go."

Peter's off in crazy Hamlet land—he leaves with barely a look. I want him to come back, now that he's gone.

I could stop now, but I've learned the monologue. This might be the only chance I'll get to give it onstage. And I'm feeling the right things—a gap's closed between Ophelia and me. We've both pushed away boys we like. We're both being watched, and embarrassing ourselves. We've both wrecked everything.

If I want to tell Ophelia's story without "acting," there might not be a better time.

"O! what a noble mind is here o'erthrown . . ."

The emotion is there, so I don't have to force anything, just shape the words like a song. I lift my eyes toward the audience and let them in. It's awkward to let them see my face when I'm feeling so much, but that's what the scene needs.

They applaud. I try not to look at individual people, but Peter walks back onstage, beaming and clapping for me, and something between us has shifted. It feels dangerous to make eye contact with him, like if I look too long, I won't ever be able to stop.

Nadia doesn't clap. Her face is blank, judging me, but there's no way to tell what she's thinking.

I stand up, mutter "thank you," and walk down the stairs on the far side from Peter, away from his arms that are stretched out to give me a hug.

14.

I make myself sit through the next few auditions even though my whole body feels like it's burning. I sit far away from Mandy and her friends. Everything seems far away—I don't think I could look them in the eyes and hide how far away I am.

I go over and over the scene in my head, where I felt like her and forgot myself, where I felt like myself except out of control, where I felt both at once . . . Peter holding me, almost touching his hand to my skin.

Shakespeare didn't write stage directions that require Hamlet and Ophelia to touch, but how could I ever think acting with Peter would be safe? I've seen how physical Peter can be in real life, and the whole point of theater is that it's bigger, more.

Maybe because it's acting, a touch wouldn't matter.

He'd be touching Ophelia, not Caddie. But Ophelia's still with me, buzzing inside, and all our nerve endings are electric. It's not just the fear of Peter touching me . . . it's the bigness of the scene. It's so big how she feels, how she loves.

I want to play her so badly, but to do that onstage again and again, so open and exposed, to want him to touch me . . . The tremor starts at my center, rumbles out through my heart, shoulders, wrists, hands, and teeth.

Nadia's going to hear my teeth clatter, going to know better than to cast me, even as a guard. I should never have let the fear get this bad or my stupid crush on Peter go this far. It's a joke to think I can act, or have friends, or a boyfriend, or anything else if performing one scene makes me shatter.

I'm up and halfway to the auditorium door before I know it, one leg swinging in front of the other, stabbing the ground and propelling me out. When my brain catches up with my body, I speed to a jog.

In the hallway, I roll against the wall and will my teeth to stop, try to steady my breathing. I'm getting too much air, enough to drown. Thinking that makes it worse, but the thought comes, and I sink against the wall.

I don't want to panic in school, but at least no one's watching.

Then the door to the theater creaks open.

Peter.

I cover my eyes with the heels of my hands, hold my breath so he won't hear my voice catch, wait for him to get that I want to be alone, but he stands there. I have to breathe, gasp, and cover it by coughing.

Slowly, Peter shuts the door. His army boots shuffle closer. "Oh, no . . . sad clown."

"I'm okay," I tell him.

He doesn't take the hint. He slides down the wall so he's crouching beside me. "You don't look okay."

"No, I'm fine. I just—I want to be alone right now."

He doesn't move, but he doesn't speak, either. I try to steady my breath, but it isn't cooperating. "I really— Do you mind?"

"I'm so glad I got to read with you," he says. "I was impressed."

I shake my head.

"Caddie, you were amazing. . . . That monologue . . ."

I did get through the monologue, and I felt like Ophelia. But everything else was a mess.

My voice gasps as I breathe, and Peter says, "Are you . . . should I get someone?"

I shake my head emphatically, and he waits while I get it together to speak. "I just— I get like this. When I'm anxious."

He waits for me to say more, then says, "I hope I didn't . . . I hope nothing made you uncomfortable. Nadia wanted us to be physical. The rest of us, we're used to it, but you're new. Maybe I shouldn't have—"

"It's nothing you did," I say. "I'm sorry. I just want to be alone."

He accepts it, just like that. I told him it wasn't his fault. He believes me. No fuss.

Because he knows that it isn't his fault. He knows that I'm strange.

"I don't believe in letting people cry alone," he says. "You don't have to talk if you don't want to, but I'm not going anywhere." His face seems perfectly steady, like he couldn't care less what I think about him joining me on the floor.

"Look, I'm embarrassed," I tell him. "I don't want you to see me like this." And he nods. He isn't grinning exactly, but his lips are set.

"That's okay, but like I told you before, I'm not going anywhere."

For a split second I wish he would hug me, crush me, so this stupid game can be over, so I don't have anywhere to go or anything to do but cry into his shirt. And then I want to smack him. But I'm not allowed to do either. I stand, wobbling a little, and he reaches out a hand to steady me.

"Don't," I say, pulling away and balancing myself on the wall. "You can stay here as long as you want, but I'm going."

"Good deal," he says, and he stands too, following me down the hall.

"God, just quit it, okay?"

He shakes his head.

"You can't follow me home." He shrugs as if to say he can. "We barely even know each other, Peter, so why do you care?"

"Is that a serious question?"

"You're making me angry."

"Good," he says. "Angry is better than what you were before."

I don't know how to argue with him, so I walk. He follows me. It's almost funny. His steps thud behind me, then speed up and he's beside me. At the stairs, I run, up and up as fast as I can. Peter laughs and races me, taking the steps two at a time, wheeling around me on the landing and beating me to the top.

We both have to catch our breath, and when his eyes meet mine, I actually start laughing. It's all so ridiculous, I can't help myself.

"Where are you going?" Peter asks.

"To the roof," I say, putting on a wild bravado. "I'm going to jump off the building. Do you want to come do that, too?"

"I did that once," he says. "Jumped off a roof. Roof of a cabin at summer camp. I broke my leg in two places and got to go home." He says it nonchalantly, as if that's a completely normal thing for a kid to do, and he sinks down on the step above me.

"Why would you jump off a roof?"

"I didn't want to be there. I was like seven years old. I was living with my dad while my mom did grad school. Dad had just remarried. He and the stepmom wanted a honeymoon. I told my cabin counselor if he didn't let me call them I would jump off the roof. He didn't. I did. It took them a day or two to get back from where they were, but they came and got me."

"That's crazy."

Peter slides down a step to sit beside me, and I let him. There's no point telling him to go away. The guy jumped off a roof.

"Did you— When you did it, weren't you afraid of what might happen?"

He shakes his head. "No. I remember being angry that it hurt so bad. It's like I thought they were making it hurt worse to punish me. I wanted to dole out some pain to every adult there."

"Wow."

"I was scared, too, like, the doctors told me I was bleeding from my bones, and I thought that must mean I was a goner."

"That's awful. Were you okay? Did you ever forgive your dad?"

"Oh yeah, I guess I did. What else do you do when you're seven? I definitely milked it for a while. I was a bratty little patient."

I can imagine.

"So, are *you* okay?" he asks.

It's a moment before I can think about myself again to answer him. "Yeah, I am," I say. "You pissed me off, but yeah, I guess I feel a little better."

"I knew you were nervous," he says. "You hide it, but I could tell."

I should tell him to stop looking so hard, keep it safe between Peter and me. But I like that he looked, that he could tell.

"It's more than that," I say. My chest's tight from saying it out loud. "My dad doesn't want me to be here. He says I have too much 'academic potential' to be an actress, like this isn't even a real school. I feel like I have to do well here or else . . . he'll have been right. I'll be disappointing my mom. Things . . . aren't good right now between them."

"I wondered," Peter says.

I do a mental rundown of the time I've spent with Peter, what I might have done to give that away. Or is it blatantly clear to everyone, like a face tattoo reading CHILD OF A BROKEN HOME?

"What do you mean?"

"Nothing. I thought something might be going on with your family. You never talk about them. You seem stressed a lot of the time."

Hearing him say that aloud is comforting somehow. I haven't talked to anyone about this stuff—wanting to prove myself to my dad, wanting to make Mom proud.

We sit there silently, listening to the hum of air sighing through the old building.

"What's the most scared you've ever been?" he asks, and right then I want to tell him everything and see how he reacts, see if anyone can understand and not think I'm crazy like I know I am. I want to tell him about our fight in March, and the hospital, about the day Dad left and not touching, about how I imagine it would feel if Peter touched me, like the worst and best things in the world all at once.

"I don't know," I say. "A lot of things scare me." He nods like he could have guessed that's what I'd say.

He's so close, our clothes touch. He plays with the corner of my cardigan that rests on his thigh, giving it the slightest tug. When he looks back to me, he tilts his head, and this might be the moment if we were two normal kids when he'd lean in and we'd kiss.

But instead he stares as if he can read something written on my skin. I'm unnerved by his ease with me, how close he came to making me spill everything.

"Okay, so am I excused?" I say. "I think I need to go."

"I think you're safe to travel. You sure you're okay?"

I don't answer, but I smile long enough to convince him I'm all better, then guard my face on my way down the stairs. I don't want to chance Peter reading more than I'm ready to say.

All the way home, I think about falling.

15.

Ophelia falls. On purpose or not, we don't know. She falls from the willow branch into the pond and drowns.

I could drown in Peter. One touch, skin to skin, and I'd fall.

I'm chopping veggies, helping Mom with dinner even though it's Friday. The others are probably out celebrating being done with auditions, but I didn't have the guts to make eye contact with Mandy after I read for Ophelia, much less call her.

"Caddie," Mom says. I've stopped chopping. "You looked so far away."

"I was thinking," I tell her.

"What's on your mind?"

I shake my head.

She faces me, her lips in the pout she makes when she

can't decide how far to push. "I know it's been hard on you with Dad gone."

It annoys me when she skirts around the words. "That you're getting divorced."

"We're taking some space. Sometimes you need that space in a relationship. Even a very good one."

Which theirs isn't.

"Mom. I understand how things are. It's okay. It's not your fault."

Her eyes soften. "I appreciate that," she says quietly. "It's not your fault either. You know that, right?"

I nod and go back to cutting, try to bottle the cry in my throat before it can grow into a full-fledged sob. I know no such thing. It's arrogant in a way to think I could have such an effect on them, but that doesn't change how it feels.

"I submitted a portfolio to the Goblet," Mom says, changing the subject. The Goblet is a bistro with a gallery. Fancy customers wander around there with decorators in tow, sipping wine while they shop for their homes. "They're open to new artists' work."

"That's cool." My voice is too flat, but the hope in her voice, the enthusiasm, worries me.

On a night like this, making dinner with Mom, it's easy to act like nothing's changed. But Mom submitting to a gallery—that's very new. And she agreed to let Jordan play football. And she's certain, even though I warned her it doesn't look good, that I'm getting a part in the play. She's got all three of us doing things that Dad might describe as "frivolous."

Maybe that's what we all need, to move on and let go. Jordan takes out his aggression on a football field. Mom gets a gallery show. I get a role in a play, a boyfriend. . . .

Peter almost touched my skin at our audition. I keep telling myself I was careful, but no amount of careful can make me feel safe because I know something new: I *want* to know what it feels like to have Peter touch me. And I want to touch him.

"Caddie." Mom takes a long pause. "You seem awfully . . . tense."

She's picked up on it, then.

"I want you to feel like you can talk to me, Caddie, when you need help with something."

A few years ago, I might have seen this look on Mom's face and assumed she was getting a migraine. Now, I can look in a mirror any minute of the day and see that same expression on my own face.

Worry.

The first time we went to the doctor for my panic attacks, we went in together, and talking about my problems made Mom start to cry. I'd only ever seen her like that because someone had died.

That terrified me, I could have told Peter, that I could be messed up enough to make Mom cry. And then, in March, when Dad found out that Mom let me audition for the academy . . . that night was murder. Mom had taken me to the audition in secret.

The night my acceptance letter came, nobody was "emotionally contained." Mine and Dad's tempers boiled over, and we shouted at each other until I started panicking and Mom screamed that we had to calm down, that this was hurting me.

Dad went down to the basement, got in his car, and drove away. Didn't say where he was going or when he'd be back. He abandoned us for twenty-eight hours—long enough for me to break.

I'd been doing better before then. The panic that had gotten so bad in middle school was under control. I hadn't been to Dr. Rice in more than a year. But that night, Mom took me to the emergency room. They gave me a sedative to make me sleep. The next day when I woke up and Dad still hadn't come back and I felt so groggy, caught in some other girl's half-dreamed life, I was sure that he never would.

Later that night, when he did come back, I knew it wouldn't last. Something had broken that couldn't be mended. By June, he was gone.

Now I work to free my face of tension. It took forever to convince Mom that my night in the hospital wasn't a relapse, just a one-night slipup, brought on by the fight. No more panic. No more doctors. If I seem all right, Mom will let this go.

I wait to see if she wants to make a thing of it, but she stares into herself and crosses her arms. "Do you want to do the dressing for the salad?" she asks, and I nod.

She's going to leave it alone, and I'm going to cooperate to thank her for it.

That night, I lie in bed waiting for sleep that won't come.

By Monday I'll know. If I'm Ophelia. If Peter is Hamlet.

The part of me that *needs* to touch is like a tiny bird I swallowed by mistake. It beats its wings against my throat, tickles my heart with its feathers, grips a rib with its claws. It tastes the inside of my skin with its little bird tongue.

When Peter looked at me—with so much need—it started chirping to get out.

Fear tugs at me and I'm falling.

I grab at the mattress, dig in with my fingers, flop onto my stomach, hold tight. Press my face into the pillow so hard it hurts. The quilt twists like it wants to smother me.

I can't scream out loud, but there has to be some release. I kick my feet against the mattress in a muffled frenzy, legs flying fast and hard enough to carry me miles away. And when it's done, nothing's changed. I'm still stuck right here.

16.

Mr. Kiernan reads the announcements during second-period chemistry: the cast list is up. We'll be able to check during the long break between second and third. Livia twists in her seat, eyes wide and sure, and reaches across the lab table—to squeeze hands I guess.

I wiggle my fingers in a wave.

When the bell rings, Livia's up fast. "We should all go together," she says, but I take my time arranging and rearranging the contents of my backpack. I'd rather wait for the crowd to thin out.

Mandy pushes through the exiting students and flies to us, bouncing on the balls of her feet. "Why so slow? I'm not going without you guys!" To me, she says, "Hey, you!" and there's an acknowledgment in her voice that it's the first time we've spoken since Friday. "Where were you this morning? Peter was wanting to talk flash mob."

"I was running late," I lie. "Hold on, I need a piece of gum."

"I meant to tell you good job after your audition," Mandy says. "That was pretty . . . intense, but then you ran off."

The way Mandy says "intense" doesn't sound entirely complimentary.

"I was weird," I say. "You did great." I go back to rummaging.

"Forget the gum. I saw Peter and Hank in the hall."

Mandy reaches for my shoulder, and I jerk away. "I didn't ask you to wait," I say, and immediately regret how harsh I sound. Mandy's face falls.

"I don't want to look without you," she says, her voice hard now too. "It's more fun if we go together."

"Okay, sorry. I'm ready."

Mandy's giddy again, walking backward to make sure I'm following. "You're just worried you're going to have bad breath when you're jumping up and down and screaming, 'Hallelujah for me, I got cast!'"

"Right," I say, letting her draw me out into the hall.

I see Drew before Mandy does. His face is alert and too tense.

Mandy sees the curiosity—the worry—in me, and she spins around to Drew.

They hold eye contact for a few solid seconds, and then

Mandy breaks off with her back to us, presses her palms to the wall. "Crap," she mutters. "Crap. Crap." She doesn't turn around when she asks, "Did I even get a little part?"

"I told you she wasn't going to like you being pushy," Drew says before putting his hands on Mandy's back, which is shaking. His words aren't comforting, but when Livia steps closer to Mandy, he shakes his head to say he's got it covered.

Livia turns to me. "Come on, we have to look," and she darts ahead.

Mandy's audition was good. If she's not on the list anywhere, then who knows what Nadia wants? As anxious as I am to check for my name, it's more important to show Mandy I care. I take a step toward her, but Drew wraps his arms around her and rocks her back and forth. He shakes his head at me. "Go on, Caddie. Go look."

"I'm so sorry, Mandy. I know you wanted it."

Mandy waves a hand to send me away.

I walk down the hall toward the bulletin board as if pressing through something heavy and wet. The crowd hasn't dispersed, but it's spread. People give one another space as they read the list over and over, looking for something they might have missed, memorizing the names.

Livia sees me and smiles big. My heart floods. I'm in the play. I'll be one of the theater crowd. I'll be a part of things . . . but Mandy won't.

April is planted in front of the board with her arms

crossed, staring at the list even though there's no way she's on it. She turns toward me and her face flinches.

"You're that new girl. The junior?"

By the time I'm done nodding, she's mastered her face. She's easy to read because she's so much like me, trying to look like she doesn't care. "Congratulations," she says. "All the senior girls are going to hate you."

My heart thuds harder.

Something in Drew's face made me wonder. I didn't believe it. It would be unlikely for a new girl to get cast as . . .

Ophelia.

My name's next to that name. I can't help raising my finger to the board to trace the distance between her name and mine, to make sure they line up.

"It's really you," April says. "It's a great part. I'd be nervous to play it."

She's saying it partly to make herself feel better, but it's the truth, too. She would be nervous. I am. And happy, and worried, and embarrassed, and a bazillion other things.

"God, don't cry," April says.

I blink hard and take a deep breath to calm myself down. I scan the other names, looking for Hamlet.

It's Peter.

I didn't need to look. As soon as I saw my own name, I knew. If I hadn't read with him, I doubt I'd have been cast. I'm grateful he's not here with me. Whatever real feelings are there, we're going to be pretending we're in love. I feel feverish as it is—with Peter standing beside me, I'd catch fire.

All the rest of them made it, one way or another. Hank is Hamlet's uncle, King Claudius. Oscar is Laertes, Ophelia's brother who swordfights with Hamlet at the end of the play. Livia is Gertrude.

Drew will be playing my father, Polonius. It's not a flashy part, but it's a major role. I wonder if Drew's happy with it, or if he's feeling exactly what I am—worried because he got a part and Mandy didn't.

We have to sign our initials to say we accept, that we'll be at rehearsals this afternoon and every afternoon.

Signing that paper means opening up to Ophelia's tsunami of feeling. It means working with Peter, closely, and trying to keep my head. There's the fear of pissing off Mandy, the fear of becoming the new Macbeth asthma kid, the risk of disappointing Mom, and disappointing Dad for sure.

I want to tell Dad, I realize. I *want* him to be happy for me, proud, want him to reassure me that this blessing doesn't mean I'm cursed when it comes to him.

I take my phone out to the courtyard, where the leaves rustle red and orange.

"Y-ello," he answers, "yes" and "hello" together, all business.

"Dad? It's—"

"Oh!" It takes him a second to realize. "Caddie. I didn't even look. I'm expecting a call."

If he'd seen me on his caller ID, he wouldn't have answered.

"Can you call back and leave a message, sweetie?"

"I have some news."

"We'll talk soon, all right, but I need to take this call."

"Dad, I—"

"Call me right back and leave a message to remind me."

Click. And he's gone.

I call right back, like if I'm fast enough, he'll still be on the line.

"You have reached the cell phone of Charles Finn."

Before it can beep, I end the call.

17.

I'd been building up some kind of power by not calling Dad, but now I've spent it, and he wouldn't even talk to me.

I go to lunch both hoping and dreading to see Mandy. I want to tell to her about Dad, see if she and I are okay, but she doesn't show. Neither does Drew.

"I don't understand why Nadia didn't give her some part," I say. "It's mean."

Hank shrugs. "I don't think she did it to be mean. Most people would be honored to do what Mandy's doing."

"What?" I say.

"It was on the crew sheet. She's assistant director," Hank says. "Nadia would be pissed if she saw Mandy acting disappointed about it."

Across the lunchroom, Peter and Oscar are making

their way through the line. Every time someone comes up to Peter to congratulate him, Oscar acts super interested in the haircut of the guy in front of him.

Soon, Peter's setting his tray down by mine and standing with his arms wide for a congratulatory hug. "I told you, didn't I?" he says.

"Congratulations," I say, clapping my hands in front of my face. "Sorry I can't stand up. My foot's asleep." The longer I play this game, the better I get at lying.

Usually Peter sits across from me, but with Mandy and Drew gone, he takes the seat at my side.

"Look at the happy couple," says Hank.

"Until he goes crazy and she kills herself," Livia says, and I'm grateful to her for dashing even Hank's snarky suggestion of romance.

"We get to be in love too," says Livia, squeezing herself against Hank's shoulder.

"Famous!" Hank says, and he takes her face in his hands and gives her a giant smooch full on the lips. Livia exaggerates fanning herself.

"All right, your turn," Hank says, spinning his finger in a circle toward me and Peter. "We can double date, the king and the queen and the prince and the . . . What are you?" he asks me.

"A courtier? I don't know. Are you so excited?" I say to Peter, to get away from the cute talk.

"Excited," he says. "And terrified."

"That's what makes it fun," Oscar says. "When I went in for my first day of shooting with Lance—"

"You shook so bad your costume glasses fell off your face," Hank finishes.

"She hasn't heard it before!" Oscar says, pointing to me. "I'm not bragging."

"Of course not," says Hank.

"If I were bragging, I would act like Lance was the one scared to be working with me."

"Lance?" Peter teases.

"You work with a guy, you get to be on a first-name basis. I'm not trying to be snotty about it."

"You're so good at it, though, without even trying," Hank says.

Everyone laughs, Oscar too. He still rubs me the wrong way—he did rub me, in a very wrong way, at our first meeting—but I get why they like him.

"Let's talk flash mob." Peter turns sideways in his seat so his knee bumps mine.

Careful.

"Cannot wait," Livia says.

Peter nods. "I was thinking we could do it at Mandy's Halloween party."

"Mandy's?" I say.

"I know it's a ways off, but it will give us time to plan."

"It's an annual thing," Hank explains. "You guys are so tight, I'm surprised you haven't come before." If anybody else said that, I'd question whether he meant to make me feel bad, but Hank has a way of being oblivious to the social dynamic.

"Will there be enough people there?" I ask.

"Half the school," Oscar says.

Peter says, "Count on a hundred and fifty people. I figure if fifteen percent of them freeze, that should be about right."

"That's like the whole cast of *Hamlet*."

"Great minds . . . ," Peter says, pointing a finger back and forth between my great mind and his. Livia claps. They're all looking at me with the same excitement Mandy used to show when I had a great idea. Getting cast makes such a difference.

I belong, even without Mandy here. I'm not glad Mandy's skipping lunch, but I'm glad to know how this feels.

"Caddie, I know you're going to beg to be my partner for warm-ups at rehearsal today," Oscar says, "so I'll kill the suspense now and say yes."

"Show of hands if you vote Oscar's banned from trust falls," Peter says.

"Trust falls?" I say. "Like, where you fall. And other people. Try to catch you?" It takes several breaths to get out the words.

"That's Nadia's favorite bonding thing to do with a new cast," he says, completely oblivious to my horror. "She's got a bajillion variations."

Livia says, "I like the one where you stand in the middle of the circle and let everybody pass you around."

"But you actually like people groping you," Hank says. "I know."

Livia giggles.

"I like the one," Oscar says, "where people put their hands on different parts of your body all at once, moving down like a waterfall. Kind of hot."

"Caddie?" Hank says. "Are you all right? You look red."

Any sense of belonging I had has fled, and I'm back in my bubble. My air's running out—one false move and panic will come crashing in.

"Yeah, I'm okay," I say. "I feel like I might be getting a fever. I'm going to see if the office will give me some Tylenol."

Peter reaches out as if to touch my forehead, and I stand up fast.

"Feel better," Peter says. "You can't miss the first rehearsal."

"No, I know. Thanks. You feel better too. I mean, I didn't mean that. I mean, see you guys later."

Going home sick is one option.

Jumping off the roof is another. Better that than drop out of the play.

My feet carry me outside, across the drive to the amphitheater. Mandy's there, on the lowest level, folded into herself and smoking. Drew sits with her, and when he sees me, he stands. "Oh, good. Caddie can keep you company while I scarf something down."

Mandy looks up toward me, indifferent. "You're leaving me?" she says to Drew.

He rubs his hands up and down her arms. "I love you, baby, but I'm hungry."

"Okay," she says in her mopiest voice. "Grab me a banana?"

"Sure thing." On his way up he mutters, "Good luck," to me under his breath.

"He's being nice," I say.

"Yeah. He still says I 'wrecked his audition,' but I guess I'm forgiven since I wrecked mine more."

"I think you helped his audition—or you would have if he'd let you."

Mandy takes an aggressive draw on her cigarette and lifts her chin to exhale.

"She should have at least asked me," she says, "if I wanted to be AD."

"What would you have said?"

She shrugs. "It might be more fun, if it were between that and a small part, but who knows? My mom's going to be pissed."

I don't feel like I have permission to sit down yet, so I hover. "We missed you at lunch."

"I couldn't deal with everybody."

"I'm sorry." I step down to the lowest level and sit, leaving one big stone seat between us.

"It's not your fault," she says, and then after a drag, "Congratulations. You must be excited."

"I am and I'm not," I say. "I'm afraid of messing up, and . . . I've been afraid you'd be mad at me."

She locks eyes with me. "I am mad at you," she says, "a little. But I know it's not fair. I'm just jealous." She smiles. "I'll get over it."

I smile too, because she looks like the Mandy I know, the one who gets over things fast.

"Let me ask you this," she says. "Did you even want that part? Because you didn't act like you did."

"I did," I say. "I didn't think I would get it, but yeah, I wanted it."

She nods. "Good. I would be madder if you didn't. Why didn't you tell me, though? I was going on and on about it like an idiot. I wish I had known that you wanted it too."

I can't help smiling. "So you could talk me out of it?"

"What? No!"

"Like you told Livia she'd be good at Horatio when she said she might be interested in Ophelia?"

Mandy inhales and takes that in, smiles guiltily. "Did I do that?"

"A little bit."

"Hm."

"I think she's pretty happy with Gertrude. King Hank

kissed her at lunch."

Mandy cackles, then shakes her head. "She's barking up the wrong tree."

"What do you mean?"

"That tree only likes cats."

It's nice talking with Mandy about her friends who are now *our* friends. Without Mandy, I wouldn't even know them.

"I'm sorry I didn't say anything about Ophelia. I didn't want anybody to know that I cared."

"Okay, but there's a difference between telling everyone and telling your best friend."

My reaction to that phrase, "best friend," makes her smirk. She holds my eyes.

"We're friends, Caddie. I want us to always be friends."

"Okay."

"You have to be open with your friends, though, or what's the point?"

I should tell her. She might even understand, weird as it is. And maybe it would take some of its power away. . . .

"I need to talk to you about something," I say.

"Yeah?"

My heart seems to tug at my vocal cords, stretching them tight. "It's about rehearsal this afternoon. I hear Nadia likes to do trust falls? Okay, well, remember when I told you I had sun poisoning?"

She nods.

If I let her in, it won't be just my problem anymore, and Mandy will want me to fix it. People change, feelings change—people hurt each other, hurt themselves, and whether or not I touch people has nothing to do with it.

"I . . . well . . . I still have it."

Nadia's kind of acting is hard, but a lie is so easy.

"Seriously? That was, like, three weeks ago."

"I know. I'm stupid." I make myself sheepish. "It was dumb, but I laid out again."

"Can I see?"

"I'm not supposed to expose it to sunlight."

"We're in the shade."

"I know, but it hurts to pull up my sleeves."

"Ow! That sounds awful."

"Yeah, well, I was hoping you could tell Nadia that I don't want anyone to know . . . or to worry about me, because it's not that big a deal, but I can't do trust falls. It would hurt too bad."

She nods. "Ouch! Yeah, okay, I'll tell her. You'd better not go in the sun again, though. You're going to have trouble being in a play and not touching anybody."

My thoughts exactly.

18.

Some kids wait in the audience for rehearsal. Some stretch on the stage, including Peter. I'm going to be acting with him; I'd better be able to sit beside him.

I *want* to sit by him.

"Hi, Ophelia," he says with a big grin as I flop down next to him.

"Hi, Hamlet," I say, stretching over one leg. "We're so tragical."

"I don't know about you, but I don't see the point in even doing the play. If we cut to the chase and do ourselves in at the top, we could be done in five minutes and go out for ice cream."

"Right?"

"Wait," he says. "Here's the kind of thing Nadia's going to want to know for your character journal: What's

Ophelia's favorite ice cream flavor?"

"Character journal?"

"You'll see."

"Did they have ice cream in Denmark back then?"

"Doesn't matter. Hamlet's taking Ophelia to the ice cream social. What does she order?"

"Um. How about lemon sorbet?"

"Ooh, I like it. Simple, clean."

"What about Hamlet?"

"I think Hamlet's got to be a rocky road kind of guy."

"So wait, is this supposed to be the kind of ice cream he would eat, or the kind of ice cream that he *is*?"

"It's an essence thing," he says. "Instinct."

"All right. I'll buy rocky road. What about Peter?"

He shakes his head. "To find that out you have to accompany me to the ice cream social."

Did he just ask me out? To a nonexistent ice cream social, but still . . .

"Do some character research?" I say.

"Sure, or because it would be fun."

Nadia's voice makes me shake: "Three fifteen. Let's begin." Normally her presence in a room is enough to turn heads, but Peter's distracting.

"Thank you for being on time," she says. "If you're late on a consistent basis, we'll replace you. Easy."

Mandy stands at Nadia's side with a clipboard. She's beaming, and if it's an act, it's a good one.

Nadia motions for us to gather on the stage and gives us the first day rundown. We'll be taking this show to Bard if school-site judging goes well, but if the judges heard about the debacle at Thespians, they'll be less inclined to take us seriously.

When Nadia introduces Mandy, she says, "I'm pleased that Mandy Bower has agreed to assist me in this process. Treat her with the same respect you give me." Mandy widens her eyes at us in a goofy, fake threat.

Nadia assigns the character journals. We're supposed to write down everything other characters in the play say about us, and lists of ways we're the same and different from the characters we're playing.

"Don't tell me the obvious, 'Rosencrantz lives in Denmark, and I live in America.' I want essential differences. Peter might find that he and Hamlet both have a lust for vengeance."

Peter laughs wickedly, and Nadia goes on, "Hypothetically. Caddie might find that while Ophelia is completely dependent on her father, she herself has trouble understanding that connection, or she understands it entirely. Either way. Think about what separates you from your character and what draws you together."

We're supposed to come up with metaphors, like the ice cream. "If Laertes were a type of weather, what type of weather would he be?" She tells us to start collecting images—real-life people who remind us of our characters, poses and gestures we might use on stage. And we're to shoot a self-portrait.

"I want to see the character in you. You don't have to put on a costume or makeup, but you should try to capture something essential."

Mandy leads warm-ups, and she takes an extra-long time with it, just for kicks, I think. She's a good leader. No one complains.

Then it's time for trust falls.

"I do this with every new cast," Nadia says, and a couple of people laugh in recognition. "Let's all make a tight circle, shoulder to shoulder."

I stand apart as the circle forms.

"Caddie," Nadia says, "come and join us."

Mandy widens her eyes at me and grimaces.

"Oh, but I can't . . ."

"Are you afraid? We'll catch you."

"No. I mean, yes, I . . ."

Mandy rushes up beside us. "I'm sorry. I didn't get a chance to tell her," she says, low.

"What's this?" Nadia says.

"I got . . . sun poisoning." It's harder to make it sound like a good reason with Nadia than with Mandy.

"It makes her uncomfortable," says Mandy.

"Uncomfortable?" Nadia says.

"I mean, it hurts her."

Nadia looks back and forth between us. She thinks

Mandy's lying for me, even though as far as Mandy knows, it's the truth. "You won't be falling far."

"I know, but . . . even a little touch burns."

Nadia freezes me with her tiger stare. "I'd like you to give it a try."

She turns back to the circle, fully expecting me to follow behind. I don't want to be difficult, but it's a lot that she's asking. Even if she doesn't know it.

When she sees I haven't followed, she turns back. The eyes of the circle turn with her, impatient. "We're not going to make you do anything you don't want to do," she says in the reasonable voice of disappointed teachers everywhere. She means she can't make me do it. But she can silently judge me for not participating.

I have the gloves. I have long sleeves. The risk of somebody touching my skin is small, but choosing to take the risk feels like a betrayal. I'm not even sure what I'd be betraying. Mom and Dad aren't showing any signs of reconciliation.

I step into the circle between Peter and Drew. Their arms are longer than mine and should keep anybody from falling against me, even if I mess up.

Nadia beams. "Step in tight."

Peter's shoulder presses in on one side, Drew's on the other. It's clothes touching clothes, nothing more.

Oscar steps into the circle, and it's all I can do to keep breathing at a normal pace as he starts falling first to one side, then the other, his arms crossed over his chest like a standing corpse with rigor mortis. As the circle gets into a rhythm, he rolls around the edges, passed from hand to hand. I hold back just enough, let Drew and Peter squeeze in so they don't need my hands at all.

One time as Oscar passes, Peter looks to me—he's noticed maybe that I hang back, but he doesn't say anything. He starts anticipating, stepping forward a bit to take the weight from Drew, basically skipping me as Oscar comes around.

It goes like that for four more people, and I keep my breath steady enough to stay blank. If Nadia could step inside my head and see how far away it all seems—there's a film between me and the rest of them, the wall of my bubble that keeps me from drowning—she'd take me out for safety.

"Caddie, step into the center," Nadia commands.

Peter's hand touches my back, a slight push forward. The circle closes in. It's too late to sell that Peter caused me physical pain, but I cry out anyway. It's easy to make a small noise out of a giant fear.

Nadia twitches; then her mask comes back. She's already regretting casting me—such an odd, stressed-out, untrusting girl.

"Are you all right?" she says.

"I can't do this."

"We're here to catch you," she says.

"No, I know. I'm just . . ."

"Have you ever been dipped? Like dancing?" someone says, popping the bubble, and they're all too close, too fast. A tug at my shoulder, and I'm spinning; someone yanks my arm, and I wheel into a chest.

Oscar.

He tips me, stupid, since I'm already falling, head over head over . . . I push away, hike my knee into his stomach so he goes "oof" and drops me, spins away.

My head hits the stage, rattling my teeth, and I find the floor under me. Breathe.

They want to know if I'm all right. They're standing back, giving me room.

Oscar's repeating, "Oh God, I'm so sorry, Caddie, I'm sorry. Wow. I'm sorry."

I pull myself up, even though it hurts my head. Peter reaches out a hand, but I wave. "I'm fine, really, I'm fine. I just freaked out. I'm sorry. I'm sorry."

"She's crying," Mandy says, and crosses toward me. I wave her away, smile.

"I'm all right. Really, please, don't worry about me. I'm fine."

"Take her to the office," Nadia says.

"No, please, I want to stay. Can I just—can I sit in the audience for a second? I'm going to be fine."

Nadia stares at me hard. "Fill out an accident report. Then come back if you can."

She motions for Mandy to accompany me, and I have to smile big to keep Mandy from scooping me up in a fireman's carry. She looks that worried.

I make it back to practice, but Nadia doesn't use me at all.

"You might as well go on home if you're feeling bad," she says, but I shake my head and watch from the audience.

She's demonstrating how Shakespeare uses punctuation to tell his actors when to breathe, when to build to a climax. When there are three single-syllable words in a row, we're supposed to slow down: Draaaaaaw. Theeeeem. Ouuuuuuuut.

The rest of the cast sits on stage and practices lines when Nadia shows a new rule. I could sit on the stage without any problem, but no, I have to "rest."

The distance between the audience and the stage is interstellar.

19.

Mom and I agreed that I would stay after school for rehearsal whether I got cast or not and tell her in person what happened. I must look pretty grim because she says, "Oh, dear," before I even make it all the way into the car.

"No, Mom, it's good. I made it."

"You were trying to trick me!" she says, and I nod, force a huge smile.

"Gotcha."

Crying and laughing are so close, it's a tiny switch to trick even myself. And I'm so close to happy—

"I have a special announcement of my own," Mom says, but she won't reveal it until we're all together for dinner.

Please let it be something good about Dad. I can't help myself from wishing it.

Before dinner, Jordan leans in my doorway, says,

"Congratulations," and plays with the corner of the Oph-elia picture on my wall. "I knew you would get it."

"Yeah?" I say. "I wish you'd told *me* that."

Jordan's actually smiling for once. "So, Mom's in a crazy-good mood," he says. "Do you think something changed?"

"I don't know," I say, but I hope, hope, hope.

At the table she says, "I want to make a toast," and Jordan and I lift our glasses of sparkling grape juice.

"To Caddie," she says, "for taking risks. You changed schools, put yourself out there; you worked hard, and it paid off. To Jordan—"

"What did I do?" he says.

"—for showing how responsible you can be, keeping up with sports practice and your schoolwork."

Jordan makes a face—he doesn't like being patronized—but he has been acting better since Mom gave him the chance to try football.

"What's your news?" he asks.

"My news . . ." Jordan's holding his breath, I think, and that makes me hope harder she'll say something good about Dad. "Caddie's not the only one who's been chal-lenging herself. I got a show! At the Goblet!"

She told me she submitted to them. I should have known.

"Mom . . . that's . . ."

I'm looking for the right words . . . fancy, fantastic,

impressive, a big deal, but Jordan says the glaring truth before I get a chance: "That's bullshit!"

Mom's face falls, and I say, "Jordan!" even though I was thinking the same thing.

Jordan sets his glass down so hard that it sloshes onto the tablecloth, and he storms out.

Mom stares after him, so I go for the seltzer water in Dad's liquor cabinet—Mom doesn't drink any of that stuff, but maybe he thought it would be tacky to take it with him.

I put a kitchen towel under the tablecloth and pour onto the spill. Mom must be rattled if she's not taking over—cleaning is Mom's happy place.

"He thought . . . ," she says.

"Yeah. I did too, or I hoped."

"I messed up."

I meet her eyes, but I'm not going to rub it in by nodding.

"Are you okay?" she asks.

I shrug. "I'm happy for you. If we hoped something else, that's our own stupid fault."

And then Mom starts crying, harder than I've ever seen. I don't know what to do.

"I'm such an idiot," she says.

"No . . ."

I try to pat her shoulder, but any second she's going to grab me, pull me into an octopus hug, wrap her hand around the back of my neck, press her cheek to mine.

And I *want* that. I want to hold her and release this

tight ball in my chest.

What if I hugged her right now? Said, screw it, and let it all go?

It would be selfish, taking comfort for myself but risking hurt for us all.

"I'm sorry, Mom," I say, blotting the stain. "You should get to be happy. This is a happy thing."

"I feel like I've had blinders on," she says. "I mean, I've known this is affecting you, but I thought, what can I do about it? I've almost had my fingers in my ears going *lalala*. I've been trying to move forward."

"That's what you *should* be doing," I say. "It's okay."

She shakes her head, mad at herself. I should find a way to comfort her, or go to Jordan, or bring Jordan back to Mom, but instead, I go to my room with Ophelia.

It will be a relief to be her for a while instead of me.

Our first task for our character journals is to write down all the things said about us in the play—see what information we get from other points of view. Plus, I'm looking for clues.

I can't touch anyone, so my Ophelia will have to be that way too. If I can justify it for the character, then Nadia will have to stage it that way.

Luckily, Shakespeare never shows Hamlet and Ophelia together and happy—their relationship's all in the past. In Ophelia's first scene, her brother Laertes tells her not to trust Hamlet's affections, and her father spends a couple of pages saying the same thing and ordering her not to talk with Hamlet anymore.

Even though she's in love, Ophelia says, "I shall obey, my lord."

My rules are ones I made up for myself, but I obey them just the same. I'm wary. I fear.

I start on my list of similarities. "Ophelia and I both follow the rules."

And the rules tell us, *look but don't touch.*

My phone sounds and I shudder, pulled back to myself.

It's from a number I don't recognize:

Ham has congrats present for O

It has to be Peter.

ME: O's not allowed to take presents from Ham

PETER: From P to C then

That's not allowed either, but I can't explain why.

PETER: Meet me in the library, first thing

I would love to talk to Mandy right about now, but she would ask for explanations too.

The best, safest answer is silence.

. . .

. . .

. . .

But I can't help myself. Ten minutes later, I text Peter back.

ME: C cannot wait

20.

My heart beats faster than I'd like as I cross the library's threshold, but I focus on putting one foot in front of the other. There's no sign of Peter, and with no bodies filling the space, the library's chilly, gray, and tired. I feel like an idiot. When Peter said "first thing," he probably meant five minutes early, not fifty.

I settle into one of the big armchairs in the reading center of the library. I *should* finish my precalculus homework, but I pull out my character journal and open to a line that's been bothering me. Ophelia's father tells her, "Lord Hamlet is a prince, out of thy star." He means "star" astrologically, like their love's not meant to be. But he's also saying Hamlet's out of her league.

Such a beautiful way to say an awful thing.

I used to like the idea of fate. It's comforting to think

things happen the way they're supposed to, but what if your fate is a bad one, like Ophelia's?

What's a person supposed to do with that?

I must believe that my fate isn't set, or else why play my games?

Something loops down through my field of vision and slides across my neck. I go fight-or-flight, throw one hand up to catch whatever's there.

Don't touch.

I can't really feel what it is through my glove, but some kind of fabric is slipping away as I turn, grazing my neck as *Peter* reels it back in.

An empty shirtsleeve.

He slings the shirt over his shoulder, over a fraying T-shirt that . . . biceps. Peter has biceps.

"I startled you. Sorry," he says. But he doesn't look sorry. He looks pleased with himself.

"That's all right. I thought . . . I don't know what I thought."

"Hard at work on Ophelia?" he says with a grin, but he's not making fun. "Over here." He waves for me to follow him into the stacks.

We're alone in a nearly abandoned building. The ridiculous thought pops in: His present is a kiss. He'll press me up against the shelves. Books will fall, and the building will crumble. The thrill-and-dread mix makes it hard to follow him without shaking, and I keep some space between us, just in case.

He leads me through a maze of shelves to a corner table where two rows of stacks meet. On the table, several books lie spread open. They're encyclopedias—one from each set the library has—and a couple of dictionaries, too. He closes a *Merriam-Webster* and hands it to me.

"Look up 'asshole' in the dictionary," he says.

"What?"

"Just do it."

I open it and flip to "asshole." There's a picture of Oscar smiling back at me.

I laugh for a second. Then I tug at the photo's corner. It sticks.

"You did this?"

He nods and gestures to the table, "The encyclopedia entries are longer, more detailed in listing his crimes."

"Why?"

"I'm on a mission. Because he's an asshole. Because he dropped you."

"He didn't mean to."

"He was being his stupid self and he hurt you, and he's been harassing you since the first day of school. Anyone can see you don't like it."

"Okay, sure, but—"

"Tell me you're a fan of getting groped by Oscar, and I'll put these back." He moves as if to start.

"I'm not a fan. Not. A fan."

Peter smiles.

"But this is so . . . elaborate." That he would do this for me, I'm overwhelmed.

"I have anger problems," Peter says lightly, as if he's said he's a fan of scuba diving. "Sometimes when I get angry, instead of punching my fist through a wall—"

"You've done that?"

He shrugs. "I express my frustration through art."

"This is art?"

He shrugs again, grinning, "Well, that's what I'll claim if they catch me, but they won't. And even if they do, I used the tiniest bit of putty. It'll peel off. That's grounds for suspension, tops."

"But for making fun of Oscar?"

"I'm not making fun of him," Peter says, "I'm defining him." His smile's contagious, dangerous.

"He'll think I did it."

"No. He won't. Seriously, you're new. You're a girl. The only thing he suspects you of is being in love with him. The guy's got a runaway ego."

"So who's he going to think did it?"

"Somebody who wishes they could *be* him. Probably the mission will backfire. Probably, it'll just feed his ego."

"Mission?"

"Yeah, Project A-hole."

I'm laughing too loudly. I'll get Peter in trouble. "Can

we put them away? Before somebody sees?"

"I'll put them away. I can't risk you getting implicated in my covert activity. Roger that?"

"I copy."

"No, you're supposed to say 'roger' back."

"Roger back."

He groans. "You'd be hopeless as a spy."

"Thanks a lot."

"No, I'm serious. Get out of here before you compromise my position."

"Okay."

"Go! Be off!" He's gathered a couple of volumes in one arm and is sweeping at me with the other. "That's Shakespearean for 'leave.'"

"Peter?"

"What?"

"Thank you."

He holds my eyes, and maybe it's my imagination—it's still dark in here—but I think his cheeks flush red. Or maybe I'm mixing up what I see in him with what *I* feel.

Peter waves me away.

"Have you seen this?" Oscar bends over the lunch table, *Merriam-Webster* in hand, open to his definition. I guess news of pranks travels fast.

Oscar's beaming.

People lean in and fall back laughing. Peter does the

same. He's a great actor because he's not hiding anything. He's not worried about getting caught, and he thinks his own joke is fantastic.

"I'm famous," Oscar says. "I mean, more famous than I already was."

Peter widens his eyes at me—see? He told me so. And he mouths the words, "Worse than I thought."

Oscar breaks into song: "You ain't nobody till somebody hates you!"

My eye contact with Peter lasts a little too long, and there's so much potential energy thrumming between us—it wants us to close the distance, fall in. It's like one of Dad's physics tricks—stretching the rubber band makes it get warmer.

Sooner or later it snaps.

I ask Mandy if we can go somewhere to talk after rehearsal. As much time as we've been spending together, it can be hard to get Mandy alone.

We pick the Dancing Elephant Café, a crunchy-granola place near Avondale Park, named for Miss Fancy, the circus elephant who used to be an attraction there. The sign out front is already lit up since the light's fading earlier these days, and there's actually a chill in the air.

On the stage in the corner, a guitarist's setting up for what looks like a punk-country crossover. "Cowboy meet fauxhawk," says Mandy. "I like."

I think she likes the guy's exposed arms. Mandy looks like she wants a private concert, but I hope he won't start playing before we're gone.

Mandy buys us tea and pumpkin bars—"Made with *lots* of *real* butter," she says, "so hush-hush to my mom."

I've got to talk to someone, but telling Mandy about Peter feels like a risky step. If I tell, it will feel more real, like this might be the start of something.

So, I stall. "You and Drew . . . that's all good?"

"It's been rough since auditions," she allows, and then brightens, "but Caddie, you have no idea how amazing it is to be in love."

It isn't her fault I have no idea, that I won't maybe ever. "I don't suppose you want to tell me about it?"

"It's like, I see things differently. Everything looks . . . more of whatever it is."

I snatch up and tuck away every word. By the time she's finished, Mandy's made love sound like a unicorn made of rainbows that cures cancer in its spare time.

"So what's up with you?" she asks.

"Well." I break off a piece of my pumpkin bar with a fork. Mandy, of course, is using her hands, but everybody's gotten used to me keeping the gloves on to eat. "Peter did something super nice," I say, and at the risk of breaking spy rules, I reveal that Peter was behind Oscar's definition. "I like him, Mandy."

She squeals. "I knew it!" she says. "I *knew*! Maybe this

is why you had to get cast as Ophelia. Maybe it's your *fate* so you and Peter can fall for each other."

"Too late on my end," I say.

"I knew it!" she says. "I was just waiting for you to admit it."

"Here's the thing," I say. "I don't know what to do about it."

"You kiss him," Mandy says. "Duh."

I think, *don't touch*, but in spite of it, I laugh.

"I don't want . . ." I'm not sure what I can say that won't reveal too much. "What if something went wrong and we couldn't stand working together?"

"That's fear," Mandy says. "You know what you do with fear? You have to crush it." For punctuation, she takes a raw sugar cube from the bowl on the table and pulverizes it between her teeth.

"That's the other thing about being in love," she says. "I'm not afraid of things so much—it's like when you ask yourself what's the worst thing that can happen? It can't be that bad because Drew is still there."

"Mandy, what do you have to be afraid of?"

"I get afraid of things," she says, "looking stupid, saying the wrong thing . . . Everybody does."

I think about Mom, how her face looked pinched for months before Dad left town. That pinched look, that was fear, the tension that comes before pain.

Maybe it's mean to ask, but I have to: "What about

losing Drew? Are you afraid of that?"

"Ahhhh!" Mandy makes an animal sound in her throat. "Petrified! I don't think there's anything scarier than losing a person you care about."

"Agreed."

It's not safe to care about Peter, but it's too late to stop— so far past too late, I almost wish I'd never started. But not caring for Peter at all . . . that, I can't even imagine.

21.

Over the next couple of days, every time I make eye contact with Mandy, she shoots a meaningful look toward Peter. Sooner or later, he's sure to catch on.

Meanwhile, *Peter* barely looks at me except when we're reading lines together at rehearsal. Maybe my reaction to Project A-hole wasn't as big as he'd hoped . . . or maybe he saw something in my eyes, too eager, too swoony, and he doesn't want those feelings from me.

"Best safety lies in fear." That's Oscar reading his line.

Nadia says, "What do we think he means, Caddie?" Of course she calls on me when my mind's wandering.

"I think he means Ophelia has to keep safe."

"Okay . . . in what way?"

I know what the line means. I wrote about it in my journal, but my understanding of it's all tied up with Peter, and I'm afraid if I open my mouth I might talk about that. I shake my head.

"Try to stay with us, Caddie."

On Friday, Nadia tells us to practice in pairs while she holds character conferences. I move toward Peter, but Nadia calls him, and Mandy pulls me toward Drew.

"Let's work on your first scene," Mandy says.

"Nadia said pairs," Drew says. "Just actors."

"As long as I'm here, I might as well help," Mandy says, and she looks back and forth between us, smiling. "My boyfriend and my best friend, making magic together."

Drew lowers his voice to speak to Mandy, but I hear him fine: "You said you'd stop trying to help. It gets us irritated with each other, and I don't want that."

"That's when we're not at rehearsal," she says, "but it's my job to help here. What if Caddie needs my help?"

Ophelia has only six lines in this scene, and they're not that difficult language-wise. Polonius, on the other hand, never stops talking. But Drew turns to me, resigned.

"Daddy's little girl," he says to me, his voice and eyes flat as he opens his arms. I don't step into them.

"We can work on the father-daughter vibe later," Mandy says.

"I don't know—it feels pretty right-on to me," I say, and Drew exhales something between a sigh and a laugh. For a moment, I'm free from his negative beam. Without meaning to, I've taken his side.

"We're just doing language right now anyway," Mandy says, eyes cast down on her script.

Nadia's told us that commas mean speed up, keep building, and on one line, Drew has so many that he runs out of breath and gasps.

"This is impossible," he says. "'Springes to catch woodcocks,' what does that even mean?"

"He means that Hamlet's setting a trap for Ophelia, making her think he loves her so she'll sleep with him. 'Springes' means traps. It's in the footnotes, see?" Mandy reaches to point at his script, but Drew shuts it.

"Nobody talks like this."

Mandy laughs. "You hear a lot of people walking around going ''tis' and 'hath' and 'prithee'? It's Shakespeare, baby."

"Don't call me baby."

"You call me that all the time."

"But you like it."

Mandy purses her lips and says, "Not if you don't like it when I say it back to you."

"Guys," I say, and they both turn their mad eyes on me. Mandy's drop back to neutral quickly, but Drew's stay mad. "Sorry, I just . . . shouldn't we practice?"

"Yes," Mandy says, and she turns back to Drew. "Let's take it again from the top."

"You take it again," Drew says, and he stomps off.

"That doesn't even make sense," Mandy calls after him.

"Baby!" Turning back to me, she says, "That went well."

"Maybe he needs some time to get used to you being assistant director."

"Yeah, I don't think Drew expected me to actually do anything as AD besides take notes and make coffee. If that were the job, I wouldn't have taken it."

"I'm sorry."

"Why should you be sorry?"

She dives back into the script. I would be so anxious to run and fix things with Drew, but she seems determined not to let him get to her.

Nadia calls me then, and Mandy pops her eyes wide.

"Thank you," I say.

"What for?"

"For working with me, being excited for me. You're a pretty amazing friend."

Mandy beams and puts her hand to her heart. I always want to shake off nice words—they embarrass me—but Mandy drinks them in.

Nadia's made a meeting space in a room off the back-stage area. Peter's coming out as I'm going in. I almost want to reach out and squeeze his hand, but he steps aside, giving me plenty of room.

"I'm so nervous," I say. An offering.

"Nervous works for you," he says. "She already loves you. You'll be great." I try to take in his words like Mandy would, let them swim through me like a drink of something warm. There's an unfinished edge between us, something wanting to be said, but now isn't the time. He waves and heads back to the stage.

"Ophelia," Nadia says with a twist to her mouth like there's something funny about it.

"Hi."

She motions for me to sit down and turns to a fresh page in the little notebook she carries. "How are you feeling about the part?"

"Excited. Nervous. Thank you for casting me. I didn't think . . . being new . . ."

"I didn't either," Nadia says. "It usually takes new students a while to feel open enough to give me the performance I'm looking for."

Open. I don't think of myself with that adjective.

"I hope," I say, "that it wasn't a fluke. I didn't expect that I would . . . I don't know . . . feel so much at the audition."

Nadia shrugs. "You were listening," she says, "letting things affect you. If you did it once, you can do it again."

And again. And again.

"Of course, we'll want a little more control."

I nod.

"So tell me about Ophelia," Nadia says. "How do you see her?"

I breathe in, try to keep it smooth, then say, "I've been thinking about how she's someone who has rules to follow—her father's rules, and her brother's rules, and Hamlet's, too, I guess, since he's a prince."

"Yes, good."

"And there's that part where she talks about Hamlet coming to her room and how he touches her face and shakes her by the arm . . ."

Nadia waves a hand as if to pull more words from me.

"Well, I think that freaks Ophelia out so much not just because Hamlet's acting crazy, but because it breaks all the rules."

"Hm. Mm-hm." Nadia tilts her head, writes something down.

"So, I'm wondering, wouldn't it be cool if Ophelia never touches Hamlet onstage, like it's this barrier they can't cross?"

"I like how you're thinking," Nadia says, "but do we want our Ophelia to be the traditional girl who goes along with everything? Because Mandy made a good point at the auditions. Ophelia might not be so innocent."

"Well, but at least, on the surface, where people can see."

Nadia nods, but I'm not sure she's sold.

"What I like about this," she says, "is that it points to a tension—between what Ophelia wants and what she's allowed."

I nod, too eagerly I'm sure, and she goes on, "I like the idea that she's holding herself together tightly. So when she breaks—which I think she does in that scene you read at auditions—it can be a striking change. What if Ophelia's proper in those early scenes with no physical contact, and then later, she might be very hands-on."

I stare at a stack of colored gels. They're only stiff, beat-up cellophane with numbers scribbled in wax pencil, but put them in front of a light, and they'll change the mood of the play, turn the scene melancholy blue or fiery red. There's a disc of metal—a "gobo" because it "goes between" the light and its beam—patterned with skeletal trees, which can turn the stage into a forest, maybe for the scene when Hamlet confronts his father's ghost.

I used to feel safe on stage, but that was silly. The stage *transforms* us, makes us *more* of whatever we are.

As long as I focus on the equipment, Nadia might believe that I'm turning her words in my mind, thinking how best to deliver the performance she wants.

"I'm not sure," I say, "if I got that far in my thinking."

When I exit Nadia's office, she calls Hank, leaving Livia partnerless. Livia's studying one of the flats backstage. The plywood wall on a shoddy frame has probably been painted a hundred times for a hundred different sets. I join her and see that the unpainted back is covered with drawings and scribbles. She gives me a sly smile.

"What's this?"

"Wall of Infamy," Livia says. "People write on it during productions."

Most of it is dirty. There's a running theme: Blank did it with Blank in blankety-blank way. "They just leave this up?"

Livia shrugs. "Tradition."

I follow her eyes to where the wall reads, "On this spot during sophomore showcase, Livia did it with Hank while wearing an Elvis mask."

Below that, in different handwriting it says, "Then he took her mask off and saw that she wasn't a dude."

"No way!" I say. "You mean that's not true?!"

"Please." She rolls her eyes. "Actually, it was a Reagan mask. Hank's got a thing for dead Republicans."

She snorts as I try not to scream.

We're silent for a while, reading the scandalous stuff on the wall, and then, because I feel like she won't make a big deal about it, I ask, "So what does it mean when a guy does something nice for you, and you say thank you, and it seems good, and then afterward, he acts like it never happened?"

"That he's gay?" she deadpans, and then twists her lips into a smile. "That's what it would mean if you were talking about Hank and me, but that's not what I think it means coming from Peter."

Am I so transparent?

If Livia catches my frustration at her calling me out so bluntly, she has the grace not to acknowledge it.

˙ "I'll tell you what I think that means," she says, and I nod, please. "I think that means it's your turn."

I let the others go ahead of me at the end of rehearsal while I scribble down last-minute notes. I want Nadia to see me working hard, but I can't concentrate. Livia's right. It's my turn to encourage Peter, let him know that I want to be friends, or . . . something. It's safer with him avoiding me, but I miss him.

When I finally get to the junior hall, the sight of Peter sitting cross-legged in front of his locker, almost like he's waiting for me, makes me stop in my tracks. He looks up and smiles—I must look funny frozen here.

I swallow my fear, walk up, and sit across from him, so close our knees almost touch.

"Peter, what are you doing this weekend?"

He shrugs. "Watering the neighbors' plants, mowing lawns. What about you?"

"Nothing. Well, working on Ophelia."

"Nice." He's enthusiastic, friendly, but he's not going to help me.

"Do you . . . would you want to get together sometime to talk about our characters?"

It's the most obvious thing, the least frightening.

And Peter says, "No."

His bluntness throws me.

"Oh."

"I'd rather do something else. But if that's my best chance of getting to hang out with you, then sure."

He's teasing me, truth or dare.

One of his hands touches the strap of his backpack, the other his knee. Mine touch the insides of my gloves. So why do I feel like he's holding me tight, like I can't look away?

"Well, we could make it fun. Send ourselves on a mission?" I say with no idea what that might mean.

"Only if the safety of several foreign countries and the fate of a small child is at stake." His answer's so perfect so fast, I'm not sure I can keep up.

"I'll see what I can do."

"Roger back," he says with a smirk, and he's up and gone.

When I'm home, I text Peter. The few lines take me nearly an hour because I want to strike a balance between super spy and silly, but it can't feel like I worked too hard, and I still have no idea what the mission is, and I don't want it to sound like I'm asking him out on a date, but I kind of want it to be a maybe date. . . .

I finally come up with this:

Agent P, you have, in poor judgment, agreed to take part in a mission. The fate of Denmark and a small section of the southern US are at stake. The only child I know is my brother, and if you decline, I will be sad, which will probably make him happy, so let's scrap this part.

Please transmit your availability Saturday through Monday.

Further instructions forthcoming.

Agent C

I hit send and panic rushes through me. Even those few lines ask too much. He'll say no, and I'll hurt, hurt, hurt. Or he'll say yes and then no, and I'll hurt worse. Or he'll say yes, yes, yes, but I'll have to say no because I'm untouchable.

It's too late to take anything back. The damage is done.

Peter doesn't make me wait or wonder. He writes back within a few minutes:

Agent C,

Nothing will deter me from my mission.

I'm free tomorrow.

Agent P

22.

Peter's truck is a true antique—an unrestored, falling-apart antique—but beautiful. The green paint's so faded it seems yellow in places, gray in others, and not an inch of it shiny; it's chalky and flat as limestone.

As I near the truck, Peter gets out and comes around to meet me. Standing there in his nubby barn jacket, raking his hair back and out of his eyes, the hint of a question in his smile, he's far too touchable.

"Ready to do some shooting?" I ask.

Peter plays dumb. "Nah, I don't hunt," he says, "to my dad's eternal sorrow."

"I learned to shoot from my mom," I say, holding up the fancy hand-me-down that hangs around my neck.

"Nice camera," he says. "Mine's point-and-shoot."

What if Peter thinks I'm spoiled? "This is a fringe

benefit of having a professional photographer for a mom."

I move toward the truck, and he stops me. "Should I offer to meet them?" he asks. "Your parents, I mean?"

"Aren't you the gentleman?" I say.

For once, Peter seems more awkward than me. It's sweet.

"My momma raised me right," he says.

"Well, it's just Mom who would be here." I don't want to get into it, but the way I said that, he might think Dad's dead or something. "My dad . . . he doesn't live here right now. Temporarily? We're not sure."

"Got it," he says. "Sorry."

"No, you don't have to be sorry."

Suddenly, this feels very much like a date. An awkward date.

"Well, so should I introduce myself to your mom?"

"No, she's working. She does wedding photography. Saturday's a big day for weddings."

Ugh, I did not mean to be talking to Peter about weddings.

"Right, well, tell her I tried?" he says. "I wanted to make a good impression."

He did?

I guess I knew what I was asking for when I invited him. I knew there was potential for things to feel romantic between us, but now that we're here, I'm not sure my heart can take it.

Peter opens the passenger door for me. "Can I give you a hand?"

I almost laugh because a hand is exactly the worst thing he could offer.

I say, "I've got it," and haul myself into the cab.

Inside, the truck smells like Band-Aids and rubber, cut branches, and wet dog. It's altogether comforting.

"Love me, love my truck," Peter says as he wrestles with the ancient gearshift and backs out of my drive.

"I already love your truck," I say.

Oh, Lord, did I just suggest I love *him*? I keep talking too fast. "I thought we could work on our self-portraits, for our character journals."

I hadn't chosen a location, but the layers of color on Peter's truck make me want to time travel, to take Peter to the Paleozoic era of my childhood. The train cars from Mom's series pop into my head.

"Let's go into old Irondale. I feel like there'll be some cool stuff there to inspire us."

For years, Mom and Jordan and I would drive this way to a pool set back in the woods against a stretch of tracks. Every couple of hours, a train would go by, blow its whistle, and all the swimmers would turn to watch something heavy and old rumble by.

We cross Crestwood Boulevard, with its dilapidated shopping plazas where only the hardiest big box stores survive. Train tracks in old Irondale stretch like capillaries from a giant artery, the rail yards that border Ruffner Mountain.

We cross one set of tracks arcing over a hill, and Peter's truck wheezes. It's too easy to imagine it stalling there.

"I have an idea for a picture," Peter says, "if we can find some tracks that aren't out in the open."

I point us in the general direction of the pool because I know those tracks go through the woods, but we make turns on instinct and once by the sound of a whistle. Something about being with Peter makes me believe we'll find just what we're looking for.

We're going through an old neighborhood—tiny houses with peeling paint and broken shutters, one with a sign advertising CHEAP DENTAL WORK, HOME OFFICE—when the sound of a train makes Peter pull up next to an overgrown lawn and open his door.

"Do you think it's safe to leave it here?" I ask.

"A, this truck is a piece of junk," Peter says, "and B, it's all families living here." He gestures toward a plastic baby pool on the lawn. Rubber toys float in dirty water, a moldy film ringing them. We're not so far from the Gate City projects and Eastlake, where people get shot. I want to tell Peter that crazy crack dealers have families too, but he's excited, so we walk between two houses and into the woods toward the sound of the train.

The woods go deeper than I expected, a buffer for the tracks when this neighborhood was new. At one point we have to cross a little creek, and Peter offers a hand to help me.

"I'm not afraid," I say and make a show of balancing on a wobbly rock before hopping to meet him, never taking his hand.

The further we go, the more we have to step over broken trees and push brambles aside. Beneath the top layer of plant matter, the ground's mushy and damp from the rain. I reach to grab hold of a tree for balance and pull back just in time to avoid smashing my glove into a slug.

"How you doing?" Peter asks.

"I miss this. I used to go exploring all the time."

Mandy and I would go. This adventure is the kind of brave, random thing I associate with her, but we used to do this sort of thing together, and it wasn't always her idea.

We see the break in the trees before we reach it, a relief from the dense tangle of branches overhead. A lane of open sky cuts across the woods as one might over a river, but here it's making way for the train. The tracks cut a wide corridor that seems to narrow to nothing as it winds away into the woods.

"Awesome," Peter says as we step onto the rise of orange pebbly dirt supporting the tracks, and he presses a palm to the rail. "Still warm. Feel it."

He takes my hand and starts to pull off my glove, but I stop him, saying, "No. That's okay. I don't need to." So much for bravery. "I don't like to think about how recently the train came through. Would we hear it coming?"

"Yeah, we'd hear it. We'd feel it," he says, stepping onto the rails and wavering for balance. "Let's find our pictures."

I step up behind him and make a game of matching his footsteps, trying not to dislodge extra pebbles from between the tracks. They seem so precarious as it is. "What are we looking for?"

He turns to face me, walking backward on the rail like a balance beam. "Hamlet can't bring himself to take action, right? Since I'm impulsive, Nadia says it might be a challenge for me to get that about him."

I smile. "Maybe *I* should be playing Hamlet."

He wobbles and pivots forward without having to step down. "Maybe you should. Ophelia doesn't really make decisions for herself."

"Well, except when she dies."

"But is that a decision, or is she just crazy?"

A pressure rises in my chest, at my throat, and my words tumble out.

"Yeah, it's a decision."

I didn't realize I even had an opinion about this till now. Maybe it's his choice of the word *crazy*, but I find myself wanting to defend Ophelia. I want Peter to see her the way I do.

"She knows what she's doing," I say. "Maybe she's out of herself enough not to care, but I think she knows."

"I think she does too," Peter says, twisting his torso to smile back at me. "I think she gives the whole kingdom a big 'F you,' and she breaks all their rules and gets free."

"And dead," I say, "don't forget dead."

"Okay, yes, free and dead. . . ."

Peter wobbles on the rail and drops down, breaking off clods of orange dirt as he slides back to level ground. I stay up on the tracks, but in line with him. He keeps his head down, and we walk quietly like that for a long time.

"When you jumped off that roof," I say, "did you think you might die?"

Peter barks out a little "Ha" of surprise—maybe he forgot he even told me about it—and then squints at the track where it curves into the woods ahead of us.

"Yeah," he says, "I guess I did think I might, but I didn't understand what that meant, so I don't think it counts."

"You weren't afraid of making things worse? That it would hurt?"

I remember him saying he wasn't afraid, but how could that be?

He twists his lips up in thought, then says, "I guess that's where being impulsive comes in—I didn't think anything could hurt worse than how I was feeling."

I get Hamlet—I get being afraid to reach out a hand and make something happen because so many bad things might follow. But jumping, not knowing or caring how I might land . . . how does a person get to that place?

"Here we go!" Peter jogs to a point on the tracks beyond the curve, any sense of melancholy instantly gone.

It's a junction where two tracks merge into the one we've been walking. The woods thin between them so both tracks can be seen for a distance beyond this one point.

Peter lies down with his head at the point where the tracks make a "Y," his arms lax at his sides, and he grins.

"Do you want to be smiling?" I ask, taking aim.

"I guess not." He tries to steady his expression, but he bursts into laughter that wracks his body so when I snap the picture, the whole line of him arcs and curls.

It's a mistake, and we shoot a lot more, but when Peter finally hops up to see the whole batch, that one makes us both stare. "That's the one, am I right?" Peter says, and I nod.

It's as if the rails are electric and shocking him—his body arched, his mouth wide and gasping but smiling. His eyes focus skyward into some middle distance, open and reaching. Peter's Hamlet has no intention of choosing one direction anytime soon. He is eager for a train to rock the rails and mow him down.

I'd like to find the pool for my Ophelia portrait; it has to be close, but we need to get back to Peter's truck before the sun starts going down. I've got no signal out here, and if Mom beats me home and Jordan tells her I disappeared with a guy . . .

"I bet it's just ahead," Peter says. "We'll find the pool, and if we need to, we can walk back to the truck along the roads."

"But we won't know which road." I hate the whine in my voice.

"We'll find it," he says. I want to believe him, but I'm also annoyed at him for pushing. I win what wasn't even a fight. We head back to the truck, and the sense of adventure is gone by the time we're back safe in the cab.

"Well, what do you want to do?" Peter asks.

"What do *you* want to do?"

He smiles, but there's a twist in it—I shouldn't have thrown the question back at him.

Instead of answering, he shifts and fixes his eyes on mine. He will lean in, any second, he will lean in close, take my face, hold my cheek in his palm . . .

"Are you cold?" he says, breaking his gaze and reaching into the space behind the long bench seat for his barn jacket.

I was shivering, shaking, still am.

"I'm okay," but he holds the jacket out for me, waits while I reach one arm in; then he wraps it around, helps me find the next sleeve. He pulls the front closed, runs his hands down the sleeve-ends, and grips the cuffs where they hang several inches below my balled fists. He tugs at those ends like he might wrap me up straitjacket style, but no, he's tugging me forward, slowly closing the distance between us. I could duck my head, let my forehead bump into his chest and stop my forward motion, or lift my face, let go, but instead, I free the sleeves, make a "brrr" sound, and throw myself back into my corner of the cab, hugging myself tight.

I belong in a straitjacket.

"Thanks for the coat," I say.

"Caddie . . ."

There's an abandon in Peter that I caught in the picture. Too much of it can be dangerous, but not enough . . . that can be dangerous too.

I speak before Peter can ask what's wrong with me. "We're losing light fast," I say. "Let's see if we can make it to the pool."

We drive in silence, only talking when we have to figure out which way to turn.

When we hit the curved drive that leads down toward the pool, it's a shock how familiar it is. It feels wrong, in a way, to bring Peter here, like we really have traveled through time and I can't promise safe passage back. As we twist down through the woods, the sinking light shoots through tree branches and blinds us. Peter takes the curve fast, and it's like we're in one of my nightmares where a car flies off the road, except we stay on track, make it down to the base of the hill.

"Are you mad at me?" I ask.

"Why would I be mad?"

His smile looks real but sad, too, and tired.

I know every inch of this place, where the aquamarine slide cracked and had to be patched with white caulk, where fuzzy caterpillars crawled all over the chain-link fence in the summer. But everything has changed.

The pool's been drained, but it's not empty. For what must have been months, leaves and pine needles have collected in soggy puddles across the bottom of the shallow end, and several feet of stagnant water fill the deep end. All the pool chairs are gone; there's a single sawed-off pipe where the slide used to be.

The pool house is chained shut and marked with a plastic-wrapped permit. There's a huge sign on the fence with a construction company's logo and, on top of that, a NO TRESPASSING sign.

Peter walks across the blacktop with me to the low fence that rings the baby pool. On the far side of the pool house, a part of the main pool's concrete wall has been blasted. "It looks like they started and ran out of money," he says, "or never had enough money to begin with. How long since you've been here?"

The tears catch me off-guard. It's been longer than I realized. "Four years, maybe five. I used to love coming here, and then after we stopped . . ."

"You didn't even think about it," Peter says. He doesn't reach toward me, doesn't try to comfort me, and why would he? I'm a fricking porcupine. I turn away so he won't see my face.

I shake my head. "Wow, I'm sorry, I didn't realize it would hit me like this."

"This is good for your picture," Peter says, his voice soft, and he swings his leg over the chain link and hoists himself up.

"What are you doing?"

"You want to go in, don't you?"

"What if someone comes?"

"Does it look like anybody spends much time here?"

Peter's all the way in by now, and he steps into the empty baby pool. It's surreal to see him stride across it like a giant. I kick one leg up and push myself onto the fence. Peter takes a step toward me, but I say, "I've got it," and he backs away—fast. My voice came out harsher than I wanted. Of course I wobble and have to start over, but he doesn't try to help again.

My jeans catch on the top of the fence, and I have to bounce on the other foot while I work them free. Peter keeps his distance and watches me struggle.

"I don't know how you're not screaming in pain right now," Peter says.

"What I lack in height, I make up for in flexiness."

"Is flexiness one of your superpowers?" Peter says.

"What?"

"The gloves."

With both feet safely down, I rest with my hands on my thighs as if I need to catch my breath. Peter's never mentioned my gloves.

"I can't figure out why you wear them," he says, his voice careful, "except that you're secretly some kind of superhero."

When I trust my face, I straighten up, force a silly expression. "Don't tell anybody, or I'll have to kill you."

"I thought that was spies. Superheroes don't kill innocent people."

"You're not innocent," I say, and I walk to the gated fence that separates the baby pool from the big people pool. There's a lock, but the gate is even lower than the outer fence and easy to climb.

Swinging up and over gives me a thrill. Maybe Peter's impulsivity is catching.

Peter follows me. We could walk straight down the steps at the shallow end into the pool. It's like a dream I'll forget upon waking.

"Where does Ophelia want her picture taken?" he asks.

It makes sense to take a picture of Ophelia by water. But the extremity of how she finally lets go is a part of her I don't understand.

I walk around the wall of the pool toward the deep end. Peter goes straight down the steps and in. He walks across the pool's bottom for as long as he can before the floor slants and he hits standing water. The trees around the pool have thinning branches, leaving clumps of dead leaves on the water—we've fast-forwarded to fall.

I lie down along the edge of the pool wall and stretch my hand down toward the dirty water. The numbers along the wall here say 10 FT, so even with several feet of water pooled up, it's a long way down.

"That looks good, the reaching," Peter says, "but I can't see your face."

I look up and try not to focus on any particular thing, but I can't stop catching sight of the camera—it makes me feel stupid. It's all so contrived, safe, and planned out, like every other thing I do.

"What do you want to show?" he asks.

"That she's choosing to fall, like she's choosing to let it all go."

"Well, right now you just look spaced out."

I kick up to standing and jog around to the diving boards. The higher one stands fifteen feet above the pavement, more from the base of the pool. I grab hold of that ladder and hoist myself up, stepping on the yellow tape that crisscrosses the steps.

"What are you doing?" Peter says.

"Impulse!"

"Caddie, that doesn't look safe." He makes a move to step closer but stops when water seeps up through the mess of pine needles and leaves. It only gets deeper from there.

"I'm pretty sure it isn't safe." I step onto the board and grip the rails—there's no way I could fall off, but everything is slippery. The rails are slick under my gloves, the board thin and mean.

Peter's wavering, I think, not sure whether to stay where he has a good shot or climb out after me and pull me back to safety. This is where my being a porcupine pays off—Peter stays away.

"I don't like this," he says.

"Oh no, sad clown."

"We can get a good picture on the side of the pool."

I shake my head. I don't want it to look safe, don't want it to *be* safe. I can't touch Peter's skin, but I can stand fifteen feet over concrete and stretch my arms out to the sky. I step to the edge of the handholds, standing over the deep end. If I fell, I would break both my legs, maybe my neck. I take one step out, one step forward, and my legs wobble.

"This is so dumb," I say. "Look at my legs shake." The shaking's supposed to protect me, I guess, make me turn back, but it only makes things more dangerous.

"Caddie, I don't like this," Peter says. "Will you please get down?"

"Hold on," I say, and I will my legs to be quiet, calm. I can't steady them any more than I can steady my hands or lips for a touch. "Ah, I hate this!"

"So get down."

"No, I mean, I hate being afraid."

"You're afraid for a good reason. You're standing on a narrow board over concrete that can kill you. If you weren't afraid you'd be dumb."

I stand with my arms at my sides for a good minute, but my legs won't feel normal.

"Am I taking a picture or what?" Peter says.

I take one last breath, breathe in the broken fence, the wrecked aqua hole in the ground, the shape of a place I can never come back to, and then I turn around.

"This isn't right anyway," I say.

Trying to make Ophelia brave in the moment she lets go, it's not true. I think she's more like Peter on his roof. She doesn't choose to fall because she isn't afraid, but because not falling is worse.

Peter and I don't talk much on the drive home. There's no mention of ice cream socials, no talk of my unfinished pic-e or let's do this again.

'e asked, with his arms and his hands as he wrapped tight in his jacket, he asked.

' no—without talking, I said it.

en I scared him, acted reckless and loud—why who does that be afraid of touching him?

sk again.

23.

The sun's low by the time Peter drops me at home, but the house is dark. For a second, I think maybe they've gone. The problem wasn't ever between Mom and Dad. The problem was me, my obnoxious disorders, my selfish insistence on getting my way. Mom's taken Jordan away to Virginia to move in with Dad. They'll let me live here to finish high school—a kindness, for old time's sake—and when I graduate, they'll shut it down, cut off all ties.

Then I smell incense, musky and sharp, and follow it to the kitchen.

There's the old statuette of a frog that holds incense cones in its back and exhales smoke from its mouth. Dad hated the smell, so the frog's been decorating the garden since I was little. There are water stains, bits of moss on its sides.

Mom has the sliding door open so cool air seeps in. She sips tea and watches the frog's breath swirl its way out the door.

"Mom?"

She looks up at me, calm. "Want some tea?"

"No, thanks."

She nods. "Have a seat, sweetie."

"I don't want to."

She smiles, so peaceful, so . . . Mom. "Caddie, sit down."

"What happened?"

"It's a good thing. It's going to be really good for all of us."

My tears burn before she even says it. I knew, of course I knew, this was coming.

"Your father and I had a talk."

"When?"

"Just a bit ago. I was working, taking pictures for a wedding—the couple looked so happy. On my way home I had to pull over on the interstate and call your dad."

While I was cowering in the corner of Peter's truck *not touching* him. I followed the rules, all the rules.

"Your dad and I finally admitted that this has been good, for both of us, being apart."

"He likes being away from us."

She frowns like I've said something mean. "He doesn't *like* being apart from you and Jordan."

"You can't say that. He doesn't even answer his phone when I call."

She says what she's supposed to say. "He loves you as much as I do, but your dad and I can't be married any longer. We haven't felt married for a long time. You don't have to understand right away," Mom says. "It's all right to be angry."

"I'm not angry. I'm sad." And I'm sobbing—it scares me how hard.

"Oh, sweetie," she says, and she reaches toward me.

"No."

I'm up and away, and her face shows she's hurt, but that's all right. She should be. If splitting up our family hasn't hurt her, then something else should.

"Where's Jordan?"

She looks away. That hurts too. "I asked Connor's mother to have him over."

"He doesn't even like Connor anymore!"

"I wanted to tell you first."

"So I can show him how well I'm taking it? So I can set a good example?"

She turns back to the frog. "Something like that."

I laugh, even though it's mean, even though she looks sadder now than she did when I walked in. I laugh all the way down the hall.

By the time I reach my room, my breath is ragged,

my laugh turned to shuddering gasps. I shut my door so Mom won't hear, fall across my bed and concentrate on breathing.

I count through each inhale and exhale like I learned in middle school, trying to slow things down.

In the dark of my room, I'm not angry at Mom or Dad but at me. It was foolish, laughable even, to imagine I had control over Mom and Dad's feelings, their decisions.

I followed the rules the best I could. Maybe it wasn't good enough—I messed up too many times—or maybe my stupid game never mattered.

Either way, the game's over. I lost.

I've lost Peter, too.

I roll onto my back, peel off my gloves, and hold my hands up to the air, exposed.

When Mom reached for me, my brain said a touch shouldn't matter anymore, but my *body* recoiled.

Maybe it's habit, but without the gloves, my hands *feel* vulnerable. Potential energy pulses around them in rhythm with my too-fast heart, the threat of a billion-trillion molecules all poised to crash in on me with a pressure inverse to the Big Bang.

It's stupid, but it's what I feel. *You think a divorce is bad news? Touch another person's skin, and you and your whole fragile world will implode.*

Don't touch didn't do any good. When it keeps me from connecting with people, from kissing a guy I like, from letting my mom comfort me, it's doing harm. So why does it still feel important not to touch?

Anyone. Ever.

It was never *only* about Mom and Dad. I knew that.

Don't touch protects *me* from pain. Like an overzealous bodyguard whose last client died shaking hands. There are so many things in the world that can cause pain, and *people*—people do it best. If I can't touch them, they can't hurt me.

There's a flaw in that logic. I hurt *now*. I want nothing more than to call Mom in here for a hug. But my games have never been logical.

I roll back to my side, and the quilt's damp and cool under my face.

I should work. Ophelia's the only good thing coming out of all this. She deserves my best. I pull my character journal out from under my pillow and find my list of similarities.

We're both young.

We are both in love.

That one's scary, but I think it's true. I feel something for Peter that's bigger than other crushes I've had. Maybe it's love, and maybe it's not, but whatever it is, it feels big.

We both have brothers.

Though I don't know that Jordan would fight to the death to avenge me.

We're both crazy.

It's scary to write that one down, but it feels true. Why

else can't I drop this stupid fear? I've heard people say if you think you're crazy, you're not, that crazy people always think they're sane. Maybe I'm not crazy like Ophelia, but I'm something.

Ophelia completely loses her mind before she drowns—she loses all her inhibitions, walks around in her nightgown, sings songs, makes dirty jokes, more or less gives the finger to all the adults around her who don't understand. It depends how you read it, I know, but I think my Ophelia's angry, like me, so I write that down too.

We've both lost our fathers.

Ophelia's died; it's not fair to call that the same, but right now it doesn't feel so different.

We both wish things could be back how they were.

I hold the pen over the page a long time before writing again. I'm not sure if this one belongs in similarities or differences.

We both hurt bad enough to do bad things.

To hurt ourselves, it should say.

I would never really hurt myself. I wouldn't.

But what if I can't touch anyone again ever? A person might start feeling so tired of herself, so exhausted with trying to keep it together. . . . I'm starting to understand how that happens to people, how a person could feel bad enough to make Ophelia's choice.

More than touch, more than anything, that makes my heart flood.

I scratch it out. Scratch it out all the way so I can't even read it, can't be reminded I wrote down those words.

It's one thing I don't want to share with Ophelia. Don't even want to understand.

ACT THREE

But break my heart . . .
—HAMLET, *HAMLET* (I.ii.163)

Too much of water hast thou, poor Ophelia . . .
—LAERTES, *HAMLET* (IV.vii.203)

24.

School passes by me like a dream.

I go. Talk and smile. I do all my work, follow the rules.

I don't talk about the divorce because it's nobody's business and because I won't keep it together if I have to say it out loud.

Mandy asks about my "date," of course, and I shake my head. "It's not going anywhere," I tell her.

"But *why*? You guys would be so cute!"

"We weren't feeling it," I lie. "We'll be better as friends."

"You were so into him, though."

"Things don't always work out."

"It's just so disappointing," she says.

I want to say, *Tell me about it.* But she doesn't press.

Peter *is* friendly, but just. He makes eye contact in rehearsal, long and brooding Hamlet stares, but outside of rehearsal, our eyes barely meet and then flicker away.

These first couple weeks of October, we're working only the first two acts, and it's easy when I remove myself from myself. Nadia tells me I'm doing a good job making Ophelia regal, untouchable.

"There's something about you that's always a little bit sharp," she tells me. I imagine my whole self scaled over with razor blades.

"I like that for Ophelia," Nadia says. "She's playing her role, but there's a part of her we'll never see."

Until she cracks open. But I try not to think about that.

Home feels like a rehearsal as well.

Rehearsal for being a family of three? That's the show Mom's directing. She makes us eat dinner together, smiles and asks questions. Jordan and I find Mom's performance unconvincing.

I haven't spoken to Dad since our brief conversation the day I got cast. Mom's stopped trying to make me take the phone.

She did invite him to my birthday, which is in the middle of October, and Dad said he'd come. If I'm honest, I really hope he'll follow through, but I don't want to call and say so.

Exactly one week before, Dad calls and asks to speak to me. I'd started to worry I'd pushed him away for too long, that I'd damaged things beyond repair. So I accept.

"Hi, sweet," he says. "Got any big birthday plans?"

"No, I'm not feeling celebratory this year."

"Oh, no? Your mom told me about your coup with the play. I have to say I'm not surprised."

Really?

"*I* was," I say, "surprised, I mean. New students don't usually get big parts."

"Well, they didn't know who they were dealing with."

He's buttering you up for bad news, I tell myself. But maybe not. Dad used to be proud of me when I'd perform in school plays, back when that meant standing on risers to sing about patriotism or Christmas.

"Dad," I say, "are you still coming for my birthday?"

"Well, that's why I called," he says. My shoulders tense. "The department wants to send me to a conference on the West Coast."

Oh, the "West Coast," like he's afraid I'll track him down if he reveals which state.

"Fancy," I say, careful to keep my voice free of expression. It takes so few words from him to turn me inside out—my nerves, my heart, raw and exposed.

"I know it's a bummer," Dad says, and then chuckles. "Or maybe it's not. I feel like I might be *persona non grata* in Birmingham right now."

"No, I *want* to see you." My voice sounds tight, and I bite my lips together to prevent stray sounds from escaping.

He goes on, "Plus, it's so soon after our big decision."

The divorce. Why can't people say what they mean?

"It might be more stabilizing," he says, "if we don't shake things up with a visit right now, let everyone get used to the idea."

I almost say, *The idea of you not visiting ever?* but I restrain myself.

Dad's a wordsmith with "stabilizing." He makes it sound like his absence is all to benefit my mental health.

"I'm thinking I'll come for your play," he says. "Your mom's told me how hard you're working."

"I am," I say. I want to get off the phone so he won't hear the strain in my voice, but I also don't want to hang up. I have this feeling like once I hang up, I might never speak to him again.

"Thanks for understanding, Caddie," Dad says.

I want to smash the phone, but instead I hold on tighter.

"No, I get it."

"I'll give you a call on your birthday, all right?"

"Yeah."

"I love you."

He's saying all the things that have to be said, back-to-back, fast, so he can get off the phone.

"Love you too," I say. In spite of him being an ass, it's still true.

"How was it?" Mom asks, and then, "Oh, honey," because I guess I look stunned.

"He's not coming for my birthday," I say.

"Oh, honey, I know."

She takes the phone from my hand and rubs my shoulder. I'm wearing a scarf, so my neck's safe, but I want to lean into her, let her cradle my face, and I can't.

She sits across from me. "You know, you and your dad are a lot alike sometimes," she says. "You don't love to talk about your feelings or problems."

"No, I know."

"Your dad . . . that was one of the problems he and I had. Sometimes, I think he'd rather pretend a problem's not there than sit down face-to-face and hash it out."

"He's afraid of us," I say.

"Oh, I wouldn't go that far."

"No, he is. He's afraid of having to deal with everybody's feelings. If he stays in Virginia, he can bury himself in work and pretend the rest of the world is all good."

Mom's silent but pained.

I take that to mean she agrees.

On my actual birthday, there's a card with a check. "I didn't know what you would like," Dad writes. "Happy seventeen!"

I don't feel like celebrating, but Mom insists we should "move forward" and "embrace the positive."

On her insistence, we invite everybody over for my "birthday feast!"

Mandy and Drew arrive first, and Drew's a big hit with Mom. He shakes her hand gallantly and says, "It's a pleasure to meet you, ma'am."

"Oh, I'm not a 'ma'am,'" she says. "I'm a Molly."

When she makes a comment about wanting to pack up some of Dad's stuff to ship, Drew says, "*You're* single? That's crazy."

"Drew!" Mandy squeals.

"I'm not trying to be crass," he says as if offended. Drew plays the southern gentleman well. "I just find it unbelievable that someone as charming as Caddie's mother would have trouble in the love department."

"Well, aren't you the sweetest?" Mom says, and offers him another ginger ale.

Jordan parks himself by Drew and they talk trucks while Mom and Mandy catch up. I'm superfluous, which is fine by me. My brain's not even here—it's calculating distances between my skin and theirs, projecting potential threats and how I'll answer them. If Mom spills her drink on me and tries to help me wipe it off, I'll grab the dishrag before she can use a paper towel, which might soak through and cause an accidental touch.

Somewhere, I know these are people who love me, here to celebrate my birthday, but the most alert, plugged-in part of me sees them as accidents waiting to happen, last straws.

I'm getting worse.

"We got lost, like, eight times!" Livia says when she and Hank arrive half an hour late. The roads around here wind in strange directions to accommodate the hills, the street lamps are spread far apart, and the signs aren't always helpful. Sometimes it feels like they're *trying* to deter strangers from visiting.

Some part of me is glad they made it—I'd started to wonder if they'd blown me off—but more of me is troubled by new bodies in the room. Eventually everyone makes it. Even Peter. He's the one I felt least sure would come, but he arrives with Oscar. Like Drew, they shake Mom's hand and call her "ma'am."

Oscar even brings me a present—something oblong and messily wrapped in Christmas paper. "Sorry," he says. "It's all I could find." Knowing Oscar, the shape makes me nervous, but it's just an eclair from a nice bakery in Crestline.

"Thanks," I say.

And he says, "My pleasure. Consider it an apology for my assholery."

He pops a grin at Peter, who smiles. Maybe they talked about Project A-hole, or maybe Oscar's sharper than Peter gives him credit for. I wonder if they talked about me, about the failed "date."

Peter makes eye contact with me, and maybe I'm making things up, but his smile seems rueful. Peter's "present" to me was only a few weeks ago. It felt like the start of something, but it didn't last.

It's started getting chilly at night, but it's still nice

enough to sit on the back porch without coats. We leave the overhead lights off and instead light the lanterns and candles. The earthy scent of damp leaves and crisp air, the flames, the whiff of smoke from a neighbor's chimney, remind me of campfires at Tannehill State Park. Dad would always pick a campsite by the stream so we could hear the water rushing by as we slept.

A pang seizes me, and I press it down. I have company.

Hank, Livia, and Oscar squeeze onto the cushioned bench facing the woods, and Peter and I sit with our backs to the wood railing, leaving plenty of space between us. Mandy and Drew take Mom and Dad's rocking chairs, hands clasped so their arms form a "V." It's sweet, but it gives me another pang.

As soon as Mom's out of sight, Drew offers to spike our sodas with a big plastic bottle of Beam from his backpack, but Mandy shoves it back in and says, "Caddie's mom isn't crazy like mine. She'd kick us out for that."

Livia teaches a game with teams where we try to make each other guess the names of celebrities. When we count off, Peter ends up on my team and the whole time we're playing, I can't keep from trying to read him, to see if he's saved any feeling for me or if I've put an end to that for good.

Dad calls in the middle of the game. Mom sticks her head out the back door to let me know, and I say, "Tell him I'm busy."

I feel Peter looking at me, but I resist the impulse to meet his eyes.

As things wind down, Peter seems to glance my way more often, and Mandy keeps looking back and forth between us. When Hank and Livia call it a night, Peter pulls another soda from the cooler.

Mandy tells Drew and Oscar she wants to show them this "really cool" portrait of a cow that hangs over the fireplace in the living room. It's Mom's great-granddad's national prize-winning Black Angus cow, Black-Eyed Susan.

Mandy isn't the most subtle. She says, "Peter, you stay and keep Caddie company."

"Do some things I'd do," Drew says as he goes.

Peter and I sit, not exactly in silence, but close. The summer tree frogs have quieted, but the crickets are still at it, and off in the woods, critters with a stunted sense of self-preservation rustle loudly in the undergrowth.

Finally, Peter says, "How have you been?"

"Okay."

"You didn't want to talk to your dad." I feel his eyes on me, but I don't meet them.

"Nope."

After that respectable exchange, we once again slip into silence.

"It sucks," he says, breaking it again.

"What does? I mean, I know a lot of things do, but what in particular?"

"Well, it sucks that you can't talk to your dad. I've been there, and that's no fun for anyone. But I meant, more than that, it sucks that things are like this between you and me. I didn't mean to make things awkward."

"You didn't," I say. I shift to look at him. He's tucked up his knees and hunched over, picking at a splinter of wood from the railing.

"Yeah, but if I hadn't tried . . . If I'd left it friendly . . ."

"I can be shy."

"I know."

"I don't mean to be."

Peter moves so he's facing me. The flicker of the candles gives his face a honey glow. "You don't have to apologize," he says. "You've got a lot going on right now."

"But that isn't an excuse," I say. "I think maybe I'm afraid of starting something. I'm always afraid something bad's about to happen."

It's the closest I've come to admitting my fears to anyone. "Maybe we need to get to know each other better," I say, "before we try anything . . . *more*, you know?"

It sounds like something a normal girl might ask for. It sounds so reasonable, even I believe it for a moment—that given enough time, I might be able to let the fear go.

"Yeah?" Peter says, smiling. "I'd like that."

His words inspire a heady mix of feeling. There's fear in there, but warmer feelings too, like hope.

When the other three come back, it's like the weather's

changed. Before, the crisp in the air felt like a warning. Now, it's possibility—newly raked leaves to be jumped in, fresh-chopped wood for a bonfire, an empty jack-o'-lantern waiting to be filled. We're still standing on the edge of something, but for tonight at least, I can hope that if the ground beneath us crumbles, we might be falling into something good.

25.

The feeling lingers for almost a week, and it's like when I first arrived at the academy—fun. Peter and I plot our Halloween flash mob—he's decided the participants should be called "conspirators" like we're pulling some fabulous con. Oscar tries to teach Hank some stage combat, and Hank decks him by accident, leading to the world's biggest pity party. Drew and I cram for our English midterm together before first period, causing Mandy to fall all over herself at the friend-boyfriend teamwork. Livia teaches Mandy and me to read tarot cards—mine say I'm learning how to cope with change. Maybe that's just Livia telling me what she thinks I need to hear, but it feels nice.

I don't call Dad and he doesn't call me, and I've decided that's best, for now anyway. My life is my life. I shouldn't have to feel bad all the time because of him.

Don't touch hovers, but it's background noise.

Until Friday, when Nadia tells us it's time that we learned about listening.

Oscar whispers, "I know how to listen."

"You don't," says Nadia, "or you wouldn't be talking right now. We're going to start an exercise called repetition. Find a partner, and . . . Well, here, let's have Caddie and Livia try."

The class forms a circle around us onstage, and Nadia gestures that we should sit down in the middle, facing each other.

"Livia, you'll be observing, and Caddie, you're repeating. When you see something in Caddie, Livia, say it, that's all. You might say, 'You're stiff,' or, 'You touched your knee,' or, 'You're happy.' Whatever feels true to you in the moment. Caddie, you repeat after Livia. So, if she says, 'You're happy,' you reply with, 'I'm happy,' first-person. Make sense?"

"When do we stop?" I ask.

Nadia smiles sideways. "Just keep going until I tell you to stop. It won't hurt . . . much."

Livia sits facing me and immediately breaks into giggles. I smile back.

"That's a change," Nadia says. "So, say what you see."

Livia tilts her head and starts in, "Okay, um, you're smiling."

"I'm smiling."

"If you don't see anything new," Nadia says, "keep repeating that until you do."

"You're smiling," Livia says.

"I'm smiling."

"Um. You're nervous."

True enough. "I'm nervous." And, weirdly, saying it makes me feel it even more.

"You look sad."

"I look sad." It feels strange to have her see that—too close, in a way. "But I don't feel sad," I lie.

"This isn't about what you feel," Nadia says. "It's about what Livia sees. Just repeat."

"Sorry," Livia says to me.

"No need to be sorry," Nadia says. "You're just saying what you see."

"Okay," Livia starts in again. "You look sad."

"I look sad."

Nadia says, "Say it like you believe it: not 'You look sad,' 'You are sad.'"

"You're sad," Livia says.

"I'm sad."

"Oh, you're so sad."

She reaches toward my shoulder, to comfort me?

"I like that you're following your impulse," Nadia says. Livia smiles.

But I've shrugged away.

"You don't want me to touch you," Livia says.

"I don't want you to touch me."

"You don't want me to touch you."

"I don't want you to touch me." My heart beats too hard. Does Peter hear it, the words and the heartbeat, and think of that day?

Livia looks a little hurt. "You're weird," she says, smiling, and that breaks the tension.

"I'm weird." True enough.

"Pot meet kettle," Mandy says, and Nadia shushes her.

Livia smiles at Mandy but stays focused on me. "You look, um . . . upset."

"I look upset."

"Less like you're reporting," Nadia corrects Livia. "Just say it: 'You're upset.'"

"Okay. You're upset."

"I'm upset."

Maybe I sound too upset, because Livia jumps to something less awkward. "You're . . . wearing a blue shirt."

"I'm wearing a blue shirt."

"Boring," says Nadia, and we all laugh.

"You're smiling again."

"You're . . . I'm smiling again."

"All right, you see how it goes," Nadia says. "Find new partners, you two."

Mandy waves for me to join her. When I sit across from her, she whispers, "I have a surprise for you in rehearsal. We're doing some physical improv to work on my scene."

Mandy's scene. The scene Mandy's directing for Bard. She told me about it when I was in a fog after the divorce announcement. I'd almost forgotten.

"I convinced Nadia to let me do an experimental memory thing. She's letting me put in a kissing scene!"

"What? Why?"

"So that you and Peter can kiss!"

"But there's no kissing in the play."

"We're adding it!"

Nadia circles near us, and Mandy stops whispering.

"You're freaked out," Mandy says.

"I'm freaked out."

26.

"I wish you had told me sooner," I say in the hall between class and rehearsal.

"She didn't okay it until this afternoon," Mandy says. "I thought you'd be excited."

"Well, I'm not."

"You want to kiss him, right?"

"I don't know! I'm still trying to figure things out, and this makes it harder." A cluster of dancers go by and I lower my voice. "Even if I *did* want to kiss him, I don't want us to *have* to, in front of people onstage."

"Okay, okay." Mandy's regrouping. "I get that. I'm sorry. I wasn't thinking about it like that. I was thinking—KISS! Kiss equals good!"

"Can you change it?"

"It's just a stage kiss. It doesn't have to *mean* anything."

"That's what makes it so horribly awkward. Mandy, you have to change it!"

"I don't know. Nadia says I'm thinking like a director. She thinks the Bard judges will love it."

I want to crawl into the air ducts and live there.

"Can we at least try it out?" Mandy says. "I mean, at first I was just thinking, how can I get Caddie and Peter to kiss, but the more I thought about it, the more it makes sense for the play. I'm kind of in love with the idea."

"Well, I'm not. And I'm the one who has to do it."

"You're in a play, Caddie. Think how physical your audition was."

"No, I know." She thinks because she's assistant director she can coach me into shape.

"Do you even want to play Ophelia?" she asks. "Because I think you're lucky to have the part, and if it were me, I'd be doing everything I could to play it better, not trying to come up with ways to get out of rehearsal."

An awkward silence falls between us. This is how my friendship with Mandy dies . . . again. Already, I feel it coming. I took the part she wanted, and now I'm too afraid to do it right. That would make me crazy if I were her.

"I want it," I say. "Don't think I don't want to play her."

"Caddie," she says. "I've been wanting to ask you something. You got *so* upset at the audition. I mean, in a good way for the scene. But you seemed like you felt it so much. I wondered . . ." Mandy's almost embarrassed to ask me,

"How much of it was acting and how much of it was real?"

"Isn't that what Nadia's been trying to teach us in class—that it's both? So what does it matter?" I hear the defensiveness in my own voice.

Mandy nods but doesn't look convinced. She catches one of my gloved hands and pinches my fingers between hers. "What are these really about?"

"Just for fun," I say, wiggling my fingers.

"They won't be a part of your costume," Mandy says. "Can you get through a rehearsal without wearing them?"

"I could if I wanted to," I say, "but I don't." I make a wide arc around her, past her.

I've got the horror-movie creeps that she might be right behind me, ready to grab at me, but I resist the urge to check.

I sketch in my Ophelia journal so I'll have an excuse to not look at Mandy when she follows me into rehearsal. My sketches have fallen into a theme: Ophelia, always falling, fallen, felled. Sometimes I write words around the pictures, but mostly I draw. Sometimes the emotion comes first and I sketch how it feels. Other times the drawing takes shape, and it hits me, Ophelia's sadness—that's when I feel most like her.

Right now, it's her face that pours from the tip of my pen—her uplifted face in a circle of water, soon to sink like the rest of her. I put a star overhead and write, "Lord

Hamlet is a prince, out of thy star."

Across the aisle and close to the stage, Peter and April are talking. She has class in the theater last period and, recently, she lingers. She sits one row behind Peter, but he leans over the back of his seat, talks too close for their voices to carry—until April laughs, sharp and trilling, knives tapping on crystal.

Ophelia's father is right to warn her about Hamlet. Hamlet toys with Ophelia. He swears that he loved her, but he says that only after she's died. Only after he's used her, made fun of her, abandoned her. She didn't stand a chance with him.

Ophelia should have had a good pair of gloves. I'll suggest it to Nadia.

Just Peter and Mandy and I are called for the start of rehearsal. Normally, anyone's allowed to watch, but today, Nadia tells April and our other observers to give us "privacy."

The four of us sit in a tight circle on stage as if we're all on equal footing. "Mandy and I have been talking about some of the thoughts she brought to the audition," Nadia says, and nods to Mandy.

"Well." Mandy talks straight to Nadia, avoiding eye contact with Peter and me. "We were talking about how I think Ophelia and Hamlet have been pretty physical with each other. It was a good thing between them, but for a whole bunch of reasons, it couldn't survive the . . . you know, the cruelty of the world! I mean, that's pretty tragic. If they never cared about each other, then it doesn't mean anything when they lose what they had."

Nadia nods.

I see where Mandy's going with the kiss, but it's not a direction I can follow.

"So Nadia and I talked about having a silent scene to show the physical relationship, so that, you know, it will be more clear what they're losing."

The meanest thought occurs to me—that Mandy knows. She asked about the gloves. If she can scare me bad enough, I'll drop out and she can take my part.

"There's the speech," Nadia says, "where Ophelia describes Hamlet coming to her room, and he's supposed to be crazed with love. We want to improvise some phys-icality to layer over that speech, like a memory. We're inviting the audience to step inside Ophelia's mind for a moment. He'll kiss her, and the moment will be broken."

"That's cool," Peter says.

Kiss. He'll kiss her. He'll kiss me.

Gloves won't be an issue. I'll need a veil, a medical mask, wax lips . . .

"All right, Director, what's first?" Nadia asks Mandy.

"Um . . . let's hear Ophelia's speech," Mandy says.

I know it by heart, but I go for my script anyway, take my time getting off the stage the proper way by the stairs, and once I reach my bag, I pretend to rifle through, touching the top of my script again and again.

"Mandy has a copy if you forgot yours," Nadia says.

"No, I have it here. I want my own. So I can mark it up." I take the long way back, not that the delay helps. My mind's wriggly, no one thought staying still long enough for me to form a plan.

At the lip of the stage, I pause, and Peter says, "Caddie, you okay?"

I stare inside myself. "I'm not feeling so hot."

Mandy looks down at the stage so I can't read her face, but her body is tense. Nadia's concerned—more about my attitude than my health, I bet.

"You'll let us know if you need a break," Nadia says. "Let's hear the speech."

"Okay." In my place, Mandy would be confident, eager. That's what I'll do—I'll pretend to be her. I sit up straight, shoulders back, and read about how Hamlet comes to Ophelia, half-dressed, and takes her by the wrist, touches her face, shakes her arm. Mandy's idea makes sense—even though the moment's passed, Ophelia speaks in present tense, in a panic as if it's still happening.

When I finish, Nadia says, "Good. Now, up on your feet, you two." She and Mandy stand by the edge of the stage. Nadia takes my script, carrying away my only shield. "Take it away," Nadia says to Mandy.

Mandy still won't make eye contact with me, but she

plunges ahead with whatever plan she and Nadia have made: "Okay, so imagine you have a set amount of space between you."

That sounds good.

"Maybe the length of a broom handle. Keep that space no matter what. Let's start with Peter leading. Caddie, it's your job to keep the distance steady. Only move when Peter moves."

He holds my eyes and takes a single step toward me. I step back. He circles me, always keeping the distance, and I hold my ground. Then he takes two big steps forward, and I scurry back.

"Good. Now . . . try to hold her," Mandy says.

"Crap," I mutter under my breath, and Peter laughs. He sends me running around the stage. I'm always the one changing direction, which makes it hard to hold the distance. He gets closer, and I grab a curtain and swing it between us. Peter's arms close around me, wrapping me up in the curtain like a mummy.

Nadia and Mandy laugh, but they can't hear the rushing. A tunnel of air, empty space sucking me down. I'm falling toward Peter, and when I hit bottom, I'll drown.

"Now, Caddie," Mandy says, sounding more sure of herself, "try pulling him. Peter, don't move any closer to her than the length of a broom, but you have to stay exactly that close. If she moves, you move with her."

He backs away, giving me space to untangle myself

from the curtain, to breathe, and when I step out, it's almost like dancing. We don't even have to look at each other to stay in sync. He senses which way I'm going and follows. It's safer this way—there's power, control, in being the one who leads.

"Now, you'll close the distance," Mandy says. "As near as you can without touching."

I stand still but Peter steps in toward me, breathing so close.

The same air goes in him and out of him and into me. Everything touches everything else.

"I'm going to read the lines," Mandy says, "and I want you to mime the gestures, but don't touch her. Keep some distance."

He runs his hand down the length of my arm, his hand at the side of my hand. And when he makes a shaking motion, I mirror it.

"Good," Mandy says. "Now, raise your hands. And then bring them together."

Her voice is so sneaky and soothing, I could almost pretend that it's not me here. It's Hamlet and Ophelia—action figures for Mandy and Nadia to play with—and if they want to wave us around in the air and push our plastic faces together, so be it. No big deal.

Peter closes the distance between our hands, and I sip air. The gloves make it safe—safer—but the warmth of his fingers, him, seeps through.

"Good. Close the space now," Mandy says. "Like magnets. No space in between."

We bend our elbows, so our arms can line up. Peter presses in close, and his chest bends toward mine. He's asking for permission with his eyes. *Is this all right? Okay?* His head tilts. His arms drop. One hand folds around my back; one hovers at my cheek.

"Stop."

Peter freezes, then abruptly backs up, like I'm a live wire in the street, the kind they warn little children about—step back, hands up, stay away.

"What's wrong?" Nadia asks.

"I can't. I'm sorry, I can't do this."

I'm back in my bubble, submerged, but it doesn't hurt. No gasping for breath in a bubble. No coming up for air ever, ever.

"Caddie." She says it. One word. A sentence to stop me, but I'm not stoppable.

"I'm so, so sorry. I have to go."

And I'm walking offstage, down the stairs, up the aisle. Mandy calls out, "Caddie, wait! Can we talk?"

When did I become this person who runs away from her friends? I'm a mess, an unstoppable mess who hurts and gets hurt, and there's no sense in trying to change that. Still, I can't help looking back at them.

Mandy stands at the edge of the stage, but she's turned her back on me.

Peter sits cross-legged, chin in his hands. He looks small.

I'm so sorry I made him look small.

I go into the restroom to pull myself together, and when I come out, I half-expect to see Mandy searching the halls for me, but instead, there's Peter. He's just left the theater, and he walks right past me. I keep thinking he'll turn and offer a smile, even a half-hearted one, but no.

"Peter, can we talk?"

When he turns, his face is polite and blank. I'm just a girl in the play. I did not, nor have I ever suggested that I'd have a problem with kissing him, or if I did, it didn't occur to him to take it personally. We are professionals, Peter and I.

"I'm not the one you should be talking to," he says. "They asked me to leave so they could conference about you."

"I'm sure."

"What do you need from me?" The coldness in his voice makes my chest tight.

"Do you have a second?"

He nods, one swift gesture, eyebrows up.

"I mean, maybe we could sit down for a second and talk?" I don't like how high and anxious my voice sounds.

He adjusts his glasses. "That's going to take more than a second, Caddie."

"Okay, so a few minutes? Please?" *Please let me make this right.*

Finally, Peter softens. "Yeah, where do you want to go?"

The halls are still busy. I realize I've pressed myself into the space between a water fountain and a locker bank. I don't even have to think about it anymore, protecting myself comes so naturally. "Somewhere away from people," I say, and Peter nods.

"It's chilly out. We could sit in my truck."

The idea of sitting in Peter's truck again, with only the gear shift between us, gives me two kinds of tingles. But Peter won't be reaching out for me. Peter's mad. I nod.

He turns his back on me, and I follow him down the hall and out, feeling pulled like we're still playing Nadia's game. I have to do two things: one, convince him that the way I reacted wasn't personal so Peter won't hate me; and two, convince him that the kiss is impossible. It's not in the play, so there's got to be a way around it.

Peter gives me space, several feet of space, as we walk toward his truck. We're like magnets with opposite poles. All the way down the hill to the lot, Peter speaks only once. "October's so tricky. I never know how to dress."

I speak once back. "I know."

When we get to the truck, Peter unlocks the passenger door first, but he doesn't hold out a hand to help me up. I use the handle to haul myself into the passenger seat and unlock the driver's-side door for Peter.

"Thanks," he murmurs, swinging himself up and in.

It's already hard to breathe next to Peter. Once he closes the door, the cab of this truck's going to feel like the last air bubble at the bottom of the ocean.

And SLAM. We're shut in.

"Thanks for talking," I say.

Peter nods. "You wanted to talk," he says. "Let's not talk about talking. Let's talk." His voice is harder, and the skin at his neck, at his cheeks, has started to flush. He's angrier than I thought. And he's struggling to keep it in check.

"If you're going to get angry, maybe we should talk later."

"Caddie." He turns to me with his lips set. "Are you *trying* to drive me insane? You asked to talk to me. I'm right here. Talk."

"The scene we were doing," I start.

"Yes?"

"It's hard for me."

Peter shrugs, listening, but unimpressed. He says, "You're a good actress. You'll figure it out."

"I mean the kissing."

"Uh-huh." He starts cleaning his glasses, *not* looking at me.

"I mean, the kissing part is hard for me because I've

never actually kissed anyone."

My heart's beating so fast, Peter might as well have his finger poised to touch my lips, my throat, as I wait for him to speak. What I said was the truth, but using this truth so he'll never kiss me makes it feel like a lie.

I want Peter to be my first kiss, I realize. I want to share that moment with him. Maybe afterward, I'll tell him that he was my first. And because he's Peter, he won't mind too much if it's painfully clear. He'll tease me and say, "We have a lot of time to practice."

It's a rush, these *possibilities* that aren't possible at all, just some lies I made up to punish myself.

"Okay," Peter's voice crashes in, scattering my thoughts. "I get it."

He's looking straight ahead, not at me, and I'd give anything to hear what he's thinking but not saying out loud.

"It's embarrassing," I say. "You must think I'm incredibly lame."

"It's not embarrassing," he says, sounding almost angry, but *for* me, not *at* me. "A lot of people kiss, and more, just for the sake of doing it. I think it's nice that you haven't been hooking up with a bunch of random guys you don't care about."

His defense of me takes me by surprise, and before I can gather my thoughts, he keeps going. "You could make out with any guy you wanted. I mean, Oscar, for one, would be all over you—he's already all over you, and you're not even nice to him."

I make a face at just the thought of kissing Oscar, and Peter laughs.

"Don't feel bad about it," he says. "I'm sorry if I reacted badly. I thought . . ."

"You thought that the idea of kissing you grossed me out."

He grins. "Something like that. So, it doesn't?"

The imaginary finger poised at my throat has moved down, a gentle stroke to the center of my heart. This is not where I meant for this conversation to go.

"It. Does not. Gross me out."

Peter could eat seven onions, eight garlic cloves, and a frog, and I'd still want to kiss him, but he doesn't need all the gory details.

"I understand." Peter nods to himself. "Who wants their first kiss to be onstage?"

"Right? It's not even real. Kissing you would not be a chore. Far from it. But I don't want to look back and remember the first time I kissed a guy was because our teacher made us, and it was super awkward, and public, and awful."

"Sure. I'm glad you talked to me about it," he says. "It did kind of bum me out, I'll be honest."

"I know, and I'm sorry for that. I'm sorry I didn't think of telling you right away, instead of stopping the scene like that."

"No, no worries. All right."

His "all right," I figure, means case closed, get out of my car so I can get out of here, please, but when I say, "All right, well, I'll see you tomorrow," and open the door, he says, "Wait," like I took him by surprise.

He reaches for me, but I scamper out faster and farther than he can reach. I stand on the pavement with the door open to let him speak.

"We don't have to talk about it now, but we can figure something out," he says.

Yes, a way to get around doing the kiss in the scene. I nod.

"I've been wanting to kiss you for a while, now, Caddie. I'm glad the first time will be real."

A tremor chases up from my stomach all the way to my fingers and toes. Peter's smile is so big—he knows he caught me by surprise—but his gaze is steady.

"See you soon," Peter says. He reaches across and pulls my door closed, starts the truck, and zooms off down the hill.

27.

ME: Crap, crap, crap, crap. Peter wants to kiss me.

MANDY: And the problem is? You don't want to kiss him? LIAR.

That's how it will go if I text Mandy. I want her advice, but I can't handle all the questions she'll have.

"How was rehearsal?" Mom asks when I get home.

"Bad," I say, and go straight to my room.

"Caddie," she calls after me.

"What?"

"Your dad called. He wanted to talk about your show."

Such good timing he has, calling just when I stand a great chance of getting kicked out.

I make my face blank and head back to the den. "What did he say?"

"He'll have to find someone to cover his Friday class,

but he thinks he can swing it." I must let some reaction slip because she says, "Caddie, he called of his own accord."

Maybe now that the divorce is a sure thing, he's trying to be Superdad. "Okay. Thanks for telling me."

"Mom made me talk to him instead," Jordan says from where he's sunk into the couch, "but for some reason he didn't like it when I called him a tool."

Mom stifles a smile at that, then says to me, "Do you want to call him back? He was sorry he missed you."

"No, maybe I'll call him later, from my cell."

"All right. Your call." She catches her accidental pun, and goes, "Ba-dom-dum!" with a big smile on her face. "Cheer up, babe," she says. "We're having tacos for dinner. Nothing some chips and salsa can't cure."

"Right."

"Now, your show, it's just Thursday, Friday, and Saturday, right? No Sunday?"

"No."

"Oh, phew, I thought that was right. That's the day of my Goblet show."

I nod. "Yeah, everything will be over by then, so it should be okay. It sounds cool, Mom. I can't wait."

I almost ask whether she's invited Dad. Since he'll be in town for my show, he could see hers, too. But the show feels like something that belongs only to Mom—Mom post-Dad. Maybe she wouldn't even want him there.

Maybe she knows he wouldn't be able to appreciate it

the way she'd want him to.

It seems wrong that something so important to Mom could go on without involving Dad at all. But I guess that's what divorce means. You get to stop pretending to care about the other person's interests, stop worrying about their feelings.

I wonder if that's a relief, or if it's sad.

Rather than ask, I leave Mom to her good mood.

I'm on my bed doing homework when my phone buzzes.

I'm afraid to look, afraid it's Peter calling to set up our "real-life" kissing scene. It's Mandy, but that doesn't make my fears go away.

"Hi," I say.

"Hi," she says back, then nothing.

"What's up? You called me."

"No, I know." Something's wrong, in her voice, I can tell. "Caddie, there's something you should know."

She's going to tell me that she and Nadia talked. It's not a kissing scene they want, it's a full-on hookup, undies only, something edgy for the jurors from the Bard . . .

"You know Nadia and I talked after rehearsal," she says.

"Uh-huh."

"She's worried."

Of course she is. How could she not be?

"Okay."

"She's afraid you might drop out," Mandy says, then quickly adds, "I told her you wouldn't."

"Okay."

Another long pause.

"Mandy, just tell me."

"She asked me to be your understudy," she says.

My heart drops.

"It makes sense," she goes on, "because I'm there every day, and because I had some stuff memorized at the audition," she says. "It doesn't mean she thinks I'm good for the part or anything. I'm just there."

"Right. I get it."

"I told her you don't need an understudy, Caddie, that you're going to be fine."

It takes me a minute to find my voice. "Thanks for saying that," I say.

"I need you to know it's not something I'm excited about."

"Sure," I say, but my mean thoughts that she planned a kissing scene to freak out her friend with the gloves seem less far-fetched now.

"Caddie, can we talk about this?"

"We've been talking about it," I say.

"No, I know but . . ."

"It's okay, Mandy," I say. "It isn't your fault I'm a screwup."

"You're not a—"

"I've got to go, okay?" I can't breathe and talk to her at the same time. "I'll talk to you tomorrow."

"Caddie, if you'll tell me what's going on, maybe I can—"

"Good night, Mandy. I'm sorry, I have to go."

"Okay. Good night, Caddie."

If I want to keep my part, and I do—*I so want to keep it*—I have to get okay with touching people.

I have to let this stupid fear go.

I cross through the bathroom to Jordan's room. "Can I come in?" My face is pressed to his door. On the far side of that is a chasm; across that, my only sibling.

He grunts, and I open the door to find him huddled in his beanbag chair, slaying orcs.

"Are you winning?" I ask.

"This isn't a game where you win. It's a game where you kill things."

I watch him play for a while—the Berserker Orcs are harder to kill than the Guard Orcs, and the Shaman Orcs hit you with fireballs, but Jordan kills them quickly.

"It looks too easy," I say.

"This is a baby world," he says. "It's fun to kill stuff fast."

"You pretending they're Dad?"

"No," he says, and he pauses the game, looks at me hard. "That's not funny."

"I'm sorry. I didn't mean for it to be. I've been feeling

262

pretty angry since Dad left."

Jordan smirks and says, "Join the club."

This is where I should reach out and ruffle his hair, but touching hair's too much like skin. I need a baby step.

"Jordan. I want to ask you a favor. Will you try something with me?"

"I'm playing."

"No you're not. You're acting out your aggression."

He sighs and hits pause. "Fine, what is it?

"Okay. This is going to seem weird, but . . . I want you to pass me the controller."

Our hands will come close to touching, but we shouldn't *have* to touch. It's a manageable risk. He frowns, but he goes along, holding the controller out to me.

I pull off my gloves.

"Those things are looking tired," Jordan says, and it's true. I've washed the gloves in the sink, but even that caused the color to bleed. They're too delicate for the washing machine.

But I can't allow myself to buy a new pair. That would be like giving in to gloves for life.

Jordan holds still while I reach forward and pinch the controller between my finger and my thumb. *Don't touch, don't touch,* ricochets, but I tell myself it's okay.

My hands feel wrong, too exposed to the air, the skin stretched and raw.

Jordan was just touching the controller. Touching it

might be like touching him. I breathe, push that thought away. I'm already living in a bubble. If I start worrying about touching things other people have touched, I'll need to be vacuum sealed.

Jordan's skin is so close, heat energy rolls off his hand in waves, burning mine. That's how it feels in my head. If there's anything real to my fears, Jordan's at risk too. Maybe this experiment isn't safe, isn't fair to *him*.

"Caddie!" he says, and his other hand clamps on my wrist, the feeling of skin touching skin and the shock of a burn, both at once. He shoves the controller up into my hand and away. "There. Are you happy?"

I bite the inside of my lip and catch a few short breaths— can't let him see that I'm fighting to breathe.

"Caddie, what's your deal?" Jordan asks. He's annoyed, but he looks concerned, too. I don't like to think of Jordan worrying about me on top of everything else. I drop the controller—"Careful! They're breakable!"—and get out of his room, leaving the gloves on the floor. No good touching them until after I've washed all the danger away.

I shut Jordan's door to the bathroom and wash under the bathtub faucet, where I can scrub all the way up my arms several times without soaking the floor.

The water hits my hand, runs between my fingers and down, and I rest my cheek on the side of the tub. Nothing's saner than clean, white porcelain. This is my life. Caddie Finn, here and now. There is nothing to fear. Nothing to do but keep breathing.

Except that this moment can't last. Another one's coming, and I have to keep going, keep doing, keep touching, messing up, getting messed with. What would those moments feel like, to drown like Ophelia, skirts billowing at her sides so she floats for a time before getting dragged down? Only that one moment left. Nothing to fear coming after.

They say that Ophelia died singing.

The water's running warm, so I stop up the drain and let the tub fill. Splashing around in the faucet won't wash away this fear—I've got to go under.

I roll over the side and let myself drop, not even feeling the water at first, only the warmth as it soaks through my clothes—jeans heavy and stuck to my skin—the warmest warm blanket swallows me whole.

This is the last moment.

I imagine it's true, try to feel like Ophelia would feel.

This is the moment. No, wait, no—this one.

My body's too long to drown in a tub, except Mom always said you can drown in even one inch if you fall asleep. I bend my knees, slide down so the water can cover my face. It's too hot at first, makes me want to come up for air, but I hold on.

My pulse thumps in my chest, in my brain, *knock, knock, Caddie, come up,* but I fight.

Ophelia's death is described as so peaceful, but real

drowning wouldn't be. Bodies fight to stay alive. What if you breathe in the water, choose it, tell your body to let go?

I bet it still hurts.

A bang on the door rattles me, and up I come, gasping. No conscious thought from my brain to my body, just instinct, popping me up and out.

"Can I get in there?" Jordan calls.

My heart thuds so hard it hurts, and its echo—it pounds from inside. I can't hear right.

"I'll be a while," I yell back. "Use the guest bath."

My lungs breathe on their own, fast. They don't need any help. It's almost like hyperventilating, but this time I *need* the air.

If Jordan hadn't banged on the door . . . What was I playing with?

I might be crazy, but I'm not suicidal.

I would have come up for air. I *would*.

I should get Mom or Jordan to take a picture of this for my journal—me, in the bath, in my clothes, wondering what it feels like to drown. "It's an acting thing," I could say. No need to explain more. But that would mean putting my head underwater again, and there's something too scary about the thoughts I just had.

I've been trying to get in Ophelia's head, but I don't want Ophelia *in me*. When I stand, my wet clothes make me so heavy, it's a struggle to lift my feet up and out of the tub.

28.

Mandy's leaning on my locker first thing on Monday so that I'll have to deal with her. She left me messages over the weekend, but I never called back. I wouldn't have known what to say.

"I know you're mad," Mandy says. "You're not being totally fair, but I understand."

Mandy gets like this when she wants something settled—direct and practical. I bite my lip. "I'm not mad. Well, maybe at myself. Not at you."

"I'm telling Nadia I won't be your understudy."

"What?"

"I told her you didn't need one, and you don't, so I'm not going to do it." She speaks quickly, driven.

"You don't have to do that."

"I do. So don't worry about it."

"Okay, well, thanks."

I didn't like the idea of Mandy being my understudy, but I don't completely trust myself, either. "What if something happens, though? I mean, what if I really do need one?"

"You won't," she says. "And now that you know there's no backup plan, you'll make sure you don't."

She smiles—all done, problem solved—and spins away, asking Livia, "Did you decide about your Halloween costume?"

Nadia doesn't use me for days. I watch rehearsal to show commitment, but she barely looks at me. Then, midway through a rehearsal, Nadia calls a break and walks up the aisle with her head down like she's on her way outside. When she gets to my row, she pivots to face me. "Are you ready to work?" she asks.

"I have been."

She tilts her head. "You know I'm worried about you."

I nod.

"I didn't cast you so you and Peter could work out your personal problems onstage."

"No," I say. Lord, she thinks my freak-out was all part of some relationship drama. In a way, it is. I guess I'd rather she think that than know the truth.

She goes on. "I trust my actors to leave outside problems *outside* and to be one hundred percent focused on the task at hand when they're in this room. If you can't do that, you need to let me know that you're not up to this. We open in six weeks."

I nod again. "I'm ready."

She stares me down, tilts her head to measure me better, and a piece of her dark, choppy hair falls in her eye. She blows it away, gives me one last good glare, then stalks back toward the stage. I wanted so badly for her to like me. Now I would settle for indifference.

Without looking back, she says, "I'm sending you and Drew to work with Mandy while I work Rosencrantz and Guildenstern."

Drew takes forever gathering his things, and Mandy and I stand side by side in the aisle waiting on him.

"This should be fun," Mandy says, her face grim.

When Drew reaches us, he tosses an arm around my shoulders. We're both well-covered, but it's automatic to try and shrug away. He squeezes my upper arm with his giant hand and pulls me in tighter. The top of my head barely reaches his armpit. "Hey, sweetie," he says. "Who's your daddy?"

"Ha-ha," Mandy says flatly, and slides her arm into his, pulling him toward her. He sways in her direction but doesn't let me go, so we walk three in a row to the top of the aisle.

It's good for practice—touching with clothes in the middle and not freaking out. I breathe deep.

"Let her go," Mandy says when the three of us have to squeeze through the door, and he does, but he lets go of Mandy, too, dropping back. The silence is horrible. Mandy tries to break it, turning and walking backward. "What if we blow off rehearsal and go out for fries?"

She's joking, but Drew says, "Might as well. This is busywork."

Mandy stops walking and shoves at Drew's chest with both hands.

When he laughs, she says, "It's not busywork for me," and turns front. We shut up the rest of the way.

When we get to our acting classroom, Mandy steps into the pool of stage light, which bounces off her hair, giving her a halo. She would be beautiful as Ophelia.

"All right," she says, stepping out of the light and sitting at the foot of the risers. "We have the time, so we might as well work."

Drew sits down at the piano on the far side of the space, plunking out sour notes. "This needs tuning."

"I get it," Mandy says. "You don't think you have anything to learn from me, you don't like me directing, you have the crappiest attitude that ever 'tuded, but I'm responsible for this scene, so will you please, for me, try to get over yourself for, like, twenty minutes and focus?"

Drew stares, his fingers poised over the keys; then he drops the lid and swings to face Mandy, placid. "I'm ready. Direct me."

Mandy exhales. "Thank you. Now get up."

She leads him to the edge of the pool of light and pulls over a small table and a chair for him. "This is the first thing we see in Act Two."

Drew snorts.

"What?"

"The first scene in Act Two is actually a nice, long Polonius scene, which got cut, just like most of my part."

"Fine. The first scene in *our* Act Two."

"Caddie, did you have any of your lines cut?"

"No."

"There are only a couple of female parts in the whole play," says Mandy, "and Ophelia doesn't get that many lines to begin with."

Drew shrugs. "I just think it's interesting who Nadia puts her faith in, when some people can't get through a simple stage kiss without having a breakdown." He drops that bomb with easy innocence, and Mandy's mouth hangs open.

How many other people did she tell?

"Can we please just work on the scene?" I say.

Mandy gathers herself. "Yes. So, Ophelia, you'll enter from over here." She leads me to one side of the playing space and lowers her voice. "I'm sorry he's being such an ass. It doesn't have anything to do with you."

"I know."

"He's my boyfriend. I tell him everything. Even when I shouldn't."

"It's okay. I don't care what you say about me."

"I didn't say anything bad, I just—"

"It's okay, Mandy, let's work."

Mandy pivots between Drew and me. She looks lost. "So, this opening part is setup for the speech where we're going to break from reality and bring Peter in."

"Because Peter's not in enough scenes already," Drew says.

"*I* didn't cast you as Polonius, Drew, so stop taking it out on me," Mandy says. "I didn't get the part I wanted either, did I?"

"No," he says, "Caddie got it because she's so good."

"You guys! Please!" I jump into the scene because I don't know how else to make them stop: "Alas! my lord, I have been so affrighted!" I run to Drew and grab his arms, gloves and sleeves between our skin.

Don't touch, I think and then stifle it.

Practice, practice.

I've caught him off-guard, which is right for the scene, and it takes him a second to catch up. "With what, in the name of God?"

"This is where we'll bring Peter in," Mandy says, "but for now let's do the reality of it."

I go into the speech, imagining Peter doing all the things Ophelia describes. The improv that we did with him chasing me—it scared me, but it did help me understand. Ophelia loves Hamlet, but he's turned into someone threatening.

"Mad for thy love?" Drew asks.

"So when you say that," Mandy says, "let's make it clear you've already decided that's what it is."

"Can we get through it once?" Drew says.

Mandy sighs but manages to make her voice positive, "Sure, yeah, keep going."

"My lord, I do not know," I say. "But truly I do fear it."

"What said he?" Drew takes me by the elbow and holds me too close, so as I tell the story I pull away and face out, pretending Peter's there.

"He took me by the wrist and held me hard . . ."

To my side, Drew's acting up a storm, nodding and making faces in reaction to everything I say. Mandy looks like she's choking. When I reach the end of the speech, Drew tugs at my arm. "Come, go with me; I will go seek the king. This is the very ecstasy of love—"

Mandy cuts him off. "Great, so let's go back to Caddie's speech."

"Really?" Drew says. "We *just* got to my part."

"Well, the whole scene is your part," Mandy says. "Not just when you're talking."

"No small parts? Only small actors?" says Drew.

"I stopped because I didn't feel like you were listening. You were *acting* like you were listening."

"Oh, my *God!*" Drew says, and lurches around to brace himself against the curtained back wall. "Do you hear this? She thinks she's Nadia."

"I do not," Mandy says. "But that *is* what she's been teaching us—if you've been listening."

"This was *not* a good idea," Drew says, spinning around to face us.

"What?" Mandy says.

"For you to direct me in a scene. For you to direct at all." He sounds like he's pleading for reason. "You're still a student."

"So are you," Mandy says, "and they're letting you do Shakespeare, but I guess *that's* okay because you're *such an expert.*"

Drew deflates, sinking back against the curtained wall, and mutters, "It's not the same."

"What's with you?" Mandy's dropped her bravado. She's just hurt.

I should say something, stop this. Mandy and Drew have their problems, but we were just talking about how much Mandy loves him, and I think he loves her. They're digging a hole they might not be able to climb out of.

But the best I can manage is, "Should I give you guys some privacy?"

They answer together in a definitive "No!"

"I'm just doing my job," Mandy says, recharged.

"Your job?" says Drew. "You mean the job that Nadia gave you to keep you from being all pissy that she didn't cast you in the play? That job?"

"She wants to mentor me," Mandy says.

"You can tell yourself that," says Drew. "Seems like a bad idea to put someone in charge of other actors when she wasn't good enough to land a part herself."

Mandy stands straight, but there's something inside her that's fallen down. Otherwise she'd be pushing back, incinerating him where he stands.

"Caddie agrees with me," Drew says. "Don't you, Caddie?"

"I don't." But Mandy's already gone inside herself. She's not hearing me.

"She doesn't want to do your whole 'break from reality' scene either. She'd say so if she wasn't terrified you'd drop her."

"I'm not," I say, but I hate that he can see my fear.

"Okay then, tell her," he says. "You don't think it's a good idea."

"It's not that I don't think it's a good idea . . ." The polished wood floor feels very far away. I'm too high above it, off balance.

"Then what?" Mandy says. "Why are you being so mean? Both of you."

"Mandy, I'm not—" She cuts me off.

"No, you are. You're both undermining everything I do, and what I don't get is why?" She looks between Drew and me, and then inhales sharply, a question she can't ask.

"Oh, my Lord, no," I say. If I'd told Mandy everything, she would know how ridiculous it is to even think there might be something between Drew and me.

"Caddie, we can talk more about this later," Drew says, and stretches a hand out toward me like we're best buds, or more. His steps seem to tip the floor, tilt me toward Mandy—I'm dizzy—and then he's gone.

She stands facing the door, not looking at me.

"I don't get it," she says.

"Mandy, you *know* there's nothing going on between me and Drew. He's trying to piss you off."

"I know," she says, "because I know how obsessed you are with Peter."

"I'm not—"

"Save it," she says. "I'm sick of you telling me things that aren't true."

Her words are a slap. "Mandy, I never said a word to Drew about the scene, I swear."

"But you don't like it."

"It's not that. It's . . ."

"Just say what you mean."

She spins toward me, making me wobble—it's as bad as standing on the diving board, this falling apart.

She says, "Look, are you still mad about the understudy thing, because I told Nadia I wouldn't do it. Even if you dropped out of the play, I wouldn't do it."

She has tears in her eyes, and I feel so guilty for not trusting her. I didn't try to wreck her scene or steal her boyfriend or whatever other evil thing she thinks I might do, but I haven't been fair.

"Mandy—"

"I tried to be so nice to you," she says. "I tried to help you fit in, even when you acted super weird."

"I know. You've been great, I—"

"I tried to help you with Peter."

"I *know*. I'm sorry, Mandy, I thought—I thought something different."

"You thought I was out to get you," she says. "That I set you up to fail."

"No."

"You did. I didn't understand till later. You should have given me the benefit of the doubt, Caddie. You should have *talked* to me."

"Yes."

"What about? *What* should you have talked to me about?"

It's an interrogation, and I'm choking.

"About . . . about Peter. About you understudying . . ."

She shakes her head. "Wrong answer. God, you can be such a fake, Caddie. You're always faking something."

"I don't . . . mean to be." My words are thin, throat tight—I'm going to lose Mandy and everything that comes with her. "I've been having a lot of problems in my family."

"You and I both know that's not your only problem. You don't like being touched," she says. "That's why you're wearing the gloves."

Zap! Mandy's zapped me—the water in me is a super-conductor. I twitch.

"It took me a while to see it, but I'm not an idiot, Caddie. What I don't get is why you won't talk to the person who's supposed to be your best friend." She goes still. "You don't trust me, Caddie, and you know what? I don't think I trust you."

If she sounded mad, that would be one thing, if she were saying it to dig at me, but she's not. She looks sad and confused.

"Mandy, I'm sorry I've been strange." I'm afraid to go to her—I'm so dizzy, the floor will tip—we'll go plummeting into the black.

She shakes her head like it doesn't even matter. "It was dumb of me to think we could go back to being best friends like we were. Things change," she says. "It is what it is."

She leaves me alone in the pool of light, one tiny piece of solid world with dark all around. I drop, press my face to the cold, tilting floor, and try to stop spinning.

After that, Mandy mixes it up at lunch and sits on the opposite side of the table from me and close to the end.

Livia gives her a look the first time—that's Hank's seat—but Mandy plays oblivious.

"What happened to the seating chart?" Hank asks when he shows up and finds Mandy in his place.

"We don't have assigned seats," Mandy says irritably.

"Well, yeah, we sort of do." He's already pulled a chair up to sit at the end between Livia and me, making Livia beam.

Usually the guys end up at one end of the table, the girls at the other, with the "couples"—Mandy and Drew, Livia and Hank—at the middle, but the turnover leaves Mandy's seat open when Peter arrives. If the change-up surprises him, it's a happy surprise. I shift closer to Hank's end.

Peter sets his tray down and sits with his knees almost touching my legs. "You figured out your costume?" he asks.

My first thought's of Ophelia. "They'll tell us what to wear, yeah?"

"Halloween," Mandy says. Her face is tense, purposefully free of expression. Actual Halloween's not till next week, but Mandy's party is on Saturday.

"Oh, right. No, I don't know."

"I'm going as a vampire," Oscar says. "You could be my thrall."

"I don't think so," Peter says. With everyone watching, he lifts one of my gloved hands in both of his. This is the definition of PDA, and my nervous system's shooting off fireworks. But the party, of course, the party would be the perfect time and place to solve our . . . "problem."

Peter bats my hand back and forth. It doesn't hurt, but the threat is there. If Peter brushes my gloves the wrong way, they'll scrape off, take my skin away with them.

Mandy's eyeing me. Her expression's impenetrable, but her lips purse in question.

Peter lays my hand down on the table. I catch my breath, but my hand still pulses.

"You're still coming to the party, aren't you?" Mandy asks. "It would be weird without you there." I hadn't thought about not going, but we *are* fighting. Now that she's asked, I wonder if I shouldn't be going.

I can't read her, but because they're all looking at me, I say, "Of course."

Mandy nods, one firm twitch, and goes back to her salad.

April is at rehearsal on Friday.

She stays the whole time and sits halfway back.

Nadia doesn't say anything about it, but I know April's there to replace me, in case. Mandy said no, so if it comes down to an emergency, Nadia will lift April's punishment and let her perform in my place.

My tears are so close to the surface. They come easily when we work the breakup scene, when Peter—Hamlet— says, "I did love you once."

"Indeed, my lord, you made me believe so."

Peter touches me, holds me close and then shoves me away, like at the audition, and if it makes me clench or gasp, that's good for the scene and good practice. I have to be able to touch him, not just through clothes . . . in a kiss.

Tomorrow night.

"What's going through your head right now?" Nadia asks when we get to my soliloquy.

"I'm losing him. I'm losing him, and I can't do anything to fix it." It's easy for me to believe I'm losing him. I am— will—if I can't get myself under control.

"Yes! In fact"—she hops up onstage and kneels beside me, looks out over the audience where she means for me to see Hamlet in my mind's eye—"all those things she says about him, how he used to be, use those to bring him closer to you. Try that."

"But they won't stick."

"Exactly—for every good thing you remember, there's the truth of what you've just seen. You're trying to hold on to something that's gone. Try as hard as you can. That's the tragedy here because no one can do that."

"But it's so sad!"

She laughs. I'm afraid she's going to squeeze me into a hug. She squints at me and says, "I knew I cast you for a reason. You understand something about loss."

"I've lost some things. I don't know if I understand—"

"Well, Ophelia doesn't either. She's in the middle of it. So that's perfect."

Perfect.

Except that Ophelia's a wreck. She loses too much— and she sinks.

29.

My hoop skirt keeps trying to escape from under the dash-board and smother me. Between the dress's boned corset and my seat belt, I can barely breathe.

This is what I get for not planning a costume. At the last minute, Mom called my older cousin Jess, who used to be a Southern belle docent on a historical plantation tour. I said no to the hat and parasol and added a shawl to protect my arms and shoulders. I'm hoping my makeup and hair steer it away from Scarlett O'Hara and toward my goal: Dead Prom Queen.

"Your first academy party," Mom squeals as we near Mandy's drive. "How exciting!"

So exciting, my hands won't stop shaking. My heart wants to make a career change and work for a humming-bird.

"I told your father that going to this school would change the direction of your whole life."

"The direction of my life" hinges on such tiny, fragile moments: What if Mom had said no when I asked to audition for the academy? What if she'd told Dad instead of keeping it secret? What if I bombed the audition? What if I never, at the age of six, saw my first play? Things can change in an instant—might be changing right now—and I won't even notice until later when I look back and say, "That night. That's the night when things changed."

"I'm proud of you, Caddie," Mom says. "I'm proud of you for asking yourself what you want in life and going after it. That's something I'm still learning how to do." I can hardly look her in the eyes. If she knew how lame I'm being, how close I am to losing everything . . .

She says, "I admire you, sweetie," and her eyes are wet at the corners, and I have to look away.

Lit up from below, Mandy's house looks like an unstormable castle, a real Elsinore. I expected a lot of people, but not this many—cars are stacked all the way up the drive and line the street for a block or more in both directions. I make Mom drop me at the street and I trudge up the drive, careful not to let my skirt drag.

My people should be here, people I know.

As soon as I go around back to the pool, there's a high-pitched scream from Hank and Livia and a guttural, "Ha-ha!" from Oscar. An eerie glow from the aqua-gold pool lamps catches the undersides of their faces. Splashes of light and shadow shift so my friends seem insubstantial, half-there. But they rush at me, proving themselves real. Oscar bounds to me in two steps, and Livia hauls Hank after her by the arm.

Livia and Hank both wear togas, hers green, his gray. Livia's clearly Medusa with plastic snakes woven into her braids, and Hank's "stone." Hank planned ahead for the cold with a gray fur cloak, but Livia wears her green pea-coat over her toga, which kind of undermines the scary.

Oscar . . . well, true to his word, he came as a vampire, but I guess he really wanted a thrall. There's a blowup doll hugging his neck.

"Ew," I say.

"Girls dig vampires," he says. Oscar reaches for me, ready to pull me in for a hug. My hoop skirt and his doll form a buffer between us, but I still have to sidestep him.

"I'd hate to make your girlfriend jealous," I say.

"Oh, Bethany? It's cool. I think she's bi."

He makes the doll reach toward me, but she comes undone and he's suddenly like a kid with a broken toy, begging Hank to fix it.

Livia reaches for one of my gloved hands. "Did you plan your costume around these?" she asks.

"Not exactly."

"I bet you'd wear them in the water if it were warm enough for swimming."

She's smiling, but I don't like the questioning tilt of her head.

"Um, hang on. I should say hi to Mandy."

She's on the far side of the pool, a classic witch with some serious cleavage. I squeeze between the pool chairs and the kids who've drunk themselves warm enough to stick their feet in the water. Mandy steps away from a group of seniors to greet me. "I was afraid you weren't coming."

"Sorry. I had to take care of some stuff for Mom first."

"Well, you're here now. Dead prom queen?"

I nod. Apparently the tiara and dripping blood did their work.

"Drunk driving accident?" she asks.

"I was thinking more serial killer on a rampage?"

"Sure."

She leads me to a table stocked with hard alcohol and some mixers. A pony keg and a Styrofoam crate full of wine coolers sit underneath. "What do you want?"

"A little bit of everything?"

She laughs, but cutting the anxiety seems like a not-so-bad idea.

"Caddie, living dangerously." She pours some ice and what looks like a lot of lime vodka into a red plastic cup, followed by Sprite. "What do you think?"

It's tangy and acidic, but on top of all that it's . . . "Sweet. Really sweet."

She watches me gulp and says, "Make sure you drink a glass of water before you have another one, okay?"

I nod. It's awkward between us, but I'm grateful to her for at least trying to make me feel welcome. We wander up a brick walk to the flat expanse of grass between the pool and the ridge. The old trampoline still sits there.

"Remember this guy?" Mandy scoots onto it, sloshing her drink as she bounces. "Oops."

"Yes, I remember this guy. This guy broke my wrist."

"Right! I had almost forgotten that. Remember that time when we moved it close to the edge of the wall so we could bounce off it into the pool?"

"It's a miracle we didn't die."

As I push up onto the trampoline, my lowest hoop flips vertical, flashing anybody who might be looking. I squeal, and backpedal to the center of the net, trying not to spill my drink in the process. Mandy's laughing at me, but she helps me wrangle the skirt, and we sit cross-legged facing each other.

"I'm glad you came tonight, Caddie," Mandy says. "It wouldn't be the same without you."

"Thanks. I'm glad you came too. I mean, I'm glad I came."

Down by the pool, Livia and Hank are doing a bastardized swing dance. He throws her away from his body and yanks her back so her Medusa snakes whip around. Then he lifts her and swings her so close to the edge of the pool that she shrieks and starts kicking her feet.

I want to shake Hank and Livia so the feelings between them come out more even.

"Why does he flirt with her like that?" I ask.

"She loves it."

"But it can't ever become anything."

Mandy sighs. "Maybe that's how they need it."

I hadn't thought about them like that before.

"Maybe some kind of closeness is better than none," Mandy says, "if you're afraid of the real thing? Or if the real thing starts making you crazy."

"Where's Drew?"

"Drew. Is. Sulking," she says, and nods toward the ridge. "Peter's up there with him, I think."

Mandy must be able to hear my heart beat in my chest, feel the trampoline pulse, but if she notices, she's too polite to say anything.

"Why the sulking?"

"We had another fight. I started it this time," she says guiltily. "I wasn't the kindest version of myself. But he pushes my buttons. We ought to break up."

She says it so matter-of-factly.

"I thought you were terrified of losing him."

She twists so she can look me in the eye. "So what?"

"What do you mean, so what?"

"So what if I'm afraid?"

She holds my eyes for longer than is comfortable and

I fall back on the trampoline, watch the dark branches frame stars then swish to the side in a sudden breeze.

"Caddie, there are worse things than feeling afraid." She lies down beside me, close enough that the wire brim of her witch hat brushes my temple, but I stay still.

"I don't know if I think there are—worse things."

"I'm going to stay in a bad relationship because I'm afraid of being alone?"

I laugh at myself. "Maybe?"

"It's like with your parents—"

"I don't want to talk about them."

"Why?" Mandy asks, propping herself up on one elbow and making her voice goofy, a kid at a campfire. "Are you *afraid*?"

"Yeah, maybe."

"Scaredy-cat."

I put on a goofy voice too. "Am not!"

"Are so!"

She leaves her drink resting on the net and pokes my arm, too close to the edge of my shawl. I jerk, and the trampoline bobbles beneath us. Mandy raises her drink to save it from spilling, but that makes her slide closer to me. The elbow that had been propping her up slips and touches my skin.

"Ow!" I'm up and scrambling to the edge of the trampoline's net before I can remind myself to play it cool.

"What?"

"I feel like . . . I think I pinched my leg in the spring."

"Yeah?" She sits up and eyes me over the rim of her drink. "I touched you."

"No, that's okay."

"I touched your arm, and you didn't like it."

"Mandy . . ." There's no end to that sentence except to say please don't make me talk about it. I scoot toward the edge of the trampoline. "I'm going to get another drink."

"Wait. Caddie, please, let's talk. I started feeling bad that I gave you a hard time. I realized you might have a good reason for not wanting to talk, like an awful reason, but you can tell me, no matter what it is. You should talk to *someone*." She's gone super serious, so concerned. "Did something happen, Caddie? You know, did somebody *do* something to you? Take advantage of you?"

"God, no!"

The idea makes me ill. Mandy's decided I'm some kind of victim. It would be easier to understand, more sympathetic, than the reality. I feel almost guilty that I *don't* have a story like that to tell. The only person hurting me is myself.

"You can talk to me about it," Mandy says, "even if it's something awful."

"There's nothing *like* that," I say as I scramble down to solid ground.

"Okay, then *what*? Caddie, I'm supposed to be your friend. I don't know why you won't talk to me."

"Look, I have to run inside for a second, and then I'm getting a drink, and then I'll come back and we can talk more, okay?"

"What are you going inside for?" Her voice gets louder as I reach the brick stairs. "You're going to wash it off, aren't you?"

"Hush, please," I say and hurry around the pool. People turn their heads to see who's fighting with the hostess.

"Caddie!" she says, loud enough for everyone around the pool to hear. "Caddie, I'm trying to be a good friend."

"Stop trying," I say. It comes out before I can censor myself. "Just drop it!"

Everybody's watching. I weave my way through our poolside audience and inside.

I take as long as I can washing my arm, as much to avoid Mandy as to scrub the nagging, anxious feeling from my skin.

When I head back outside, Mandy's at the center of a tight circle saying something funny enough to have the whole group doubled over and cackling. She catches my eye, midsentence, and there's the tiniest hitch as she dismisses me and smiles at her audience.

I walk to the edge of the pool and hold my arms out, let the aqua-gold lights dance in patterns on me, one set of colors for my skin, another for the lavender gloves, like with one of Mom's filters. I could take the gloves off, glide my hands through the water, let it tunnel and fold through my fingers.

The feeling of falling—that rush that comes from standing at the edge of something—makes me step back. I'm too full of potential energy. The impulse is there to dive in, to be reckless and giddy, but it's cold and I'm wearing heavy clothes. I've been drinking and you should never, ever swim after drinking.

I give myself a task to steady myself—get some water—and float over to the drinks table. Everything's a bit off, like my motor skills are on holiday. I take an ice cube from the bucket and suck on it.

"There's a scoop for the ice. You don't have to use your hands," Peter says, startling me. He puts a big scoop of ice in his cup and rattles it around.

He's all in black with a half-mask under his glasses, a headscarf—and black gloves.

"The Dread Pirate Roberts?" I guess.

"Pity, now I'll have to kill you."

"Already dead." I point to the blood at my temple.

"Oh, right, my bad."

Why did Peter have to be a pirate? I used to have the biggest crush on that character from *The Princess Bride*. I crack down on the ice in my mouth and give my best all-things-are-good grin.

"Chewing ice? They say people do it when they're sexually frustrated, like it helps with that or something."

I spit the ice into my hand. "It helps with babies

teething, too." If promised a room full of rubies for coming up with something more inane to say, I couldn't do it.

Peter pauses, stuck on whether I'm joking or not. I wasn't, but he decides I was, and laughs like I'm a comic genius. "Hey, baby, you want some . . . ice?" he asks with a fake leer, and my laugh comes out high-pitched and bouncing.

Peter steps closer. "How are you doing?" he asks.

"I'm okay. Still working on my character journal."

"Right now?"

"No, not right now. Right now, I'm chewing ice to get over my sexual frustration."

Ack!

Witty?

Yes . . . Peter is laughing.

Suggestive?

Extra yes . . . Peter is coming closer.

I walk toward the brick steps that lead up to the yard.

"Where are you going?"

"Nowhere. Elsewhere. I feel like stepping away from the pool, is that allowed?"

He tilts his head like he's considering. "By the power vested in me as your castmate, I decree that ye may step away from the pool."

"You are such a dork."

"Shh," he says, ducking like he's looking for spies. "They'll hear you. I try to keep the dorkiness under wraps.

Otherwise, it tends to overwhelm people with its awesome power."

"The awesome power of dorkiness?"

He shrugs. "It's some pretty big dorkiness."

"Let's hope no one alerts the authorities."

"Right? They'd rush over to neutralize me for sure."

"I feel safer just having you here."

He bends his head toward me. *Oh, no.* I spin, face away toward the ridge and say the first thing that comes to mind. "I want to go see the bats."

They swoop and dive up there, fleeting shadows against the orange-purple sky. There's something other-worldly about how they skim through the dark.

"Bats," Peter says, shaking the ice in his cup. "Bats are exciting. I can't compete with bats."

I turn back to him. "No, it's not . . . You're not compet-ing with bats. You can look at bats too. I just—I haven't been up to the ridge since I got back to being friends with Mandy."

"Well, let's go."

I invited him to the ridge. I didn't mean to do that. I wanted to do it, but it's not a good thing to have done. I trudge up the hill with Peter at my side, trying to hide how the heels and alcohol make me wobble.

"You were up here with Drew," I say. "Is he okay?"

"He's fine. They fight every now and again. That's how relationships go, you know?"

I don't know. I know that my parents fought every now and again, and I know how that went.

When I stumble, Peter reaches out a hand and I take it. Now that he's gloved, too, it's doubly safe. His grip is firm and warm, and he's just enough taller than me that I feel like he's lifting me slightly as we walk to the top of the world.

The top of our little-city world, but still, it is beauty.

Bats tilt overhead like they're as tipsy as me, drop down and swoop back to daredevil heights, a show of bravado for Peter and me.

Below us, way down in the valley, gold- and pink-tinged lights make our tiny downtown kingdom shine. A dance of red and green lights streams through the city's veins.

"It's like Christmas," I say, "all the lights."

"I don't know about that," Peter says. "It reminds me of one of those sci-fi space shows with a city floating in the darkness—all stars and vacuum except for this one flat, robotic chip. Maybe it's robots down there."

"Maybe the robots took over," I say, "while we've been at this party. Maybe we're the only people left free and alive." I kneel at the edge of the world, and the hoop skirt collapses around me.

"There are worse places to be," Peter says, "if the world had to end." He sits down beside me and grins. "Worse people to be with."

Peter lifts his mask out from under his glasses, which causes his headscarf to slip, freeing a few messy tufts of hair.

I would like to touch that hair.

"Thanks," I say. "Thanks, I'm sorry I'm . . ."

"What?"

"I'm sorry I'm so weird."

I don't want to see the echo of that in his face, the "yes, you are weird," so I stretch out on my belly and prop myself up on my elbows facing the city. My shawl shifts in the process, giving the damp grass an opening to tickle my skin.

"You're not weird," Peter says, stretching out and leaning on one side to face me. "Or maybe you are, but not in a bad way. You're great."

"Thanks." My voice comes out in a whisper. But everything else is amplified—the prickle of grass, Peter's breath sighing across a charged space to touch me.

"I like you, Caddie," Peter says, low.

"I like you, too."

It's not acting. It's un-actable, the truth of those words.

"Sometimes, I think . . . you're afraid of me," he says.

I twist to my side, facing him, and I nod. "I think so."

"You don't need to be," he says. "I don't want you to be anymore."

Space shudders between us, full of potential—begging us to close this distance, to *move*.

"I don't want to be afraid," I whisper.

But fear's rising, a wave.

Peter touches me. Touches my face. And the ridge starts to crumble, ready to drop me and him off the edge of the world.

"Peter . . ."

He touches my lips with his lips.

And I scream.

30.

I push Peter away, roll to my side, up to my knees. I lose a shoe as I try to stand and get caught on my skirt, hear it tear. "Caddie, wait—"

He reaches for my arms, wants to pull me up. "I don't need help!" My words knock him back. I try to stand myself up, trip and slide halfway down the hill.

"Dude, what happened?" That's Oscar's voice, coming closer.

Livia and Hank follow Oscar—all three of them pressing too close.

"Oh, God, Caddie, are you okay?" Livia asks.

"Stop, stop, stop, please." My throat's tight, mouth dry.

"Caddie, I'm sorry." Peter's voice comes from above. "I thought it was okay. I'm sorry."

"Caddie, are you all right?" asks Oscar.

A sob—no, it's a scream—tears out before I can stop it. *Just leave me alone! Why can't all of them leave me alone?*

"Caddie!" Peter's voice shoots out, hard and anxious.

"I'm okay! I'm fine!" I yell, but it's too late. He hovers over me, reaching out his hand. *AHH! Stop it!* "Don't touch me!"

He drops his hand, looking shocked as if I'd punched him.

"Dude, what did you do?" Oscar asks Peter.

"Nothing," says Peter, his voice clipped and low. Then he makes eye contact with me. "We kissed."

"Whoa," says Hank under his breath.

"I thought you wanted me to," Peter says, his face flushed.

"I'm sorry," I say.

"Caddie, it's all right," he says, kneeling too close. "Whatever's wrong is going to be all right."

"No, it isn't. Just LEAVE ME ALONE! Please!" And I roll away from him, feel for my shoe.

"Maybe not right now," Hank says, his hand on Peter's shoulder. Livia stands over me, hands open and useless at her sides. She wants to try and heal me, but I'm a lost cause.

"Caddie—" Peter starts. His voice cuts off as Oscar yanks him up by the back of his shirt. The blowup doll hangs between them, and that makes me laugh, but it comes out like hitching sobs.

I can't get enough air.

"She told you to leave her alone."

"Caddie, I'm sorry," says Peter, leaning toward me as Oscar moves to block him. "I don't know what—"

I'm wiggling my shoe on when Oscar shoves Peter hard.

"Stop it!" I scream. "Stop it! Stop it!" The words don't come out right. There's not enough air for my voice.

Livia puts her hands on my shoulders, no skin touching skin, but too close. I shake her off.

Peter's tumbled back and is trying to right himself, but Oscar steps forward fast and shoves him. "Stay down!" he says. "Till she says it's all right."

Peter stands fast, looking ready to lunge at Oscar.

"Hey, hey, hey," says Hank, coming between them. "I know stage combat."

"What the hell!" someone—Mandy—calls. She's stalking up the hill, all wicked witch. "Tell me you are not having a fight at my party!"

Other people have started to gather. Drew jogs up and puts an arm around Peter's shoulder while Hank and Livia stand on either side of Oscar, ready to hold him back. Drew talks low, right in Peter's ear. Peter's eyes go away from me as he listens to Drew, but he still looks like a dog who's been kicked and wants to make things right again.

He looks back to me one last time, all questions, before Drew turns him away.

"Caddie, what happened?" Mandy asks, keeping her distance. She knows better than to touch me.

It takes me a second to breathe, to speak. "I'm okay."

"I didn't ask if you were okay. I asked what happened to make all my friends start acting like lunatics at my party."

I try to hide the panic. "Mandy, I need to go home."

Faintly, I hear Livia: "Oh God, it's almost time."

"Caddie," Mandy starts, ready to argue, but I see something break in her eyes. She gives up on me. "Fine, then. Let's get you home."

As I hobble down the hill toward the pool, Mandy follows my steps with her eyes as if they might catch me if I should cut and run, as if eyes are as good as hands.

Just as we reach the pool, the party seems to suspend with one held breath. A taut anticipation ripples down the lawn, around the pool, as one in every five or six people freezes. Mandy curses under her breath and goes rigid beside me. One guy holds a chip between his teeth but doesn't bite down. A girl who's bent over to hike up her tights stands caught in a gesture that's meant to be quick and discreet.

The ones who aren't in on the joke stare in wonder, then laugh, poke at their frozen friends. One very drunk girl's yelling, "What the hell? What the *hell*?"

On the other side of the yard, Peter's surrounded by statues who rest their steadying hands on his shoulders to show that it's me and not him who is strange.

When Peter steps away from their circle toward me, no one stops him. Their hands hang in midair, comforting his ghost.

They'll stay still for three minutes. That was the plan. Peter and I made this together, but because of me, we missed the cue.

That's all right. I've been frozen for months.

Now I need to move.

I feel Mandy shift ever so slightly as I step away from her and closer to the pool, but she stays put. I *feel* Peter coming closer but can't look at him.

The pool lights make the water angelic, blue ripples lit up from inside. It looks clean.

All my fears have come true, but this anxious residue still smothers me and coats my skin. I've been holding on so tightly to what, at the end of the day, is a lot of pretend. I'm not normal, and nothing is fine, so why act like it is? Why not let my crazy show?

I twist, put my back to the water, and drop like a felled tree.

Gold and blue wash me inside and out.

My enormous skirt accordions and reverses itself, forming a cage of hoops around me. I bat at them, upend myself so they unfold around my legs, and I'm free.

Underwater, I laugh, spend the last of my air with the echoey sound.

I could let the chlorine burn my skin away. There'd be

nothing to touch, nothing to keep me from touch. Bubbles burst. Everything touches everything else.

When the need to inhale seizes me, I resist.

The water is clean. I want more.

My heart beats at me, pummels my lungs, ribs, screams at them, *make her breathe, make her come up for air.* I flap my arms to keep from surfacing. It's giddy to fight against breathing like this, to fight *against* air instead of for it. *I decide when I breathe. I'm the one in control.*

There's a crash at my side. Through a spinning cloud of bubbles, Peter reaches toward me, come to save me from myself. My feet stab at the bottom of the pool. Arms push down. And I kick away from him. My skirts drag, but I'm strong. I kick at the water, up and out, coughing, gasping.

Peter pops up after me and treads water, holds my eyes but keeps his distance. His lips are pale, and his teeth chatter—from fear or from cold, I'm not sure. I cough, take one more sharp breath, and then mine start chattering too. The party's broken its freeze. People stand at the edge of the pool watching us. Peter and I float in a bubble—two people and the freezing water and the black sky.

"You can't touch people," he says, loud enough for only me to hear. "You swam away from me so I wouldn't touch you."

I nod, and it feels cleaner than the water, sharp and as easy as breathing, to let Peter know, *Yes, you figured it all out. I'm crazy.*

He looks away, sorting it out for himself, how this changes things.

"You might just have saved me from drowning," I say.

He laughs, but it's hollow. "How's that? You're so horrified at the idea of touching me, you had to come up for air?"

He looks up, away.

Overhead, chilly stars prick the blue-black sky over the pool, fading in with the purple wash that bleeds over the ridge.

Peter floats and I float, lots of space in between.

"Caddie, *what* are you doing?"

Mandy's voice pops the bubble around Peter and me, making me shake in a more violent way.

The reality of what's gone on tonight works its way in. I'll be a good story tomorrow—the crazy girl playing Ophelia who got acting mixed up with real life.

I tread toward the pool ladder, where the underwater lamp makes my skin glow tissue thin. My skirts are heavy, but they don't drag me down. Ophelia would have had on heavier clothes, and she probably didn't know how to swim. My body wouldn't let me drown. I knew that. Of course I knew that.

I meet Mandy's eyes. I think she's more angry than worried.

"Get out," she says, her voice tired and short, and she turns her back to the ladder, giving me space to climb, but she doesn't reach out her hand. "Come on. Somebody get her a towel."

Halfway up the ladder, I look back toward Peter. He doesn't take his eyes off me, but I can't read his expression.

We tell Mandy's mother I fell.

"Her shoes," Mandy says. "The strap at the ankle broke. Caddie tripped."

"Bless her heart." Mrs. Bower pulls off this southern ladies' slogan with a perfect blend of insincerity and disapproval.

Mandy does all the talking because I'm still underwater, can't breathe right. The big picture window in Mandy's living room is like one of those giant tanks at the Chattanooga Aquarium, and the party's crowding in to see the show. They might as well press their hands and cheeks to the glass.

Except for Peter. He sits on the brick wall beside the pool and stares straight at the water. He never looks up.

"Well, I guess we should call your mom," Mrs. Bower says. "I hate to trouble her, but Dad is . . . indisposed." Mandy's dad gets indisposed often with this terrible condition called scotch on the rocks.

Mrs. Bower leaves, but it only increases the pressure in the room. Mandy exhales heavily and sits straight as a rod on an ottoman. As soon as she's landed, she's up again.

"Do you want some of my clothes?" Mandy asks, maybe

just to have something to say. Her voice is flat, and her eyes don't meet mine.

"I would love something dry," I say, then, "I'm sorry, Mandy."

She shakes her head as if to discourage some buzzing fly, and disappears upstairs.

When she brings me the clothes, she lays them across the ottoman where she'd been sitting, and says, "I'm going to try and enjoy the rest of the party. I hope you feel better."

She says it like I'm a dying stranger in a nursing home, someone she has to be polite to, but who makes her uncomfortable—someone we both know won't ever feel better again.

31.

I stay in bed.

On Sunday, Mom asks, "Did something happen at the party?"

"I just don't feel right," I say.

When Mom insists on taking my temperature, I run the thermometer under hot water, and she assumes I caught a cold.

"You're going to need a doctor's note," Mom says on Monday. "I think we should take you in."

"They can't do anything for a virus," I say. "There's one going around."

When she tries to make me talk about the party, I say, "Please, can I sleep? I'm so tired."

On Tuesday, Mom says, "You're so worn out. What if it's mono? Have you been sharing drinks—or maybe a kiss?"

She says it slyly, like we're best buddies and she's onto me.

I laugh, one sharp, "Ha. I haven't been kissing anyone," I say, though that's not exactly true.

Peter kissed me. Our lips touched. If there were ever a more awkward, horrifying first kiss, I'd buy tickets to see it.

Mandy calls on Tuesday afternoon, and Mom brings me the phone. I shake my head, but Mom sets it on the blanket and leaves me alone.

"How are you feeling?" Mandy asks.

"Not so great."

She pauses. "There are all sorts of theories. People are saying you got so drunk you broke all the blood vessels in your face, and you're not coming to school because it's red."

"Ha."

"And then I heard one that you slept with both Oscar and Peter that night, and that's why they were fighting, and now you're having the baby of one or the other, but it's too early to tell which one yet, and that's why you're not coming to school."

"Creative."

"Well?"

"Well, what?"

"Which one is it? Or is it what I think . . . that you're so mad at me you can't stand to see my face."

This takes time to absorb. "Why would I be mad at

you? I wrecked your party."

"Okay, so you think I'm so mad at *you* that you can't stand seeing me, one of those two."

"No."

"Or you're embarrassed about Peter."

Yes, yes, and yes, and more and more.

The other night at the party, it's like a wall that hid my darkest self fell down. Even if I was drunk, even if I was acting out or getting my life mixed up with Ophelia's, there was some tiny, impulsive part of me that thought it might be nice to drown.

"Mandy, I don't—"

"You don't want to talk about it. I know." She sighs, but she sounds as frustrated with herself as with me. "I'm really calling for something official."

Here we go.

"Nadia wants to know how many more days you're going to miss. She has April playing your part—as an understudy, for now—but if you can't come to rehearsal . . ."

"I know."

"Well, she *wants* you to know. And she wants you to come back. She'd rather have you in the part, she told me."

"Mandy . . ."

"Yeah?"

"Nothing. Never mind." I hang up the phone.

❦

On Wednesday, Mom tells Dad I've been sick in bed for four days and asks him to talk to me. "I hear you went ice swimming," he says.

"Something like that."

"Well, you know, it's not really being cold that makes you catch cold, I was telling your mom, so it doesn't make sense that you'd catch it that night."

"Did you make Mom feel stupid for believing me?"

"Did I— No, no."

I almost miss his stubborn rationality. Nothing can't be fixed with a bit of logic.

"Maybe someone at the party gave it to me."

"Maybe." He doesn't sound convinced. After a dead space, he says, "You know your body loses heat in cold water nearly four times faster than in air?"

"Dad, what does that have to do with anything?"

He makes a sound somewhere between a cough and a sigh—a fizzle. "Nothing, nothing."

Dad wears a mask too, it's so clear to me now. When he can't handle reality, he retreats into science. I swear, he could look at a ten-car pileup on the highway, fourteen people killed, and he'd start comparing the tensile strength of the cars' metal frames.

I'm sick of the stupid masks, sick of pretending.

"I don't think I'm doing very well," I say.

"No? Do you think it might be time for you to see someone again?"

A cold hand squeezes me, colder than under the water. Dad always said my problem was an overactive imagination, that I'd outgrow it. He calls psychology a soft science. He must think I'm a mess if he's suggesting a doctor. Or maybe he just wants someone else to sort me out so he won't have to worry.

"I'd be fine if you were here," I say. "I wish you were here right now. I wish you could give me a hug."

If he would come back, maybe things would go back to normal. I'd drop all my games.

"I'd like that," he says.

"No, you wouldn't," I say.

He goes quiet for a long time, clears his throat. "You know what?" he says. "I *do* wish I could give you a hug. I would like to do that very much, and I'm sending a hug to you over the phone. Can you feel it?"

He sounds like an ad for a long-distance carrier. "Nope, I can't."

"Well, I'm sending it to you." He clears his throat again. "And maybe things would be better if we were all in the same city and could see each other more, but I don't wish . . ." His voice trails off.

"What?" I don't try to keep my voice from sounding hard. I let it be as angry as it wants to be.

"I don't wish that I was back living there with your mother because it seems to me like this is a change for the better."

"Ha! Of course things seem better to you. You're not here and never call."

"Caddie, your mom and I weren't so good for each other. Doesn't your mother seem happier to you?"

I don't have anything to say to that, so we stay on the line in silence. I listen to him breathe. It's better knowing he's taking the time to be silent with me, even if we don't have anything to say to each other, than to hang up and go weeks wondering if he'll ever call the house again.

Finally, he says, "The work I'm doing here, Caddie, has the potential to help a lot of people."

I know how much Dad cares about his work. I always loved that about him, that his work was important, noble.

"And the funding, the support, is incredible. You know how you're working to prove yourself, Caddie, at your new school? I'm working to prove myself right now too."

"You should call us more often," I say. "If you care."

"I guess I thought it might make it easier for everybody to get used to the new situation if I weren't calling every day."

"Or every week?"

He goes quiet again.

"Maybe it made it easier on me," he says. "Maybe I needed some space, to make this new life here feel real, like mine."

I think of the night Dad drove away, never telling us where he was going, when or if he'd be back.

He stammers on. "I . . . I should have made more of an effort. I get caught up in work. You know me."

I do. I know. But it's not an excuse.

"I'm still planning to come see your play."

"They're going to kick me out for missing rehearsal," I tell him.

"Oh." He sounds surprised, and maybe I'm imagining it, but he also sounds disappointed.

"I know you thought giving me the academy was going to make everything a-okay," I say. "Like that would magically replace you or something."

"Nobody thinks that," Dad says.

My face flushes hot and suddenly I need out from under the covers.

"It seems like you've been able to replace Jordan and me with your work just fine."

"Sweetie, I know you're not so happy with your dad, but you want to give me some kind of a break?"

"Not really," I say and hang up.

An hour later, Mom sits at the foot of my bed to one side of my legs. Her arm pins me down on the other side, too close. Her weight stretches the quilt tight so my toes point. I'm caught.

"Caddie," Mom says. "I think we need to check in with Dr. Rice."

I wriggle under the covers to face away from her.

"Your dad told me what you said, that you're not doing well."

"I was trying to upset him."

"Well, you did. He's worried about you."

If that's even a little bit true, I'll take it.

I twist to face her. "I love how when you two think I have a problem, the first thing you think of is getting me to talk to somebody else about it."

"Caddie, I've been *trying* to get you to talk to me. Do you want to talk?"

Her jaw's set, eyes sharp. She examines me for signs. It's like we're in a movie about the spread of some zombie plague, and she's looking to see if I'm still her same Caddie.

She smoothes the quilt, pressing it down around me even tighter—it's supposed to be soothing, but I'm blinded by aqua-gold lights again, holding my breath.

"I think I'm going crazy," I say.

"No," she says, firm.

"But I was doing so much better. It's so much worse than it ever was."

"Things have been stressful. You know how that works. Anyone who has a problem with anxiety—when you get stressed, it's going to make it that much worse. I should have anticipated."

Maybe it's finally talking to Mom, or maybe it's the sadness in her eyes—like that first time I had to go see Dr.

Rice, the sadness that something was broken in me that she couldn't fix—but I'm crying and it feels like I might never stop.

I kick at the covers, slide up to sitting, and Mom gives me room.

"I'm afraid I'm not going to get any better."

"You will. With a little help."

"I *had* help. I'm supposed to be better. I'm not supposed to *be* like this anymore."

"Hey," she says, and there's some of Dad's practicality in her voice. "Life doesn't work that way. If it did, your dad and I would have come to our senses and broken up years ago."

Would that have been better or worse? Or maybe that's a dumb question. Maybe these things just *are*.

"Why do things have to break?" I say.

"I don't know," she says. "I don't like it either. Have you ever seen me on a bad cleaning spree?"

I give her a look. Everybody knows how she gets.

"That's my way of coping," she says. "Some people throw fits. Some people run away. Some people drink. I scour."

"At least yours is practical," I say.

She laughs softly. "It's more than a little OCD. I think you get it from me."

I always thought of myself as having more in common with Dad—his need to control things. His avoidance. Dad tries to control other people. Mom tries to control her environment.

I try to control *everything* by controlling myself.

It's like the things in Mom and Dad that grate against each other met in me. If they couldn't live with each other, how am I supposed to live with myself?

"I'm sorry," I say to Mom.

"What for?"

I'm not even sure. I'm sorry for being how I am, for making her worry, for not being able to help things between her and Dad, for the dark thoughts I had underwater.

"Can I sleep now?" I say. "I'll go see Dr. Rice, but right now I just want to sleep."

When I wake to see Peter filling the doorway, at first I'm embarrassed he caught me dreaming about him, which doesn't make sense. If I'm awake, I'm not *dreaming* about Peter at all. Peter's real.

I hate to think how I must look, all pasty and red-eyed. My sleep shirt's medicinal green, and I haven't brushed my hair for days. But Peter doesn't look at me. He sits in the rocking chair by the side of my bed and stares at his boots.

A bunch of flowers hang between his knees. They're warm and cheery colors—red, orange, and yellow for a girl who's feeling blue.

"Your mom said you might be asleep," he says.

"Sorry."

"What? No . . . Do you have . . . I don't know . . . a vase?"

I shrug and he sets the flowers on the night table. A few petals fall.

"My mom let you up here?"

He nods. "She said company might do you good. I thought she should warn you, but she said you'd tell me to go away." He grins and looks me in the eyes for the first time. "Sorry to take you by surprise."

I don't answer. I can't say it's okay, can't say I don't care, and I don't trust my voice.

"Happy Halloween," Peter says.

It's actually Halloween. I love Halloween, but I hadn't even realized it was today.

"I heard a crazy story," he says, "that the strap on your shoe broke, and that's why you fell in the pool."

"Hmm." My throat is too tight. If I let one word out, who knows how many might come tumbling after?

"Everybody was watching the flash mob, but I was watching you."

"Yeah, I'm sorry for wrecking that."

"Why did you jump in?"

"I didn't jump. I fell."

"But you let yourself fall."

I shift on my pillow to face him. "You jumped off a roof."

He looks toward the door. "That was stupid of me."

"Are you calling me stupid?"

He almost smiles at that, but he checks himself.

"You were drunk . . ." He trails off. He knows there's more to it than that.

I hold his gaze.

He pulls a flower from the bunch and picks it apart so its orange petals drift to the floor. "You stayed under so long. Did you mean to?"

I look up at the ceiling. Tired as I am, it hurts to hold my face still for so long, to pretend I'm okay when I know that I'm not—it's like holding my breath underwater.

"I don't know," I say, and I don't like how ripped up and raw my voice sounds. "I don't know what I wanted. I hope I didn't mean to, you know, stop breathing. I just—I had an impulse and it felt right, so I did it. It made me feel free."

I shut up then, because he's too close. I've already told him too much. The space in my room closes in on itself, filling up with bad feelings and worry, no air.

"You can talk to me," Peter says, but what he's really saying is, *Let me help you. Please, please, let me in. Let me touch you, squeeze you, press you. Let me breathe all your air.*

I love that he came here, *love* that I haven't totally scared him away. But he should be with a girl who can hold his hand, kiss, maybe more. He shouldn't get stuck with my problems.

"I don't think I can explain it," I say.

Peter pulls the last petals from the stem in his hand and watches them fall to the floor. Any second he'll stand up and leave me alone, let the bubble close up around me again, let me breathe.

He reaches down to pick up a few of the petals and holds them toward me as if he means to press them into my bare hand that lies open on the quilt. I haven't been wearing the gloves to bed. I pull my hand back. "Don't—"

"No, I know," he says, gentle. Those words make me flood. My heart pumps hard, extra blood heats my face.

He holds the petals in the space between us. "If I promise not to touch, is that okay?" he asks, and his hand doesn't move. I let mine fall open, cupped on the quilt at the edge of the bed. He moves his hand closer to mine, slowly, tentatively, giving me plenty of time to pull away.

I close my hand into a fist and press it down into the mattress, but I stay.

He's almost to me when the words come: "It's scary," I say. I laugh at myself even though it's not funny. It's safer to laugh than to cry.

Peter pauses but doesn't pull back; he exhales a few little breaths, his own nervous laugh. His hand shakes. My breath catches. The sheets feel like they're on fire, but I still dig my fist into the mattress, fight the impulse to scurry away.

He tilts his head and touches the petals to the back of my hand. Peter considers my hand like he's taking an

X-ray of my bones and knows exactly what he'll see.

I unclench my hand, and Peter brushes the petals along my fingers. He's still shaky, but careful and slow. When he reaches my fingertips, I turn my hand up and let him drag the petals down all the joints to my palm. It tickles and twitches so much I have to flex my fingers back, extend to resist squeezing shut.

He traces the lines on my palm—the life line, the love line, the ones of lesser consequence—and I concentrate on relaxing my muscles, letting go, so my hand folds back into a cup.

I take a deep breath, feeling . . . proud, and I meet Peter's eyes. He smiles. Not a grin, but a full smile.

He lets the petals go, lets them fall into my open hand.

32.

Peter waits downstairs while I shower and change.

My whole body feels different under the water. Everything is sharper, more sensitive and alive. It almost hurts, but in a good way—a why-haven't-I-showered-in-four-days way.

I pull on jeans and a top with long sleeves, and I put on my gloves—one scary step at a time, please.

Peter's in the den, checking out Jordan's costume—a mask that fills up with blood when he presses a pump. Next year, Jordan might be too old for trick-or-treating. It almost makes me sad, but I check myself. He has horror movie marathons, visits to haunted houses, and parties, so many parties, in his future. Not every change is sad.

"All better?" Jordan asks me.

"Working on it."

"I thought maybe you caught some kind of sleeping sickness, like from a mosquito."

"No such luck," I say.

"I'm not kidding. I was worried about you." Jordan looks a little offended.

"I'm sorry I made you worry."

"You ready to get out of here?" Peter asks.

"Yeah, I guess I'm feeling brave."

I can't fix everything all at once, but there's one important thing I need to fix as soon as possible, maybe even tonight. As Peter pulls out of the driveway, I confess, "I think I've been a bad friend to Mandy."

"She'll forgive you," he says, "once she understands."

But how to make her understand? Peter seems to accept my fear without needing to ask a lot of questions, but Mandy will want to know a clear reason why. I remember how she talked about Peter's "nuttiness" after I first met him. I can't bring that up to Peter, obviously, but it makes me worry that Mandy might shun me now that I've let my crazy show.

Peter parks at the top of Mandy's drive, and we walk in and out of the cones of harsh area light that surround Mandy's house. At the pool, we find Mandy and Drew on lounge chairs.

Mandy's up like a shot with her arms spread dramatically as if to block me from leaping in. "Step *away* from the pool," she says like an agent in a cop show.

"Swimming season is over."

"I'm done swimming," I say.

She relaxes her arms, takes a drag on her cigarette, and considers me. She doesn't look angry but poised—at any moment she could shift into attack mode. She turns to Peter and says, "This is my surprise?" He responds by walking around to take Mandy's seat next to Drew.

"Can we talk?" I ask, and Mandy shifts her pursed lips to the side. She's not going to make this easy.

"You want something to drink? *Non*-alcoholic."

"No, thanks. I'm good." She leads the way to the upper lawn, removed enough from the pool that Peter and Drew won't be able to hear us.

I perch on the edge of the trampoline, but Mandy chooses the grass.

"I'm sorry," I say.

Mandy nods.

My words spill out in a rush, things I've waited too long to say. "I'm sorry I freaked out. I'm sorry I haven't been a good friend. I've been keeping things from you, and I haven't been able to talk about why, and that sucks. And I'm sorry I missed rehearsal and messed up your scene. I'm sorry I'm interrupting your . . . date, or whatever, right now."

She nods again. "Okay. Apologies accepted."

But she doesn't look at me.

"Are we still friends?" I ask, and waiting for her to

answer is as scary as holding my hand still for Peter. She doesn't respond for a long time.

"I think you and I will always be friends, in a way," she says. *In a way.* "We have a history together. That's important."

I nod, but my mind's racing, thinking how to make it up to her.

"I don't know, Caddie," she says, and she ashes onto the grass. "We don't even know that much about each other—not recent stuff anyway."

"I *want* to know," I say. "I want to talk about it."

"About what?"

"About . . . you and Drew. About my weirdness. About the state of affairs in the Middle East. About how to get Livia to give up on Hank. Whatever you want."

Mandy's quiet for a long time, staring out toward the ridge. Bats dip and play, and at first it takes me by surprise to see them there. In my mind, they came out special for the party—atmosphere for Peter and me. But here they are, a week later, not caring about me and my little drama, just doing their own batty thing.

"She's really making an ass out of herself," Mandy says.

It takes me a second to register that she's talking about Livia.

"I don't know if I'd go that far."

"No, it got worse after you left. Hank knows that she likes him; she knows that he knows; he and Oscar make faces about it as soon as her back's turned. Maybe . . ."

"What?"

"Maybe we could get Livia to go for Oscar."

"Honestly? I think Oscar and Hank might do better together."

She sniffs out a, "Ha. Yeah, you're probably right."

"Not everybody has to be coupled up."

Mandy's turned back toward the pool, where her eyes follow Drew as he paces beside Peter's chair. Peter's laughing; Drew isn't, emphatic about whatever position he's taken, per usual.

"I think I'm afraid of being alone," she says, and she looks to me, eyes full and dark. I used to think of Mandy as never being afraid of anything.

She breaks away from watching Drew and lies back, looking up to the sky. I slip from the trampoline and lie down beside her, leaving maybe half a foot between us. "You're thinking about breaking up with him?"

She takes a long drag, lets it out. "I love Drew, but we aren't always nice to each other. We're too much alike. But the thought of letting him go . . . it makes me want to jump out of my skin."

Crickets sing, and I don't have to say anything. Just listen.

"Did you ever think about how brave your parents were," Mandy asks, "to split up?"

"Maybe there's something to that."

"You're looking very couply with Peter."

"Am not."

"Are so."

We both laugh. I haven't felt this much myself since Dad left, nothing forced or performed. Mandy rolls onto her side, propping up on one elbow to face me.

"So, you and Peter? How's that going to work, if you can't . . ." She holds a finger in the air between us, and I raise one gloved finger to meet it.

". . . touch anyone? Yeah, it's a problem. For the play, too. I was hoping you might help me work on that."

ACT FOUR

And as my love is siz'd, my fear is so.

Where love is great, the littlest doubts are fear;

Where little fears grow great, great love

grows there.

—PLAYER QUEEN, *HAMLET* (III.ii.117-19)

33.

I tell Mandy everything, and she doesn't look at me like I'm contagious. She listens like I'm the most important person in the world, nodding and saying a sympathetic, "Oh, Caddie," when I get to sad parts.

"It makes so much sense now that I know," she says.

"You always suspected I was crazy?" It's a joke, but I realize I'm eager to hear her answer.

"No, no, I never thought you were crazy, but you used to space out sometimes."

"I'd be going through things in my head, making deals with myself, trying to make sure I didn't think the wrong thing."

Mandy nods. "And I knew you had panic attacks. My mom told me."

"She did?"

"But she told me not to bring it up to you, that it wasn't polite to talk about. I should have said something."

"I should have told you. I was always so freaked out, and . . . when we were drifting apart, I thought maybe it was because you could tell something was wrong with me, that I was weird."

"No!"

"It seems dumb now."

"I could tell there were things you weren't sharing with me. I thought—"

"You thought I didn't want to be your friend."

Mandy wipes her eyes with her scarf. "God, it's so dumb."

I shake my head. "I'm not going to hug you right now—because I can't—but Mandy, when I'm better, I may hug you to death, okay?"

She nods, sniffling. I never imagined, back in middle school, that it might have hurt Mandy to lose me.

Dr. Rice offered to squeeze me in first thing Thursday morning, and Mom jumped on it. Waiting in the office isn't as nerve-racking as I remember. For one thing, Mom's not crying.

She actually makes a joke when I'm called. "If she gives you a hard time," she says, "just blame it on your parents."

When I first met Dr. Rice, she terrified me. Not because she's particularly scary—she looks like a soccer mom and her office smells like cinnamon—but because I feared she might know more about me than I did about myself. She might have figured out horrible things about my brain that she'd tell Mom and Dad but not me.

But now, she seems more like a regular person, a lady with a job. A job that involves listening to me babble for an hour about my problems.

"Your mom mentioned the divorce and your new school," she says. "You've been under a lot of stress."

"I guess." I feel a bit patronized, like she's trying to win me over with her understanding.

It's true there's been a lot of stress. But Mom and Dad are the ones splitting up. The academy's a change for the better.

"A lot of folks would have needed to come see me sooner," she says, and the smile lines around her eyes, the one giveaway to her age, crease. Her voice is neutral, but that smile says, *Come on, Caddie, what took you so long?*

It's a fair question.

"I'm pretty good at hiding it when things upset me," I say, studying the faded tips of my gloves.

"Well, I'm glad you came back to see me," she says, "when you weren't feeling right."

She helped me before, when the panic grew so frequent and fearsome that even a hint was enough to make an attack start in force.

"I didn't exactly come right away," I say. "Things have been bad for a while."

The first half hour is mostly me talking. She asks whether the exercises she taught me still help with the panic. And she asks about my "unwanted thoughts." She gives me an assessment for OCD, and I tell her what Mom said about her cleaning.

"That doesn't surprise me at all," she says. "Anxiety tends to run in families."

She makes it sound like eye color, or shoe size, the luck of the genetic draw. Nothing any individual person can control.

And that actually makes me feel a little better.

Maybe the looks are my imagination. I can't trust it after all, but I feel like everybody in the hallway is staring at me—even the musicians. And I refuse to believe that the cast of *Hamlet* called up the horn section to dish about my swan dive. It's just. Not. Likely.

Sane people don't assume everybody cares what they're doing.

I'm nearly to my locker without a single mention of my midnight swim, when Livia pounces. "I can't stop thinking about you!" She blocks my path so I almost run into her. "Sorry, sorry! I just wanted to say, I was impressed by what you did at Mandy's party."

"Impressed?"

"You did what came to you and didn't care what anybody thought."

"I should have cared. I wasn't thinking straight."

"Exactly!" she says. "You were thinking curvy." She waves her hands in a double helix in front of my face. "I've got to get better at that."

"Livia," I say, "you're one of the curviest-thinking people I know."

Her smile's solar powered. "Thank you!"

"Not a problem." She walks at my side to my locker.

"So." She takes a long pause. "Have you figured it out yet?"

"Figured what out?"

"*You* know," she says, bringing her pointer fingers together. *My heart. My heart.* She knows I can't touch.

"Oh, God. Does everybody know?"

Hank and Drew are talking at their lockers, but they stop and look our way.

Livia waves her hands. "No, no, no. I'm sorry. I shouldn't have said— I just— I picked up on it a while ago. I thought you knew that I knew."

"No!"

"Well, I don't think everybody knows, but it's not hard to see if you're paying attention."

I wonder if I should tell her how equally obvious her secret is. "I know something about you too," I say.

She lights up. "Ooh, go on!"

I whisper, "You're in love with Hank."

She smirks and without taking her eyes off me, says,

"This was sometime a paradox, but now the time gives it proof."

Facing away from me, he says, "I did love you once."

"Indeed, my lord, you made me believe so." I want him to come back, touch me.

But I know that he won't. Hamlet won't. And Peter won't.

Not my skin. Not without permission.

"It was quieter," Nadia says, when we finish the scene, "but more tender, too. We'll probably bring back some of the fireworks from the audition, but for today, I'm happy."

"Me too," Peter whispers, and he squeezes my gloved hand. "Good job."

"Thanks," I whisper back, but anxiety gnaws at the edges of this small success. It's one thing to avoid touch in a scene, but in real life . . . Peter is patient, but if our places were reversed, I'm not sure how long my patience would last.

"When is your friend coming back?" Jordan asks.

He leans into the kitchen island across from me and steals a pinch of grated cheese.

"Careful, Jordan. You'll make me grate your finger." My fingers, of course, are safe in my gloves, but that means I have to hold the cheese in plastic wrap.

Taco sauce bubbles on the stove behind me, filling the kitchen with the cheery scent of chili powder and paprika.

We're on our own for dinner since Mom was invited to some art thing—like a book club, she said, but in a gallery. Dad would never have been okay with that. He was always highly protective of "family time," except when he decided to spend it in his office.

Mom made me swear up and down that I didn't mind her leaving us, but how could I mind? Watching her get ready to go, humming to herself, made the house feel like Christmas.

"I don't know when Peter might be back," I say, "but I hope you'll see him again."

Jordan drums on the counter with his hands. "Me too."

"He's fun, right?"

Jordan nods. "You should make him your boyfriend."

I laugh. "Simple as that?"

"Yeah. I think so." He looks deadly serious.

Jordan must know something's wrong with me, but I don't think he knows exactly what. If I told Jordan about the not touching, he might try to torture me with it, but maybe that's good. If he touched me and nothing bad happened, that would be a sort of proof.

Just this morning, I had my second appointment with Dr. Rice. She wants to see me once a week, at least until I'm willing to touch other people. We talked about how anxious it makes me to tell people what's going on with me. "Silence is your enemy," she said. "Your fear wants to stay secret so it can be as big and scary as it likes. As soon as you share it with other people, it starts losing its power."

I push past my "big, scary" fear and keep talking. "I've been kind of weird since Dad left, have you noticed?"

Jordan nods emphatically.

"That bad, huh?"

"Yep. Real weird."

"Ha. Well, part of it is, I got this stupid idea . . ." I focus on grating the cheese for our tacos—swipe the yellow brick down and up, down and up. What I'm talking about doesn't matter. "I got this idea that if I could keep from touching people—touching their skin—that maybe Dad would come back, or they'd fix things or something."

Breathe, have to breathe, but not too much . . .

Jordan looks toward me, but not at me, like he's sorting through moments of me being strange, putting pieces together.

"That doesn't make any sense."

"No, I know. Like I said, it was stupid, but it felt real."

He looks as if he's trying to figure me out, but also, maybe, feeling sorry for me? For us. "But it didn't work," he says, almost a question.

"No."

He rolls along the counter, facing away from me. "I thought there might be something I could do, but I didn't try anything like that." He sounds wistful.

"Well, that's good you didn't, because it was a bad idea.

And it's still got me messed up."

I'm waiting for Jordan to flip my confession back on me, lunge across the counter and grab me, but he's quiet, staring at my gloves. "Do you still think he might come back?" Jordan asks. "You think that's why you're still messed up about it?"

I told Dr. Rice this morning that I don't think Dad will come back. I still hope it a little, but in my heart, I *know* he won't.

I shake my head. "Now it's more like if I give it up, I'm afraid for myself."

When I told Dr. Rice my theory that it's mostly myself I'm protecting, she said a wry, "Knowing is half the battle."

"Okay, so the thing is, if you touch people, Dad won't come back? Or some other horrible thing happens. But what can you do that makes everything okay?" Jordan asks.

"Nothing."

"Well, that's a bad deal."

"I know."

"Because you could stop touching people forever and it won't make a difference."

"I know."

"And then if you *do* touch somebody, and some new bad thing happens because it's supposed to, because . . ."

"Bad things happen all the time." We say it together.

And Jordan continues, ". . . then you'll always wonder if you caused it."

"Right. I know."

"Caddie, that's stupid."

"Yeah, well, that's what I said."

I've grated way more cheese than two people could ever eat, but something makes me keep grinding away. I want to see it all in shreds.

"You've got to quit thinking that," Jordan says.

"Yeah, I know." I've grated the cheese down to my fingers. It would be satisfying to scrape right through the plastic but not helpful. Instead of forcing the last tiny wedge through, I say, "Catch," and toss it to Jordan.

"So, you don't believe it?" I say. I feel silly even asking, but I still have to check. "If I took the gloves off and shook your hand right now, you'd be okay with that? You wouldn't be mad at me for taking the chance?"

"Chance of what?" Jordan says, his mouth full of cheese. "There's no chance Dad's coming back. I know that. You know that. And I don't believe that my sister has magic powers to make random bad things happen."

"You don't believe I'm magic?" I feign shock.

He shakes his head, emphatic again.

I turn to stir the sauce. It's bubbling now, threatening to splatter, so I turn down the heat. And on impulse, I peel off my gloves.

I mean, really, who cooks wearing evening gloves?

"What, no gloves?" says Mom later that night.

"Fashion is fickle."

From her smile, I'm sure she gets this is more than a fashion choice.

Even touching objects without gloves feels new and strange. *It's okay. It's allowed,* I tell myself, as I grip the fridge handle. But my heart's still thudding like it's trying out for drumline.

I pour myself a glass of juice, making a conscious effort not to slow down in case Mom decides she wants one too and brushes her hand against mine.

"You're going to get that song stuck in my head," Mom says.

I've been humming Ophelia's crazy song, the one she sings after her father dies and Hamlet is taken away. Nadia gave me a singsong tune that won't leave me alone, but the words are sticky too: "An' he'll not co-ome aga-ain, an' he'll not co-ome aga-ain."

When we blocked that scene, I got "hands on" like Nadia asked, dragging my fingers along Livia, Hank, and Oscar, but I was wearing my gloves. I already convinced Nadia that gloves should be part of my costume, but it's exciting to think that one day soon I might not need them. Exciting and scary. My humming turns shrill, and I cut it off.

"Has Dad said anything more about the play?" I ask Mom.

It's been more than a week since he promised to call more often, but the phone has been silent. I try not to think too much about that, but the idea's already there. If he comes to the play, it will be a sign that taking off the gloves was the right thing to do. And if he doesn't . . .

Mom shakes her head.

"Caddie, your epidermis is showing!" Oscar pulls out that old joke when I arrive gloveless at the lockers the next morning.

Mandy's more direct. "You're practically naked!" she squeals.

I make eye contact with Peter. His eyebrows are raised in question, and his lips curl up at the corners.

"I'm trying something new," I say.

Oscar steps in as if he means to take my hand.

"Nope. No," I say, tucking my hands under my armpits.

Peter's smile falters.

"I'm working on it," I say to Peter.

"Working on what?" Oscar asks.

He doesn't look snide, just curious. I bite the inside of my lip, focus on the pain instead of my nerves.

Friends know things about you, Livia said. And Oscar *is* one of my friends. Talking about fear takes its power away. Trembles shudder from my heart down my arms, and my legs feel unsteady, but I say it. "I have trouble touching people. I'm afraid of it, but I'm trying to get over it."

"That. Makes. So. Much. Sense!" Oscar says.

"Oh yeah?"

"Yes, I *knew* there had to be a reason you weren't jumping my bones."

He doesn't come any closer, doesn't try to tease me or make it a game like I feared he would. Instead, he says, "Stay right there for one second."

He pulls his coat from the hook inside his locker and tosses it over my head like a net.

"Hey!" Mandy says.

I say, "Oscar, what the hell?"

I can't see a thing, but Peter's laughing, which reassures me. He knows how big my fear is. If he thinks this is funny, it must be okay.

And before I can panic, Oscar's bony frame and wiry arms are squeezing me tight. The force of it steals my breath, and the coat smashes my nose flat. It's a ferocious bear hug, but the coat protects me.

"I'm sorry you're having a hard time," Oscar says close to my ear, his voice muffled by the fabric. "Soon you'll be all better, and you and I will have so much sex."

"Oh, Lord," I mutter.

"Hey now," says Peter.

"Or you and Peter," says Oscar. "You'll be having sex with someone soon, Caddie. Don't worry."

"Please, please, stop," Peter says, choking on laughter.

"Please, I'm going to pee myself," Mandy says.

Oscar just squeezes me tighter. As obnoxious as he can be, I'm kind of grateful for it.

I haven't been hugged in the longest time.

34.

Mandy's insisting on cutting the kiss even though it changes her "vision." I didn't want her to compromise on my account, but she said, "Caddie, when you're ready to kiss Peter in real life, I will do backflips, but I'm not going to complicate your mental health for the sake of a play."

Part of me wants Mandy to push me so I'll have no choice but to work it out, but she's right—no matter how much I want to embrace Mandy's vision, I don't think I'm ready.

So, on Saturday, Peter picks me up for a private rehearsal at Mandy's house. He doesn't honk from the driveway when he comes to pick me up. He comes right up to the door—fifteen minutes early. "I thought Jordan and I might get in some man time," Peter says, and they hole up in Jordan's room with video games while I finish lunch.

"He's great," Mom says, and I nod, chewing. "Just a friend, or . . . ?" She's a little too hopeful. She should know that me having "more than a friend" would be nothing short of miraculous.

When Peter pokes his head back in the kitchen, Mom tries to feed him, water him, plant him as a centerpiece and sing to him to make him grow.

"Wow, good with moms?" I say, when she finally lets us go.

"I'm good with parents in general," Peter says, "as long as they're not my own."

"What happened?" I ask as we pull ourselves into the truck, and there's one of those monumental silences, one that has to be filled with talking, but in its own time.

Peter backs out of the driveway and puts a country station on low. "Sorry," he says. "I'm just thinking about it."

"That's okay. You don't have to tell me."

"No, it's not that," he says. "Please. I would tell you anything you asked. But I want to get it right. We—disappointed each other," he says. "That seems like the best way to put it."

"How could they be disappointed in you?" I say.

He flashes me a cocky smile. "No wonder I like you."

My cheeks burn.

"I was a 'difficult' child," he says. "I told you about the roof. I think my parents spent a lot of my childhood wondering what they did to piss off the gods. My mom loves to tell this story of us in a Target. She was trying to empty her cart because she couldn't take it down the escalator to the parking lot, and she lost track of me. She heard some commotion; turns out I was at the bottom of the escalator, flipping birds at everybody as they rode it down. When she tried to get to me, I hopped onto the up side and kept flipping birds and saying, 'Come and get me! Come and get me!'"

"Oh, Lord."

"Yeah, my parents are saints. And with the divorce I got worse, or at least angrier. When it was just me and my mom, I could be hard on her. We did family therapy, anger management, the whole deal."

"And you're better now?"

He shrugs. "I've got a temper, but I'm 'channeling it in productive ways.' That's counselor speak for 'I do theater instead of break things.' And I've got a sense of humor about it. That helps."

"Do you still go for counseling?"

"Not for a couple of years. My parents and I get along. They're both remarried now, and I've made peace with the stepparents."

"I'm seeing somebody now," I say. It just comes out and I immediately wish I could suck it back in. "A doctor. Mandy knows, but nobody else."

Peter nods. "That's good, right?"

"I guess. I wish I didn't need it."

"Think about it this way—it makes you way more interesting. Problem-free people are boring."

Knowing he knows, and that it seems to be okay, is a relief. I swell like a bright wave, like I could pour out past the boundaries of my skin. I want to know all about him, want him to know me. And I hope we'll have time to fill in all the gaps.

"Do you remember when you invited me to the ice cream social? You were going to tell me what your favorite ice cream flavor is. I still don't know."

"You remember that?" He gives me a look like he's ready to tell me the most solemn secret he has, but he can't even look at me while saying it. He has to turn back to the road. "It's butter pecan."

Mandy tells us her new "concept": we'll perform the same actions, but with distance. "So it will be like you want to touch each other, but you can't," she says, "because it's a memory, see? It might even be better this way."

"Maybe we could work up to the touch," Peter suggests. "You can touch through clothes, right?" he asks, holding his arm out toward me. Because it's unseasonably warm, we're outside on the flat lawn above the pool. Peter's wearing short sleeves.

Mandy doesn't say a word, but her eyes are fixed on me. They want to know how bad my fear is. It will disappoint them if I don't at least try. I reach out a hand, touch

Peter's T-shirt sleeve, take a breath, and without giving myself time to think, place my hand on his shoulder.

Baby steps.

"Keep it there," Mandy says.

My heart's in a rush, but I'm still breathing. "It's uncomfortable," I say. "But I'm okay."

"Yeah, you are," Peter says. "What are you thinking about?"

"It's so close. I feel like I'm asking for trouble."

We stand still. I wait for the anxious wave to stop churning inside me as it tries to push me away from Peter.

"See, I can do it," I say, "if I make myself. It's okay."

"Now try touching his skin," Mandy says.

My hand pulls back—a reflex I can't control.

"I've seen people touch you," Peter says, "and you got upset, but nothing happened."

"But I didn't choose it," I say. "They touched me. And I still had to wash it off after."

"What are you afraid of?" he asks.

"I've always been scared of lots of things." Even thinking about it makes me feel off balance. "In middle school, when my parents were fighting, I was always afraid that my dad would leave, or that one of them would die—it didn't always make sense. This most recent stuff started with Dad. But it's bigger than that now. Just . . . I don't know . . . that the world's going to end?"

"Oh, only that!" Mandy laughs. "Well, if it's only that!"

I laugh too, because it's silly. I know it is. But that doesn't change how it feels.

"So, back to the not-touching plan . . . ," Mandy says.

Mandy has us start with Nadia's exercise of keeping distance between us, never less than six feet.

"It's kind of like in middle school, when you have to dance with your arms stretched all the way out," Peter says, and we hold our arms out and sway in time, not touching.

"You guys look like zombies," Mandy says. "Arms down." She pulls our focus back to work.

I speak my lines as Peter "enters" from the brick steps by the pool:

"To speak of horrors, he comes before me."

Once Peter gets within six feet of me, I start walking backward. He circles around, and I maintain the distance.

Mandy reads Polonius's line, "Mad for thy love?"

"My lord, I do not know; but truly, I do fear it."

"What said he?"

"He took me by the wrist and held me hard . . ."

"So mime the action," Mandy says, and sticks her arm out straight to demonstrate, "as if he's pulling you."

". . . He falls to such perusal of my face as he would draw it."

"It's like the mirror game," Mandy says, "where you follow each other's actions. You do what she says in the air,

Peter. And Caddie, follow him."

Peter's a good actor, but when he starts waving his hand around in the air like he's petting my face, it looks more than a little silly.

"Here, you need to be closer," Mandy says. "Step in, Peter."

He does and sculpts the air close to my face. Mandy moves his hands closer, keeping only a couple of inches between my skin and their hands so I have to stay still. "Is this too much, Caddie? Am I freaking you out?"

"You are, but I think Ophelia is freaked out, so maybe that's okay."

Peter won't touch me without asking, but Mandy might. Mandy might tap my cheek just to see how I react.

"Ophelia says, 'Long stay'd he so,'" Mandy says. "So she just stands there. What's up with Ophelia while Hamlet's rubbing his hands all over her face? And he's barely got his clothes on."

"She's scared," I say, looking at Peter, "but it's exciting, too."

Mandy nods.

"Here, close your eyes," she says.

She says it with so much authority, I almost obey without thinking. "I don't want to," I say.

Mandy cocks her head. She didn't ask me if I wanted to. I close my eyes.

"Here," Mandy says. She whispers something to Peter, and then she says, "Caddie, Peter is going to touch your face."

Already, I'm shaking. I open my eyes.

"Keep them closed," Mandy says. "You want to be able to touch people without having panic attacks, right? You don't have to do anything. Just go on with the speech."

This is more than a baby step. "I'm scared."

"Yeah, I know, but so is Ophelia. You just said."

If I let Peter touch me and I can stand it, maybe that will be the break I need. Take power away from the fear.

I speak.

I'm shaky, but not entirely in a bad way. My nerve endings tingle and twitch like they're waking up after a long sleep. Peter shuffles on the grass. His hand hovers close to my face—the air trembles with its nearness—and his lips approach mine. His breath troubles the air I breathe, but he doesn't touch me.

I lean in, oh so slightly, and inhale. His breath is warmer than the air and crisp. Smelling lightly of sharp mint and salt, it reminds me of the ocean right before a storm.

I catch myself leaning and straighten to finish my line. But I get it, what Mandy whispered. She told Peter *not* to touch me.

I wanted him to.

"That was amazing," Mandy says, when I open my eyes. "That's what I want. Just like that."

"I couldn't see what Peter was doing."

"He was so close to you but not touching, and you were so keyed up. It's amazing to watch."

"Okay, but now that I know Peter's not going to touch me, how am I supposed to repeat that?"

"I don't know," Mandy says, smiling. "I guess you'll have to act."

"Oh, right! Acting!"

"Don't you think you could get to that place?" Mandy says. "Where you're not sure what's going to happen—"

"I do," I say.

"—and you're afraid he's going to touch you?"

"Yes."

And afraid that he won't.

"Excellent," Mandy says. "Let's run the whole thing a couple more times, and then I'll feel good to show it."

When we're finished, Mandy invites us to stay. The sun's already slipping, but for November, it's balmy. We can sit by the pool.

"I invited Drew to come over later, but we can all hang out," she says. "I'd *really* like it if you stayed." She sends me a meaningful look. After I ditched the gloves, she told me I inspired her. That if I could quit something, she could too: Drew.

When Peter goes inside for a minute, I ask, "Are you going to do it?"

She plays with a strand of her pink hair. "I hope I can. I think it would be good for me, to prove that I'm strong enough."

I want to squeeze her hand. With the gloves, I would have. Instead, I tap my hand to my heart and say, "You've got super strength, Mandy. I have no doubts."

Peter returns with an armful of sodas, and we shift topics fast. Drew's still Peter's best friend.

There's only a little sun left, when I get an idea. "How's the camera on your phone?"

I tell them what I'm thinking . . . I still have to take a self-portrait for Nadia where she can see Ophelia in me and me in Ophelia. And the time I felt most like Ophelia, there's no question. It was on the edge of Mandy's pool, on the very edge of falling in.

"Well, it's actually warm today," Mandy says.

"I'm not going in."

"Promise?" she says, and she pulls out her phone. "Where do you want me?"

"I think at the side there is good." I kick off my shoes.

"Is Peter ready to play lifeguard?" Mandy asks.

Peter moves to the edge of the pool and pulls off his boots.

"You don't need to do that," I say.

"You don't know what it's like to walk around in wet boots."

"I won't go in. I promise. And anyway, I can swim."

"When you choose to," Mandy says.

I've earned their distrust, but I still wince.

The metal railing of the diving board ladder is warm from the sun, the board, too, and my feet have no trouble on the gritty surface. The board bounces, but that's nothing. That's normal.

I walk to the edge.

I have stood here a gazillion times, but it still feels scary. Even though there's no way to get hurt. The slightest breeze teases me. The fact of my clothes, that I'm not dressed for swimming, reminds me this is not a normal moment on a diving board.

I stretch out my arms, lift my face to the sky. "How does that look?"

"It's cool," Mandy says, "but I don't feel like you're about to go in."

"Do I need to step closer to the edge?"

"Maybe. Try it."

"Please don't," Peter says.

"I'm all right."

His eyes are worried and fierce.

I'm trying, I tell him with my eyes. *I'll try harder.*

And for a second I feel just like Ophelia. Standing at the edge of a diving board doesn't scare me. I know I can swim. Standing at the edge of Peter does.

He's as afraid as I am—afraid of falling for a girl who might drown.

"I took one," Mandy says, "when you were looking at Peter. It's pretty badass."

At my request, she snaps a few more with my feet hanging over the edge, with my arms out like angel wings, ones where I look like I'm singing.

But Mandy is right. The one where I'm looking at Peter—that's the one.

35.

Just as the sun is setting, Drew shows up pissed. I actually think Drew likes me, but he hasn't loved sharing Mandy's attention with me—or with Nadia.

"You didn't tell me you guys were all getting together," he says.

"We were rehearsing," says Peter. "We would have called you, but we figured you'd be bored."

That's a blatant lie, but it soothes the savage beast. Drew actually snorts, like an animal blowing off steam. "I would have been bored. I'm so sick of this. Polonius is the lamest character in Shakespeare."

"It could be fun," Mandy says. "If you'd let Polonius be funny—"

"See, and I don't need your opinion about everything."

Mandy pulls herself up straighter, and I swear the air

between them crackles. "I would give you my opinion, Drew, whether I was AD or not. Just like I ask your opinion on things that matter to me. You don't have to take it, but you should respect me enough to at least listen."

"Respect you?" Drew says. "You make it sound like you're my teacher or something."

"Next you're going to say, 'You're not the boss of me.'"

Peter moves closer to my side. "We should let you guys have some alone time."

"No!" Mandy whines. "Please stay! He's making things tense. Before you got here, Drew, we were having a good time."

"So you want me to leave?"

Mandy doesn't answer right away. She looks to me, quirks her mouth to the side. Maybe she's ready.

"Don't fight," Peter says. "Or do, but work it out. We'll go."

"No, stay," Drew says. Maybe he realizes that Mandy's less likely to can him in public. "You guys can entertain each other, can't you, if we go talk?"

Peter chooses to ignore the suggestive way Drew talks about us "entertaining" each other, so I do too. Drew holds out his hand to Mandy. She takes it, so easily, and lets him lead her up the hill toward the ridge.

Without talking about it, Peter and I walk over to the trampoline. Peter heaves himself up, but I hesitate.

"I won't bite," he says.

There's something about hoisting yourself onto a trampoline. It's one of those few things that's always too big for you. It makes me feel like a little kid. There's plenty of room between Peter and me, and I sit cross-legged beside him, hands folded in my lap.

He tilts his head and studies my hands. "Before I knew what the gloves were for, I kind of liked them. They made you look like a superhero," he says.

"They made me feel a little bit like one, too, but I think it takes more than gloves."

Peter lies back, propped up on his elbows.

"No, because so many superheroes hold their power in their hands—if you touch people, maybe you steal their power, or maybe you freeze them to death or give them electric shock."

I'm laughing. It's stupid, but I'm laughing.

"I can't do any of those things."

"Have you tried?"

"No."

"What do you think might happen? Aside from the world ending?" He rolls onto his side toward me, getting into it. "Hey, that's another way you're like a superhero! You're super paranoid about the end of the world!"

"It's coming, Peter, it's coming soon," I say in my best doomsday voice, and curl up on my side facing him. I wonder aloud, "Why would anybody want to be a superhero?"

"I don't know, to fight evil?"

"Okay, I'll be fighting evil while everybody else around me is making out and having boyfriends."

We go quiet. Peter shifts to rest the side of his face on his arm. His slightest move makes me wobble.

"This isn't a superpower," I say. "It's more like a super weakness."

"Well, every superhero's got her Kryptonite."

"I hate Kryptonite."

"No, Kryptonite's great. See, if Superman didn't have Kryptonite, he'd be perfect. He'd be too good for the world to sustain."

"Whatever."

"No, seriously, think how bad it would be for self-esteem. We'd all be comparing ourselves to that guy—that *super* guy. How annoying would that be? You want to be perfect?"

"Yes."

"You want to be annoying like Superman?"

"Yes."

"No, you don't."

He reaches for my ribs.

"Owww! Don't!"

Peter pulls back sharply and rolls flat on his back, facing up to the darkening sky.

"I'm sorry."

"No, I'm sorry."

"I didn't even think about it."

"No, I know."

"That was stupid, Caddie."

"*I'm* sorry. It's dumb."

"I thought clothes were okay."

"Yeah, that's mostly it. I don't like not having control. If I choose to touch you on the edge of your sleeve"—I do it, to show I can—"you might suddenly move, but I'm paying attention. I trust myself to react in time. If you touch me—"

"Who knows *what* I might do?" He's being playful, but there's an edge to it. If our places were reversed, I'd feel rejected, maybe even offended, that he didn't trust me.

"God, Peter, I'm sorry."

"Don't be."

He exhales, long and slow . . . "You know I would like to."

Don't say it, don't say it, don't say it.

"Touch you." He says it. "If it didn't freak you out so much, I would really like to touch you."

The first emerging stars are pinpricks, so far away. They don't care what's going on down here on a stupid trampoline between a boy and a girl who can't touch.

"You know I would never hurt you," he says. "Not on purpose."

"No, I know. Not on purpose . . . Peter . . ."

"Don't say that you're sorry, okay? I didn't say that to make you feel bad. I really didn't. The last thing I want is for you to feel bad." He turns to his side to face me again. "I just want you to know."

Peter's gaze draws me out of myself and into the space between him and me. Underneath us, the trampoline rises and sinks with our breath.

"I like you," I tell him.

He smiles. "I like you."

I nod and roll away. I can't look him in the eyes anymore. It's too much. My heart's full of him.

We lie shoulder to shoulder, no more than an inch of air between us. We lift our hands over our heads as high as they can reach, and even though they're still several inches apart, it almost looks like they're touching.

"So if not being able to touch people is my super weakness, what do we think is my superpower?" I ask.

"Well, if your weakness is that you can't touch, it stands to reason that your power is related. Like, if you ever did touch someone, it would be . . ."

"Super?"

"Well, yeah, in a word. I think . . . when you touch someone, it's like all the best parts of you pour into them."

"I think that's part of what I'm scared of," I say.

"But maybe that's your power, that you don't lose anything. You get to give someone else all of that, and you also get to keep it for yourself."

That *sounds* so nice.

"I don't know what I have to give that's so great, though," I say.

"Shut up. Now you're fishing for compliments."

"I'm not. I just— Peter, why do you even put up with me?"

He props up, leaning over me. The hand holding his weight could slip; he might fall down on me any moment. I inhale sharply, can't help it. He looks away like he's thinking, but I also feel like he's giving me a chance to get used to this closeness.

When he meets my eyes again, I can breathe.

"I like talking to you, Caddie," he says. "When we talk, I feel like you're really here with me—like for a minute, I'm the only other person in the world. And I know you won't talk about what I say or laugh about it after because you get it. I trust you. I like your smile and your laugh"— he brings a finger to the corner of my mouth, so close without touching, and he draws it through the air in a line that follows the line of my lips—"especially when you're laughing at something I said that nobody else thinks is all that funny."

He draws his finger down, hovers over my throat . . . "I like watching you work. I like how much you care about making the play good." Over my heart . . .

Then he moves his hand to the side of my face, millimeters away and so warm. I could tilt my head to the side and meet him. My face burns, blood rushes. It's like rehearsal, but this time my eyes are locked on his.

"I like what happens," Peter says, "when we almost touch. There's all this energy between us, this good feeling. I think that's your superpower," he says, "all of this, times a million, when you touch someone."

In the space between our eyes, Peter and I hold each other so tight. It is almost like touching, almost like Peter described.

I remember to breathe.

When Mandy and Drew make their way down the hill, they're holding hands and Mandy's hair is a scandal. She runs a hand through to sort out the tangles and gives me a guilty look.

I shrug. I feel a little scandalous myself.

Drew picks a couple of dead leaves off Mandy's back and shreds them.

"The happy couple!" says Peter, lifting his arms in a victory "V" overhead.

"Momentarily," says Mandy. "You're too distracting," she says to Drew.

"My specialty," he says.

"Maybe that's your superpower," I say, and Drew crunches his face in confusion.

"Huh?"

"Nothing."

I feel Peter's hand rising behind me as if to touch my back. It hovers there, but he catches himself and then drops it again to his side.

A few seconds later, I realize that when I felt Peter's hand hovering, *don't touch* never entered my mind.

36.

"I'm thinking about disinviting my dad," I tell Dr. Rice.

She nods. "Okay, what are your reasons?"

"Well, he won't be able to disappoint me," I say. "If I don't expect him to come, I can't be upset when he doesn't."

"So you'd be protecting yourself from a painful situation?"

"I guess."

"That's kind of pessimistic," she says.

"Or realistic."

"Do you *want* him to see the play?"

I have to think about that. "I do," I say. "If I knew he would come and keep an open mind and maybe be proud of me, then yes, I would like him to come. I want him to see what I can do."

"Is it possible that will happen?"

"That's what I don't know."

She purses her lips in thought. "It's not always a bad thing to protect yourself, Caddie, but you've told me that you overdo it."

"Right."

I don't love where this is going. Dr. Rice's superpower is reason, and I haven't yet figured out how to deflect it.

"If telling your dad not to come is your way of trying to control things, maybe it would be good practice for you to give up that control, roll with whatever happens."

"Roll with it?" I picture myself getting rolled over *by* it. Flattened.

"Would you survive if your dad disappointed you again, if he didn't show?"

The idea makes me sad, but, "Yeah, I guess I'd survive."

"Great." Dr. Rice smiles and makes a note. "Then Dad gets to keep his invitation."

Dad would appreciate Dr. Rice's practicality and efficiency. I'd appreciate them a lot more if they weren't so good at punching holes in my resolve.

Rehearsals go fast. Nadia keeps adding in props and set pieces so we'll have less to get used to in tech week. She gives me flowers to rip apart when I'm crazy. Oscar and Peter get real swords to fight with—well, real slabs of dull metal, but still, not a joke.

Nadia calls Oscar over after their fight call on Wednesday. "I don't know what you did to prep for this scene, but it's working."

Oscar beams and circles the stage in a big arc. Peter intercepts him, "Good scene, man," but Oscar brushes him off.

"Big actor-man Peter thinks I did a good job. Woo-hoo."

Peter rolls his eyes and smiles to himself, but Oscar seems full of contempt. They were getting along fine yesterday.

Nadia moves on to rehearse Peter stabbing Drew, and I slip backstage to find Oscar writing on the Wall of Infamy, not so far from the bit about Hank and Livia "doing it" with a mask. I read what he's written out loud: "Oscar Morgan of *Monkey Boy* fame would have made a better Hamlet, but his Laertes rocked the stage!"

"Too stuck up?" he asks, and scratches out "of *Monkey Boy* fame."

"A better Hamlet?"

"Just the facts, ma'am."

"What's your problem with Peter?"

He leans in close. "I'm being method, like Daniel Day-Lewis," he says. "I have to be mad at Peter till the play's finished. That way I don't have to act."

"You just said you're not really mad at him. So you *are* acting."

"And it's working."

"Okay. That's so weird, though, Oscar. Aren't you worried you'll mess up your friendship?"

"It won't mess it up. Peter's cool."

"Even coolness has its limits."

That night as Peter's driving me home from rehearsal, I ask, "Did you know Oscar's only being mad at you to do better in the play?"

"Oh, yeah, he told me. He's excited about it."

"He *told* you. That's nutty."

"That's Oscar."

We pull up to my driveway, but Peter doesn't get out like usual to walk me to the door. "I wondered," he says, "if you might be doing the same thing. The thought crossed my mind."

"What do you mean?"

"Well, Ophelia gets pretty crazy. I thought maybe all your stuff helps you relate to that."

So what if it does? That doesn't mean I want it. My skin goes tight.

"Are you saying you think I'm crazy?"

"No, I don't! That's my point—"

"I'm not like Ophelia," I say, but I hear the defensiveness in my voice.

"Well no, I just mean—" Peter's treading water. "You've been doing so much better. I guess I've been hoping that after the play, when you don't need to feel afraid or upset anymore, you might let it go. That we could be normal."

"Normal." The cab of Peter's truck feels too small for two people.

"Not normal, but you know what I mean. So we could . . ." He holds out his hand, palm up.

"You think I'd still be like this if I could just let it go?"

He presses his lips in a line. *Try*, his eyes say, *try a little harder.*

"I want to," I say.

His open hand is a dare. "You want to. So . . ."

I don't like being dared—it's aggressive, a trap to make people feel foolish.

"Caddie, I know it's hard, but I know you can do it," Peter whispers.

I want to do it, for both of us, but it's so much he's asking. My teeth clack together. The feeling of falling, this dizziness, won't go away.

But I have to try. I place my hand over his, only inches away, and I hold his eyes, willing him to close the distance. "It's okay," I say, with a breath to steel myself. "Touch my hand. It's all right."

"But it's not," Peter says. "If it were all right, you'd touch me."

"I'm working on it," I growl, and Peter lets out a breathy laugh at my frustration. "It's not funny," I say.

"No, you're right, I know."

I reach past his hand and take him by the wrist,

touching only his sleeve. I lift his hand toward my face, and Peter watches, letting me move him. I feel the warmth of his hand where it floats in space close to my cheek.

"It's on you," he whispers. "Your call."

I hold his eyes—this look is as close as a touch—but still I can't pull his hand closer.

I let go.

Slowly, Peter sinks back in his seat, facing forward.

"Say what you're thinking," I say, even though I'm not sure I can stand to hear it.

He takes his time trying to choose words that won't offend me. "You don't like feeling afraid, I know, and that's normal, but have you thought maybe you're afraid of the wrong thing? What if the way you are right now is what you need to be afraid of?"

I am afraid of it, but knowing that isn't enough. He wants things to be simple, easy, and I'm not those things.

"I think you're afraid, too," I say, my voice tight. "I think that's why you're stuck here talking with me. Why else would you be with a girl who can't touch?"

He thumps the back of his head against his seat. I am impossible. That's what that says.

But I'm right, I think, at least a little bit. It's like Livia with Hank . . . a person who can't say yes won't make you open up more than you want, more than you fear.

"I won't see you again till Monday," Peter says. "Will

you think about what I said?"

That's almost a whole week away. We're off for Thanksgiving, but I figured Peter and I would see each other at some point in all that time.

As if he's read my mind, he says, "I'm going to my dad's. It will be all family time."

"Right, of course."

"I should have mentioned it. I didn't . . ."

He didn't want to make me feel bad. Jordan and I visiting Dad in Virginia wasn't even discussed as a possibility. I suppress a pang of jealousy.

"Okay, well, Monday, then," I say, stepping down from the truck.

It's felt so easy talking to Peter these last few weeks; I don't know what to do with this awkward chill that's swept in between us.

As I start up the walk, the damp air seems to soak through my clothes, and I wrap myself tighter in my coat. If I were normal, Peter would be walking beside me, holding my hand or playing with my hair. We would stand at the top of the porch steps and kiss.

When I'm halfway up the walk, the truck rumbles, and I turn to see Peter backing away. Usually, he waits until I get inside safe.

My throat tightens, and I swallow the pain welling up in my chest.

It doesn't matter.

Mom says we're going to "free ourselves from the pressure to have a traditional Thanksgiving."

"It's going to feel strange without your dad no matter what we do," she says, so we take Meemaw to a fancy hotel buffet and gorge ourselves on someone else's "home cooking."

Meemaw keeps ordering mimosas and sneaking me sips. According to her, the national drinking age treads on states' rights, and if she wants to get her teenage grand-daughter drunk, that's her own damned business.

The waiters here would probably bring me my own glass if Meemaw told them to, but it's fun to invent new ways of hiding my sips: a folded napkin barrier, a quickly dunked soup spoon. Mom flashes me warning looks, and Jordan keeps complaining that he should get some too, but neither of them can stop laughing.

After that, we watch a stack of rented movies—all thrillers and action, not a single romantic comedy or melo-drama among them. Mom makes bowls of kettle corn, and it's actually fun.

Dad calls in the evening and says all the things he's supposed to say. He went to a grad student's house for Thanksgiving. The free cocktails were great, but the food wasn't as good as Mom's. He missed Jordan and me.

"See you in a couple of weeks," he says, "for your play."

I think again about disinviting him, but I promised Dr. Rice I wouldn't.

"Looking forward to it," Dad says.

Over the long weekend, I try to obsess about the play rather than Peter, but it's no good. I can't stop thinking about our talk.

"He's so into you, Caddie," Mandy says when I go to her house for a sleepover. "Don't stress it."

"He thinks I'm crazy."

"Of course you are," she says.

I glare.

"Caddie, you won't let people touch your skin. That's crazy. But you've been that way since he met you—and he's into you."

But Livia's more somber. "I don't know," she says. "It's like you have a choice to make. Are you going to start something with him, or are you going to play it safe? I think Peter's starting to get scared that you're not going to choose him."

We've circled our sleeping bags, a big bowl of popcorn in the middle. It's not so different from that seventh-grade slumber party at Mandy's, except this time I'm not hiding anything.

"I've chosen him," I say. "I *want* to be with Peter."

"Okay," Livia says, but she sounds dubious.

"He knows how I feel."

"Does he? Because sometimes you have to *show* it."

She nibbles at a popcorn kernel demurely, taking the puffed part and leaving the shell. She's making a collection of them on her napkin—for an art project.

"It's not like I'm choosing to be afraid," I say. "Peter knows if I weren't so afraid, I'd have my hands all over him."

"Okay, but think of it like this," Livia says. "What if a guy had to slay a dragon to be with you? How would you feel if he said, 'Sorry, I can't, too afraid'?"

"That's fairy tale stuff. *And* it's sexist."

"It's not necessarily sexist," Livia says. "It's—"

Mandy cuts her off. "Livia, she's trying to distract you with feminism." She turns to me and says, "Livia has a good point. Because it is a choice, right?"

"I'm not *choosing* to be afraid," I say again.

"No, see, that's not the choice," Livia says. "The *choice* is what you do *even though* you're afraid."

I throw a popcorn kernel at her head.

She catches it in midair and starts dissecting it with her teeth, grinning at me all the while.

37.

Tech week begins on Monday with longer rehearsals focused less on acting and more on lights, sets, and sound. We're called every night this week until nine and won't even get a chance to run the show without stopping until Thursday.

That all makes me nervous but not as nervous as seeing Peter again does.

He approaches me casually at our lockers in the morning, says, "How you doing?"

"Okay. I'm a little stressed out about how we're supposed to do homework *and* prep for Ms. Avery's test on top of tech."

"The academy strikes again. Hang in there," he says, and rushes off even though we have plenty of time before first bell.

His voice was too light. It's as if instead of suggesting that I'm clinging to crazy, Peter asked whether my sniffles might be the first sign of a cold. And it's too friendly— even if we make up, what's waiting on the other side for us couldn't possibly be a kiss. We *might* be headed for a hug or a tousling of hair.

Peter's so genuine, I never thought things could feel this fake between us, but we're like two bad actors playing the part of friends.

Later in the week, I get up the nerve to approach him during a rehearsal break. He's doing the reading for history. "Are you mad?" I ask, low, and he looks up, holding his place.

He smiles. "I'm mad that I can't read more than two sentences before the words start blurring together."

"I mean, are you mad *at me?*"

Peter closes the book. "Mad is not the right word."

"But you're something."

He sighs. "You weren't fair to me when we talked."

"I know. I got defensive. You were trying to help."

"Caddie, do you believe that I'm your friend?"

"Yes."

"No matter what, I will be your friend. I may not understand everything you're going through, but I'm trying. I'm sorry if I've been acting weird. I wasn't sure if we were still fighting, or what we were even fighting about."

"I know."

"I'm sorry I suggested you were putting on an act for the play. That didn't come out right. I know it's more than that. I guess I was hoping—"

"It's okay. I'm sorry I got mad."

He shakes off my apology. "I don't want to push you."

Push me, I want to say, *please, please, push me, and I'll fall into you.*

But it's like Livia said—it has to be my choice to touch even though I'm afraid.

An hour before our first dress rehearsal, Livia and I sit in one of the tiny dressing rooms trying to figure out how to meet the "Nadia Hair Challenge." Livia got a picture of a Ghanaian queen with her hair in huge twists supporting gold talismans. It looks regal but challenging. Mine is of a girl with so many twists and braids, her head looks like a maze.

"I don't think you can do that by yourself," Livia says.

I run out of hair for my current braid, and it slips from my hand before I can pin it down. "I don't think I have enough hair anyway."

Mandy swoops in, her face flushed.

"What's wrong?" I ask.

She crouches beside my chair and meets my eyes in the mirror.

"I need a pep talk."

"What's going on?"

"It's Drew. We had another fight."

"Oh, no," says Livia, but Mandy shakes off her sympathy.

"It's nothing new. He's just begging me to dump him. I gave him an acting note *from Nadia,* and he called me a bitch, which he knows I *hate,* and I smacked him, which—not my proudest moment, I know—but then *he* said, 'Walk away before I do something we'll both regret,' and I said, 'What, like hit me? Dump me? Because I'm *this* close to dumping you,' and he said, 'Just walk away. I'm too mad.'"

"So much drama," says Livia.

"Right? I have to break up with him."

"I'm so sorry, Mandy," I say. I pet her shoulder, far from her neckline, but she meets my eyes in the mirror and smiles.

"Don't be sorry. It's for the best, right?"

"Well, yeah."

"Yeah." But she's making a doubtful face in the mirror. "I just keep thinking, if we could figure out how to not fight, or how to fight nicer, everything could be okay."

She sighs and stands with her hands on her hips. "How goes it with Peter?"

"It doesn't," I say, and start another braid. "I guess it's a little better. We sort of made up. I don't get why I can't let it go." I shake my head. "Peter thinks I'm holding on to my fear to be better at playing Ophelia."

Mandy looks at me in the mirror again. "That's dumb."

"I know. She's like the opposite of me—she lets go of everything."

"Except—"

"What?"

"Well, I don't think you're holding on to it to be better at playing Ophelia. And I don't think it's an act. Don't misunderstand."

"But?"

"But I do think you're holding on to something. You're holding on so, so tight."

I look to Livia, who's been focused on her hair in the mirror. She keeps working with her hair pick, but she nods. "It's in your face, Caddie. Relax your face for a second."

I can't see what she means right away, but I take a breath, try to let all the tension go. My eyebrows are pinched, and I spread my fingers along them, try to make them relax. My eyes—there's the feel of a sigh at the corners; I have to blink them to keep them from tightening again. Another breath. And my mouth, I open it wide and gasp. It's like I'm drowning. All of a sudden I can't get enough air. I put my hands on the dressing table to hold myself steady, to push away that feeling of falling. I drop my head, hear myself make a whimpering sigh.

"Oh, God," I say. I can't look at them.

"It's okay," Livia says, and I feel her hand at my back before she touches me, not my skin, but she presses her palm to my shoulder blade. "It's going to be okay."

I gasp again.

"Here, let it go. Breathe."

I breathe out and take a shuddering breath in, trying to release the tension in my chest, shoulders, face. "I feel like I'm going to break apart into little pieces."

"You won't," Livia says. "You can't."

"It's okay, Caddie," says Mandy, my oldest friend. "We're here with you. You're not going anywhere."

We sit like that for what feels like hours, me trying to breathe without squeezing my lungs in a vise, and the two of them waiting, Livia's hand a constant pressure at my back.

Footsteps make Mandy shift beside me.

"Is she . . . ?" It's a girl's voice, April.

"She's okay," Mandy says. "She's just nervous."

"I came to see if you need help with the hair."

"We've got it," Mandy says. "Thank you."

There's a pause, and I can feel April looking at me with my head practically between my legs. "Caddie," she says. "You're really good as Ophelia. It's normal to get nerves, but you don't have anything to worry about."

The surprise allows me to pull it together. I lift my head. Already it's easier to breathe. "Thank you, April." My voice sounds shaky, but it's a voice. "That's nice of you."

"I'm not saying it to be nice," she says. And she's gone.

The three of us hold still for a few seconds, testing the waters, and when I catch sight of them in the mirror, they both look concerned. Mandy's still crouched beside me looking ready to spring and catch me. Livia's hair is half out and half still in braids, a lopsided 'fro. We all look completely bonkers, and at the same time we all bust out laughing.

Once we can keep straight faces again, I thank them, and Mandy swipes a pair of gloves for herself from the costume room—"If people see me, they'll think I caught your fashion trend"—and has my hair done in less than ten minutes. She goes for a curling iron to do the loose ends, but I say, "Thanks, I can do those myself if there's time. I have to make a phone call."

"You've got less than half an hour till Nadia calls places, and you've still got to get dressed."

"This won't take long."

I grab my phone and jog through the downstairs halls, where a lot of the actors are already in costume. I pass Oscar and Hank going over the bit where they poison Laertes's sword. Hank is making a thing out of spreading the poison down the tip. "Caddie," Oscar calls out as I pass, "can you help us get my sword wet?"

Normally Oscar's talk makes me anxious, but I'm full of abandon. Without slowing down I yell, "Sure can't, but I know where you can stick it!"

Hank's laugh bellows out and bounces after me.

Mandy would be proud.

Most of the space below the theater is completely underground—no hope of getting a signal—but there's an exit at the back that leads to a small parking lot and the woods.

I'm afraid the door will lock behind me, so I kick off one of my sneakers and leave it as a doorstop. I must look ridiculous, hobbling with one sock foot in my jeans with my old-timey hair, but feeling ridiculous helps. A little crazy is right for this scene.

Dad doesn't usually pick up when I call, but I'll catch him off guard, calling when I'd normally be at rehearsal. He'll think there's some emergency. As it rings, over and over, I practice what I want to say: "You're making me feel crazy. I know you've said you're coming, but you never even pick up the phone when I call, so what am I supposed to think? I've been holding on to this idea that you might come back. I've been doing crazy things to make myself believe it, and I realize how stupid that is, that you're not coming back to live with us, but it's more than that. I'm not sure you're my dad anymore. Please show up and be my dad."

Even as I'm rehearsing to scold him for failing to pick up the phone, I'm still surprised when he doesn't pick up. It still hurts.

After the beep, I should leave my message, but it's not the same talking to a machine. I consider hanging up without speaking. Consider dialing and redialing until he has to pick up and react to what I say.

After an awkwardly long silence, I say the only words left: "Are you still coming?"

I hold nothing back for dress rehearsals. They say a bad dress rehearsal means a good performance, but I don't buy it. It's just that dress rehearsals tend to go badly, and people have to tell themselves something to get up the courage to go back on stage.

It's strange to act with Peter when I feel like I'm losing him, but then again, we never see Ophelia and Hamlet happy together—they're at the end of love.

I feel it during final dress.

"I never gave you aught."

"You know right well you did . . ."

I try to make Hamlet remember his love, and I understand something new. Ophelia has to wear her mask because others are watching, but if they weren't, she would drop the act and fight for Hamlet. Right now, I'd give anything to be able to drop the script and hash it out with Peter.

"I did love you once." The line is more real to me than it's ever been, and I'm afraid it is real, afraid it's Peter saying it instead of Hamlet.

I reach for him—it's in the blocking now for me to take his arm, to try to pull him back to me, and it's safe with his long sleeves. "Indeed, my lord, you made me believe so." I let my hand slide down his arm toward his hand. What if I guide his hand to my face as Ophelia? Maybe the play will end differently. Maybe they'll make up, elope, run away from stupid Denmark, go somewhere warm.

But before Peter's hand touches my cheek, he yanks away. Maybe I've conditioned Peter to avoid my touch.

The show opens tomorrow, and then we have three performances together. During those performances, Peter will make eye contact with me, hold me close, let me see his feelings. So much of the intimacy between us has been on stage. Lately, that's the only place we're connecting. Once the play is over, that connection might be gone for good.

When I get out of rehearsal, I have a text message from Dad:

Course I'm still coming. Wouldn't miss it for the world.

The OCD part of my brain tries to explain it. *You almost made Peter touch you at rehearsal, but you didn't, and that's why Dad says he's coming.*

I want to cancel out that thought, think *don't touch*, but that's not healthy. I don't want to believe I have any control over whether or not Dad shows up.

Instead, I concentrate on my breath, think a mantra like Dr. Rice suggested. *I let go of control. I let go of responsibility for anyone but myself.*

38.

Thursday afternoon we get out of class for one last rehearsal, stolen minutes to tweak scenes and adjust to the set. Some people still need to run lines.

Peter finds me in the middle of the auditorium looking through my Ophelia journal, and he stands over me without speaking. There's the picture of me on the edge of the diving board, at the edge of Peter, of falling in love. My face in the picture is eager, and terrified.

Falling in love can't break bones, but falling out of it—that has the potential to break so much more.

"Are we okay?" I ask.

He shrugs. "Sometimes it's hard to tell what's real with you." He answers the question I don't ask. "Like last night, you almost touched me."

"I tried to."

"But you were playing Ophelia. Would that even count, by your rules?"

"I don't know what my rules are anymore."

He's quiet, then changes the subject. "You're going to do great tonight. I have complete faith in you."

I smile at him. He's smiling back, and I want to close the distance between us, relax this rubber-band feeling that's always tugging between him and me.

"Wow." He breathes out the word. "I know I said I would always be your friend, but . . ."

"But what?"

He breathes out again and turns away toward the stage. "You make it hard to keep things . . . friendly."

"I felt that too."

Nadia calls for Peter. "Hop onstage, pronto!"

"You have to go."

"I have to go."

It's like Nadia's repetition exercise. He's lingering and I want to say wait, but another thought creeps in.

Dad won't come. If you break the rules now, it's over.

"My dad's coming tonight."

"Oh?"

"I'm more nervous about that than about the judges."

He nods. "I don't blame you."

Nadia's not looking at us—a papered wall on the set has started peeling, and she's chatting with one of the techies about it.

"I can't tell what makes me more nervous . . . thinking he might not show up, or thinking he will—that he'll sit in the audience and hate the whole thing and not get it."

Peter tilts his head. "Won't he be proud anyway?"

I shake my head slowly.

"I'm not sure."

"That makes me sad," Peter says. "Dads are supposed to support you. It's, like, part of the job description."

"I know."

"Peter!" Nadia's tiny, but she's got some serious pipes. "Caddie will be there when you get back. In fact, you're going to be on stage with her in a mere half an hour. Don't make me come get you!"

"Sorry," I whisper.

He shakes his head. "No, I'm glad we're talking."

"Me too."

I should touch Peter. I *want* to. Now. And if I wait until after the play to find out whether or not Dad's come, it won't be as brave.

"This is the most we've talked in a while," he says.

"Right?" I lean toward him slightly.

I would slay a dragon for Peter. I would.

He grins sideways, amused by how blatantly I'm drooling over him, I fear. He holds a hand toward me in parting as if to say, *More later.*

I take it and press it between mine.

My palm touches his palm, which is dry, but soft and

warm. His pulse surprises me, how clear it is. My other palm presses into the back of his hand, the long bones and ridges, the soft grooves in between them. His fingers are longer than mine, the palm wider, and something in that sends a rush of blood to my heart, to my cheeks. My own pulse must be pounding his hand—he'll have bruises.

I let go.

The space between my hands, where Peter's was, feels charged, hot and tingly. My own hands radiate, pulse the sensation of me touching Peter into the surrounding air. I could almost believe I'm a superhero. With this energy, I could start fires, freeze lakes, read minds.

Before I can decide that this feeling's bad, tainted somehow, I press my hands to the sides of my neck, to my cheeks. I grip my forearms and run my hands down their length till I'm holding my own wrists tight. *Don't let go. Don't let this feeling go and turn into anything bad.*

I've been staring at Peter, staring into his eyes. And he's frozen—his mouth slightly open, his hand still extended toward me. For a second I think maybe my touch really did something to him, stole his power, made him weak. But then he breaks into the biggest smile.

His eyes say *more*—more of this, more than friends— more and more and more and more.

I dare a look at Nadia. She's still, watching us, hands on her hips. But she's patient. Most of the actors are watching us too, not sure what they're seeing beyond a brazen defiance of Nadia and a little PDA. Me looking away seems to unfreeze Peter. He jogs to the stage.

Mandy's in the front row, and she's twisted her whole body to sit on her knees. She's tugging her hair, making two super-stressy pigtails. Her mouth is a huge, *I-can't-believe-you-just-did-that* smile.

Nadia keeps her eyes on me as Peter takes the stairs and finds his place. It's hard to know what she's thinking when she stares like that, but just when I think she's mad at me, she purses her lips into a bemused smile and whirls back to the stage.

Watching Peter rehearse is easy. Rehearsing with Peter is easy.

I'm on a cloud, a tingling, floating awareness charged with the spark of that one touch—eager and dangerous and delicious.

As soon as Peter's out of my sight, though, the cloud takes on water, sinks down, and I'm swimming in stress. It's an effort to breathe, and I'm certain the pinch in my face has come back with a vengeance.

What have I done? The thought chips away at my nerves. Nadia orders pizza for our dinner break, but my stomach's in a twist. While people eat, Mandy grabs me by the sleeve and pulls me out the stage door toward the tree line.

The flood lights give us an artificial stage that drops off into dark woods.

"You're the bravest," she says.

"No, I'm not. I'm freaking out."

"That. In there. That was brave."

It feels good to hear that from her. I smile. "Thanks."

"Tell me I can't smoke," she says.

I shrug. "You *can*. But you shouldn't."

"I'm quitting," she says. "I'm quitting that, and I'm quitting Drew. Two things that aren't good for me. If you can do it, so can I."

She takes her pack from her purse and tosses it into the woods. I almost mention litter, but this isn't the time.

"Cold turkey?" I say.

She nods like a bobblehead. "Gobble gobble."

"I'll be really proud of you if you quit," I say, "but, Mandy, I'm freaking out."

"You did it," she says.

"Yes."

"Are you okay?"

I walk in a wide arc, shake my hands. "It felt good. It *was* good. It was the right thing to do."

"But?"

"You know, I made this deal with myself about touch, that things with my dad would work out. He'd come back, or . . . I don't know if I even want that now, but, at least he'd still be a part of our lives. He'd stop acting like a jerk."

"Oh, Caddie. Can I give you a hug?"

The idea of a hug from my oldest friend sends shivers

of needy fear pulsing through me. It's not allowed, or it wasn't allowed, but I want it.

"Might as well," I say and let Mandy wrap herself around me. Her curly mess of hair presses into my cheek, and I have to blow out air to keep it out of my mouth. It's an overdue hug, and it nearly pops my lungs.

"Okay, okay," I say. "Thanks."

She lets me go but keeps her hands on my arms. "I'm so proud of you," she says. Then she has a thought, drops her hands, and looks to the tree line. "I don't even want a cigarette anymore. That's how proud of you I am!"

"Dad's supposed to come tonight. Mom bought him a ticket."

"So he'll come."

I catch myself chewing on the inside of my cheek. I could almost bite through.

"Or he won't," Mandy says. "Either way, it won't have anything to do with you touching Peter's hand."

But what if I should have waited, just until after the play? I'm pacing between the stage door and the trees, and a good part of me wants to hunt down Mandy's pack and take that cigarette for myself if she doesn't want it.

"Caddie!" Mandy's using her best director voice, and it stops me cold. "Stop torturing yourself. At least give it a rest until after the show." I nod, but she keeps going. "You worked hard for this. You earned it. And I'm not going to let you spend what should be a happy, exciting time obsessing about how big a jerk your dad can be."

I almost want to defend him, but she's right. I've been making a deal with myself that if I can take part of the blame onto me, I won't have to face up to how maddening he's been.

Mandy senses a moment of weakness and pounces. "March yourself down that hall, young lady. Put your hair up and get pretty. You're playing Ophelia, and every theater student at the academy will be here to watch, and the judges from Bard will be here, and some of them are professional directors who work at the best Shakespeare theaters on the planet."

"Are you trying to stress me out more?"

"Not at all," she says. "I'm trying to get you to stress for the right reasons. This is your thing. I won't let you wreck it by stressing about your dad. Or Peter, for that matter. Move! Do your thing!"

We're walking fast down the hall, and when I turn to look at her she gives me a playful shove—forward march. I lose my balance and stagger forward into a guy coming out of a dressing room. His chest is like a wall, and my head whips back.

It's Drew. He moves me to the side, saying, "Watch it. Mandy, I've been looking for you. Nadia says she gave you two bottles of Dippity-do, but you put them somewhere no one can—"

"We're done," she says, and then looks to me as if my

presence makes it official.

"Huh?" Drew manages.

"Done. You and me. Our relationship."

She starts back down the hall, but Drew and I are still frozen with the shock of it. He looks to me—no help—and then calls after her, "Wait, what?"

"It's not hard to understand," she says. "We fight all the time. I'm tired of it. I won't be making out with you anymore." She pauses to consider something. "We have a lot of friends in common, so I figure we should try being friends. No guarantees."

The reality of the situation seems to be sinking in for Drew. "What?!"

"The Dippity-do's in the supply cabinet above the costume racks. Where it's supposed to be." Then she turns her director stare back on me. "Caddie. Your hair."

Drew looks to me, lost. "What is this?"

Poor guy. I want to say something to comfort Drew— "So sorry," or "She won't be mad forever," or "Hang in there"—but that would be fake.

"It's for the best," I say, and I'm so proud of Mandy, I don't even have the decency to wipe the goofy grin off my face.

39.

The time between Mandy starting to work on my hair and the stage manager calling us to take our places backstage flies—we're freefalling toward the audience, nothing to catch hold of, nothing slowing us down.

"All we can do is tell the story," Nadia says as we stand in a circle in the green room. "Don't even hope that they like it. It isn't about that. It isn't about you. It's about telling the story. Each person will receive the story differently. That's their right." I can't help thinking about how Dad will "receive" the story, whether he'll be there to receive it at all.

Mandy stands next to Nadia. She's sending me crazy-good vibes. And beside me stands Peter. We haven't had much time to talk, but he's like a radiator sending out warmth and concern. The touch tuned him up in my awareness.

As we take hands to pass a silent squeeze around the circle, I leave Ophelia's gloves on. I think I could do it without them. After this afternoon, what harm can one more touch, two more, do? Dad's either in his seat upstairs, or he isn't.

Still . . .

When the squeeze is done, Nadia calls places, but April's at her shoulder saying, "Wait. They need the gummy worms."

Nadia rolls her eyes as she spins away from the circle. "Can't you people do this earlier?"

"It has to be right at places," April says. "That's tradition."

She starts passing around the sacred gummy worms. Mine's electric green and yellow. "Break a leg," she whispers as she puts it in my hand. Nadia continues to signal impatience, but April doesn't speed up her pace. "If I can't be in the play as a senior, I'm sure as hell going to see that tradition is observed."

All around the circle, gummy worms dangle over open mouths. Even Livia, who "doesn't believe in" refined sugar, doesn't hesitate. It's magical thinking that the gummy worms ensure a good opening night—a superstition everybody can agree on.

"Better eat it," Peter says. "Bad luck if you don't."

"I'm trying to stop believing in bad luck."

"Fair enough," Peter says, "but you'd better believe April's going to tackle you and shove that thing down your throat if you don't."

"Fair enough."

I've never liked gummy worms. There's too much resistance, like biting into a finger, but I break this one down into manageable lumps, and there's something comforting about letting it slide down my throat and knowing everyone around me is doing the same. Maybe a little superstition is okay, if it's not mine alone.

The show is a rush. It's impossible to know how it feels for the audience, but from inside, good energy's bouncing around. And a story.

There's a boy who has lost his father. He mourns his loss longer and harder than he's allowed. He doesn't know how to do anything about it without hurting himself. He hurts the girl he loves, or doesn't love, it's hard to tell. And she . . .

She is not me. I get her, get why she does what she does enough to play her. But I don't want to *be* her. She's a sad girl, a sad girl in a bad situation without anybody to help her.

I used to think that was romantic.

I used to picture Ophelia drowning, her skirts spreading around her body, her hair twisting in bits of dead leaves and branches, her face turned up toward the cold sky and waiting. I think she was waiting—*I* was waiting—for Hamlet to run down the hill and scoop her up out of the water, take her away to an island where they could sunbathe naked, make babies, die happy.

Somehow I missed the part of the story where Ophelia dies.

It's fun to play her, knowing I'm not her, knowing she'll end when the story ends, and I'll have myself back, stronger than her.

The acting feels like a ride. I imagine what I need to make the ride start, focus on the differences between Ophelia and me. Ophelia doesn't have a Mom or a Mandy or a dream of an acting career. She has no power—super or otherwise. She's got a bossy brother who leaves and a nutty father who controls her life, and all this life-or-death hope wrapped up in Hamlet.

Mandy's scene is so overwhelming, I'm afraid we'll forget ourselves. When I close my eyes—it might be the warmth from the stage lights, or the audience's bodies compressing the space, or the fact of Peter and me, unsure of each other—the space between his fingers and my skin pulses and crackles with potential energy. I'm sure he'll close the distance this time, but he doesn't. And I cry.

The wall of light at the edge of the stage, the fourth wall, keeps me from seeing whether Dad's sitting next to Mom, or if Jordan sits between them. When I'm on stage,

"Please don't break your neck," I say. "I'm here."

He stomps his way toward me, then stumbles with a sound like wood screeching hard on the floor.

"You okay?" I ask.

"Prop table meet pelvis."

"Ouch."

"A narrow miss. Prop tables should have rounded corners, don't you think? If they're going to be sitting around in the dark?"

"That's what glow tape is for."

"The glow tape has stopped glowing. I think we should fire it."

"I don't know. I hear the glow-tape union holds a lot of sway."

"Damned union," Peter says, and slides down the concrete stage wall to sit by me.

"People are wondering where you went," he says.

"I'm hiding."

"Who from?"

"Somebody who's not even here."

He knows when to be quiet.

"I don't think I'm crazy," I say, "but if anyone can make me feel crazy, it's my dad."

"Why is that?"

"Well, for one thing, he doesn't like theater. He doesn't understand why anyone would want to act."

"Ha. My dad doesn't either." That's part of Peter's story,

one more gap filled in.

"So you understand."

I feel Peter shift. "Yeah, I do, but I have to give my dad some credit. He still came."

"I just want to impress him. I want him to see why I care about any of this. But the other part . . ." *is embarrassing*, I think.

"You don't have to tell me if you don't want to."

"No. I do. I do want to, and I do have to. You were right; I wasn't fair to you. I complained about you not understanding things, but I didn't try to help you understand it either. When my dad left, that's when I got the bad feeling about touch—the fear. It started with him. When he left."

"I don't get it." Then he laughs, because that's the whole point of this talk, to help him get it, and I smile.

"I had this idea," I say. "It sounds crazy even to me, but it felt real, that all the bad stuff I felt when he left would stay feeling that way if I let him touch me, if I touched anyone. It was kind of like a superstition: that if I touched someone, we would never be a family again."

Peter thinks a long time before speaking. "But it sort of is that way, right?"

I nod. "I don't believe that they'll ever get back together. I don't even really think they should anymore, but . . ."

"But it's hard to let go of that hope."

"Something like that. Like I'll be guilty if I do."

Peter nods. "I can understand that."

"I know that it's all in my head."

"But that doesn't make the idea go away."

"No."

We sit quietly, side by side, but it's not an awkward silence. I move my shoe close to his boot, tap the toe against his. He rests his toe on mine, and I slide it out, let mine rest on his.

"Thank you for helping me understand," Peter says. And a thought smacks me—hard; if I were a cartoon, I'd be flattened. At some point, Mom and Dad stopped helping each other understand.

Maybe they tried and they couldn't, or maybe they stopped wanting to try. I've been thinking about it like magic, some kind of a curse, them falling apart. But there's nothing special about it. Coming together, that takes magic maybe, but falling apart—it's the easiest, simplest thing.

Moving a shoe away from a boot.

I swivel away from the wall so I'm facing Peter. I can just pick out his features in the shadowy light that slips between cracks in the curtains. "Hold out your hands," I say.

"What?"

"Just hold out your hands."

Ophelia's gloves have to go, fast, before I can think about it. I whip them off—all strip, no tease—toss them over my shoulder. They make barely a sound as they hit the flat behind me and drop down, a sigh.

I let my hands float over Peter's.

When I touched him earlier today, it was on impulse. This is a choice.

"You don't have to do this if you don't want to," he says.

I shake my head. "I do have to, for me. I need to."

We're as jumpy as if we were playing the hand-slapping game; the potential energy sizzles and sparks between us.

I lower my hands, touch my palms to Peter's, and the warmth of his touch rushes up, up my arms to my heart, to my cheeks, to the back of my neck, flooding me, but my nerves still have me shaking.

Closing my eyes makes the moment a little less real, but it still feels like falling. Any second, I'll break, fly apart, but I keep my hands pressed against his. I'm still breathing, so what's the point of this tension and fear? "What's the point?" I whisper out loud.

"We're friends," Peter says, and he sounds so concerned. "We don't have to be more than that. I'm happy to have you here being my friend."

"I don't mean what's the point of us . . . I mean what's the point of being scared?"

There's no sense in looking for the end. Endings are simple. Beginnings are hard.

Peter's eyes hold me up, pull me in close, and make me forget to hold tight. I lift my hand to his cheek, feel the tickle of stubble at his jaw, and he exhales sharply. His breath plays at my wrist, and that pulls me closer. Peter wraps his hands around the back of my ribs, not to pull, but to keep me from losing my balance.

I don't fall into Peter. I leap. Our lips touch and they touch and keep touching, as if kissing is how we breathe now. People talk about "coming up for air," and I always thought kissing would feel like that, like a struggle to breathe. But that's wrong. I've been holding my breath for months. Kissing Peter is breathing.

When it's finally enough, not forever and ever, but for this one moment, we are silent and still in the dark for a long time. We float there.

"Hey," Peter says, in a whisper. "The world didn't end."

"No," I say. "No, it didn't."

When Peter and I finally emerge, the theater is empty. We hold hands and walk side by side up the red-carpet aisle, and with the crowds gone, the theater feels like it always has—like a sacred place where people come to tell stories and ask questions.

While we were kissing, all the people spilled into the lobby to drink punch and eat pastries.

When we join them, the crowd applauds, and Mandy claps her hands together so fast I'm afraid she'll catch fire. She runs up to us. "It's official. We're going to Bard!" She hugs us both and then takes us each by an arm and shakes us, making an adoring growl.

Peter asks how badly damaged Drew's ego is, and I

leave them to join Mom and Jordan by the punch bowl. Jordan's eyes are still red but angry, too. "You going to be okay?" I ask.

He shrugs. "Probably not."

"We're here for Caddie," Mom says. "Let's not forget that."

"You were good in your play," Jordan says.

"It's all right to be sad," I say. "I was sad."

"I feel so stupid for thinking he was coming," Jordan says, shredding his napkin to pieces.

I reach out and ruffle his hair, and he actually cringes from the surprise of it. "Don't say that. You're not stupid," I say. My touch isn't magic. It doesn't make it all better, but Jordan sets his lips into a tight line that's almost a smile.

"Thanks," he says.

"Congratulations on the Mountain Bard Festival," Mom says. "Maybe Dad can come see that," but I shake my head.

She starts to apologize for him again, but I tell her to stop. Part of what hurt so bad when he left were all the excuses I made for him, the belief I had in him, the expectation that under the right circumstances, he would be different, better. But he won't ever be different.

Whether or not I forgive him, I have to accept that.

ACT FIVE

Lord! we know what we are,

but know not what we may be.

Doubt thou the stars are fire;

Doubt that the sun doth move;

Doubt truth to be a liar;

But never doubt I love.

40.

Being with Peter is easy. Easier than not being with Peter ever was.

Mom and Jordan continue to love him. The Sunday after *Hamlet*, he went with me to Mom's show at the Goblet. We held hands by the punch bowl. He introduced himself to Mom's friends as my boyfriend. Mom beamed at us all night, and when Peter said her work reminded him of Sally Mann's, she cried.

I met Peter's mom and stepdad. His mom was polite but shy. His stepdad was a joker, more like a big kid than a dad. They let us go down to the basement where Peter lives without even a warning to behave ourselves. That first day it was raining, and Peter's room needs a sump pump to keep it from flooding. We lay on his bed and listened to the spatter of the rain, the hiss and gurgle of the pump, and pretended we were kissing underwater.

We spend lots of time together, but not too much. I need time with Mandy and Livia, and if Peter spends too much time with me, Drew gets grouchy. Sometimes we go out as one big group. We've even tried hanging out as a foursome with Mandy and Drew. They make fun of each other nonstop, and sometimes that gets ugly, but mostly they're friends.

In a month, in a year, we might fight, we might lose what we've found. An infinity of bad possibilities hang in the balance, waiting to hurt us. But not tonight.

Tonight, we dance.

It's our one night at Bard, the night of the party, and the music's already pounding when we get there. The room is so dark, it's impossible to make out faces more than a few feet ahead. Lights with pink and purple gels catch people from the side, making them glow but distorting them too. Way off in the distance a band plays on a raised platform, lit by lights that change color and spin. Disco balls send silver haloes dancing around the walls.

I like being able to step into this flood of swirling bodies, not minding if one or two of them brush against me. The music is its own kind of flood, sucking us in at the door, while the dark promises there won't be consequences for anything that happens in this space. That's a lie, but a nice one.

"All right, ladies," Hank says. "Who wants to dance?"

Livia smiles and holds out her hand. He tugs it so she spins into him, her green skirt flaring. When she hits his chest, he dips her with all the brooding swagger of a black-and-white movie star. It's hard to tell how much is from the lights, and how much is from Hank, but Livia's cheeks are flushed, her smile silly.

He starts up a swing step and leads her deeper into the churning dancers.

April turns to Drew—Nadia brought her along to reward her assistance—and says, "Don't let the gay boy show you up. Dance with me."

"She doesn't waste any time," Mandy mutters to me, and I nod.

Drew looks intimidated but willing. April yanks him, and he stumbles, bumping into a couple of kids from another school. "Sorry, so sorry," he says. "Forced dancing happening here."

He allows April to drag him after Hank and Livia, shooting one last desperate look at us.

Mandy turns in a sulky circle. "I don't see any cute, straight boys," she says.

"Thanks," says Oscar.

She sticks out her chin. "I will dance with you if you promise that your hands will stay at ten and two." She indicates her shoulder and her hand.

Oscar bobs his head up and down with great enthusiasm. "Promise." He takes Mandy's hand and follows her as she weaves her way through spinning bodies.

"We've been abandoned," I say to Peter. "Should we dance?"

"Not unless you want your toes to get flattened."

"I'll risk it."

"Look who's brave." Peter holds out his hand.

We walk past the pocket of light at the entrance and slip into the swimmy darkness, scoop out a space where we can slow dance even though the music's fast.

The urge to say something tickles my tongue, the same way the energy between us tickles my skin, telling me to pull him close. "I feel so good here with you. I didn't know I could feel like this," I say, and we kiss.

"I didn't either," Peter says, close to my ear. "You were right. I was afraid, a little bit, of falling for you." He meets my eyes. "I thought . . . I don't know what I thought. Now it seems silly." He winds his hand in my hair.

This morning, after the short drive from Birmingham, we did Mandy's scene on a spindly stage in a rehearsal room. It wasn't as grand as I'd imagined, performing at Bard, but we transformed that stage into Denmark. The scene was for Mandy, and Drew committed himself to every second. He scared me a little. Peter and I did the scene as directed, no touch, but there was fire between us, as if a fleet of twirlers tossing sparkler batons marched between our lips. The audience gave us a standing ovation.

After that, we did a series of scenes on the Festival stage, including "Get thee to a nunnery," and that was almost too grand, overwhelming. The heat from a hundred stage lights spilled down on us, blinding us, so we could barely make out the box seats and balcony. Past the light, hundreds of judging eyes waited to swallow us up, but we focused on each other, and we must have done well, because at the banquet they gave out awards, and we won more than once. We all sat at long tables. Peter played with my hand while they called out the names. They called his name twice and Mandy's and mine at one point, too. Mandy had to get up to take a trophy. Peter stood and brought one back for all of us and a scholarship certificate for himself. I didn't have to stand up, but Nadia reached across the table when they called my name and squeezed my hand.

In the downtime between our performance and the banquet, Peter and I watched another school do some scenes from *A Midsummer Night's Dream*. We laughed at the fairies' costumes, but they were supposed to be funny, so that was okay. Peter played with my fingers while the lovers fought. We kissed a lot there in the dark. We were supposed to be learning by watching other schools perform. I learned that Peter has a scar on the scoop of skin between his finger and his thumb, that his fingers twitch when someone yells onstage, that the skin on the inside of his wrist is as soft and as warm as his lips.

I like touching him there.

Author's Note

Hi, friend.

I love you for reading Caddie's story. *Don't Touch* is Caddie's story, not my own, but it did have its spark in experience.

I wrote this book for anyone who's felt the kind of fear that keeps us from pursuing what we love or that separates us from other people. Most of us feel that at some point, right? But for readers who might be dealing with an anxiety disorder or other mental illness, there are a few more words I'd like to share.

Here goes . . .

My own fun OCD symptoms started at age ten. My parents saw the raw skin on my hands and took me to the doctor. I didn't want attention on my problems and did *not* want to talk about them, so I hid my symptoms for four more years.

By eighth grade, my inner landscape was a minefield, every thought dangerous. I feared that I was going crazy, that I might completely lose myself. I don't remember telling my parents this. I remember locking myself in a bathroom, knowing it would scare them. That was the only way I knew how to ask for help, but it worked.

And when I finally did get help, things changed for the better—quickly. I don't want to suggest that everything got better all at once. I needed medicine, and it took a while to find the right one. Even after my symptoms went away, fear and shame lingered. It took me years to feel okay about what had happened in my brain. This brain that allowed me to write a novel—that lets me teach and perform and fall in love and consume too much reality TV—has a few quirks. That's part of me.

But—and this is the important part—*so much* got *so much better* the moment I knew I had help.

We all know—or we've been told—that the pain and challenges of life make us stronger, and that's often true. But that's a long-term view. In the short term, pain is pain. And as a cause of pain, mental illness carries so much confusion. So many questions.

Is what I'm feeling real? Is it normal? Could I be doing something to fix this? Will I ever feel better?

These are big questions, and I can only answer from

my own experience, but I'm going to give them my best shot.

Is what I'm feeling real?

Yes. Absolutely. Whatever the cause, if you're feeling it, you're feeling it. And if what you're feeling hurts, or if it's messing with your life, you deserve help in making it better.

Some mental illness stems from "organic" problems— biology. The brain is an organ like any other, and sometimes it needs support, just like the heart or the lungs or the eyes. Sometimes, stress or trauma causes mental illness. Sometimes both biology and experience are at work. It really is a spectrum.

Like Caddie, maybe you're dealing with something stressful and painful, the kind of thing any person would find difficult. Is what you're feeling mental illness or a healthy emotional reaction to trouble? Is it somewhere in between?

To some extent, it doesn't matter. Like I said before, pain is pain. And if you're in pain, you deserve help.

Is what I'm experiencing normal, or is it something more?

Trick question.

What is normal anyway?

Normal is a fiction, an exact average of every scale or

as close to that as a person can get. Is a person who needs glasses normal? Or a person with acne? How about someone with *perfect* skin?

As Peter says, "Problem-free people are boring." And they don't exist.

Nobody's normal. If normal is a perfect five, the most normal person in the world might be a 5.001 or a 4.999. My math team days are long over, but I'm guessing even that degree of normal doesn't exist.

Whether you're feeling great or awful or somewhere in between, what you're experiencing is unique and particular to you. But if you're dealing with mental illness, you're also not weird or rare or alone. According to the National Institute of Mental Health, about 11 percent of teens have a depressive disorder and about 8 percent have an anxiety disorder. About 25 percent of adults in the United States suffer from a diagnosable mental disorder in any given year.

If by normal you mean common, then, yeah, it's pretty normal.

Is there something I could be doing to fix this?

You can probably guess my answer to this question: Get help. Talk. Talk to people who love you, and if that doesn't help, to a professional.

That's right, I said it. Talking to the people who love you most is a great starting place, but it isn't always enough.

I have amazing, supportive parents and friends who've encouraged me to get help when it was needed, but I've also gotten bad advice from friends.

People may tell you to "suck it up" and "learn to live with it." They may suggest exercise, more sleep, less sleep, vitamin supplements, a change in your diet, a hobby. Some of this advice might even help. Getting regular exercise rarely makes us feel *worse*, BUT—and this is a big but— when you're suffering from mental illness, this kind of advice probably won't be enough.

And if it isn't enough for you, that's okay. That's not unusual, and it's nothing to be ashamed about. The people who love you aren't always well-informed about mental health. Almost none of them are experts. Some of them may be grossly misinformed. The people who love you best may not always know what's best for you.

If you thought you were having a heart attack, and your best friend got out a stethoscope and tried to diagnose you, you'd tell him or her to stop playing doctor, and you'd get your butt to the emergency room, right?

If the people who love you are asking you to get help, listen.

If the people who love you are telling you that your pain is your own fault or a sign of weakness, that you have to learn to live with it, or get over it, or be stronger, or . . . I could go on for a while . . . seek professional help. Find someone with training in mental health—a counselor, a school psychologist, a social worker, or a doctor. Tell them your story and ask them your questions.

You may not love the first therapist or counselor you talk to, but that doesn't mean talking can't help. Finding the right person to talk to can take time—it's a little bit like dating—but don't stop talking.

And if you're ever feeling suicidal, like you might hurt yourself, then it is extra important to reach out for help. Call a suicide hotline or go to the emergency room. Put yourself in a room with other people. Even when we feel most alone, there are always people—some of them strangers—who want to help us.

Will I ever feel better?

Oh. Yes.

So much better. I believe this with all my heart. There is help, and you will find it, and your life will be magical—not all the time, but enough of the time that you will love it.

But you have to talk. You can't keep it all inside.

That is hard, I know. I know. Oh, I know.

But you can do it. And it is worth it.

If I could tell my younger self one thing, it would be this: People want to help you and love you, but you have to open up and let them.

The things that you fear may be worthy of fear. They may come to pass, and they may cause you pain. *Or* you may wake one day and discover those fears have lost their power to worry you. No matter what, keep talking—keep asking for help and helping yourself—and not one of those fears will be stronger than you.

For more information about mental health, try these sites:

National Institute of Mental Health:
www.nimh.nih.gov
TeensHealth:
http://kidshealth.org/teen/your_mind/
Mental Health America:
www.mentalhealthamerica.net

National Suicide Hotlines:

1-800-SUICIDE
1-800-784-2433

1-800-273-TALK
1-800-273-8255

Deaf Hotline: 1-800-799-4TTY (4889)

Acknowledgments

A debut book needs many friends, and mine has been blessed with the best.

Thanks to the entire fantastic crew at HarperTeen for championing *Don't Touch*. I'm particularly grateful to my production editor, Alexei Esikoff; Kim VandeWater and Lindsay Blechman in marketing; my publicist, Olivia deLeon; and production managers Charles Annis and Ray Colon. And thanks to designers Laura DiSiena and Heather Daugherty for the dreamiest of jackets!

Special thanks to my editors, Rosemary Brosnan and Andrea Martin, who asked the best questions and gave me hope to meet every challenge in revisions, and Jessica MacLeish, who has embraced this book as if we'd been working together from the beginning.

Special thanks as well to my brilliant agent, Sara Crowe,

for her wisdom, support, and contagious enthusiasm.

This book found its shape while I studied with the incredible community at Vermont College of Fine Arts. Thanks to my workshop groups who saw this book, led by Tim Wynne-Jones and Cynthia Leitich Smith; the Super Secret Society of Quirk & Quill and our retreating friends; the "big kids" I look up to, especially Sarah Aronson, Marianna Baer, Gwenda Bond, Jandy Nelson, Micol Ostow, and Trent Reedy; and the best writer roomie, Jessica Leader.

Endless gratitude to my VCFA advisors: Kathi Appelt, Sharon Darrow, Uma Krishnaswami, and Martine Leavitt. Your insight is boundless, and I am better for knowing each of you.

Thanks to Ginger Johnson and Erik Talkin for helpful readings, and to Amy Rose Capetta and Mary Winn Heider for writerly camaraderie and emotional support late in the game. Long live TOOCF!

Extra-special thanks to Varian Johnson, for reading early and late and for being a mentor and friend to this fledgling author in more ways than I can name. I'll do my best to live up to your example.

Thanks to Dr. George Ainslie for an insightful reading from a psychiatrist's point of view, and to Genevra Gallo-Bayaites, M.S. Ed, NCC; Lane Merritt, LGSW; and Pam Watts, for thoughtful feedback on my author's note.

Thanks to Philip Markle for actor training inspiration

and for reminding me to "live epic." And to Caleb Willitz for a much-needed push to send this book out into the world.

Thanks to two instrumental teachers, Cecil Castellucci, who gave early encouragement and pointed me to VCFA, and Corey Mandell, whose screenwriting workshops taught me tons, but especially how to finish a first draft. And thanks to the Altamont School for the strong foundation in all things bookish.

Thanks to my high school theater director, Mary Jean Parson; my Forensics and Thespian coach, Kim Crockard; my college acting teacher, Kim Rubinstein; the Theatre Cherubs Program at the National High School Institute; and the Theatre and Performance Studies programs at Northwestern University. These people and places fed my early love of theater, helped my younger self find a place in the world, and led me to writing.

Thanks to the Barrel of Monkeys community—students and my fellow actor-educators, you are a constant source of inspiration, renewing my enthusiasm for writing and theater on a daily basis.

I'd like to acknowledge a few individuals for helping me through rough times and teaching me the basics of friendship and love. Yours has meant the world to me: Jay Porter—my first confidant, June & the Mees, Ashley & the Maddrys, Annie Lanier Steur, Larissa Lury, Nicholas Rains, Kevin Hogan, Roger Ainslie, Joseph Schupbach,

and Jen Johnson. There are flashes of your magic sprin-
kled throughout this book.

My many, incredible friends not yet named, I often
wonder at your goodness. If anyone reads this book and
questions whether Caddie's friends are too good to be
true, I promise they're not. My friends prove that every
day. Rather than try to name you all, I'll represent you
with one shining example whose words touched this
book: Mr. Tom Malinowski, who always reminds me,
"You're nervous because you care."

Finally and fanatically, my family in all its extensions,
and most immediately, Joe, Janet, and Laura, I can't thank
you enough for your support and love. This year has made
me even more aware of how much I rely on you all. There's
no place I'm more at home than at Dad's handmade bar in
the basement in Birmingham, Alabama.